George Lewis Platt

The Platt Lineage

a genealogical research and record

George Lewis Platt

The Platt Lineage
a genealogical research and record

ISBN/EAN: 9783337313333

Printed in Europe, USA, Canada, Australia, Japan

Cover: Foto ©Andreas Hilbeck / pixelio.de

More available books at **www.hansebooks.com**

By George Lewis <u>Platt</u>

.

T. Whittaker, 1891

CONTENTS.

I.

WHY?

———

Wherefore? Let Lord Macaulay answer when he says that those "Persons who take no pride in the noble achievements of their ancestors, will never achieve anything worthy to be remembered with pride by their remote descendants." When an angry dispute arose in the House of Lords between a peer of noble lineage and one of a new creation, it is reported that Bishop Warburton made this remark, "That high birth was a thing which he never knew any one disparage, except those who had it not, and he never knew any one to make a boast of it who had anything else to be proud of." In the spirit of these passages, is it not a duty to aid in preserving any worthy memorials of one's ancestry and kindred? In this instance, the writer testifies, it has been a special and an absorbing pleasure. He was led to undertake this work by finding a manuscript of a relative highly esteemed, in which there were many interesting details gathered together some twenty-five years since. He thought a full record would be valuable as a matter of history and awaken interest in family groups now widely extended.

II.

OUR FATHERS.

WHO were they? Where did they live? and what inspiriting influence for good have they left their descendants, as a help in life? These enquiries will find some answer in these pages. Yet, imperfection must in some degree mark any work of this kind. for the heads of new families go out from every home circle, like the rays of light from a luminous centre. What has been done herein may stimulate others to a more extended research, and to a more complete record. There has been a special effort to secure accuracy in the details, so far as they go. The writer or compiler, like one of Virgil's characters,

"Patulae recubans sub-tegmine fagi,"

has been reclining at his leisure, looking up at the wide-spreading branches of the family-tree, which has been planted in our soil now over two hundred and fifty years. The result of his studies, he hopes, will interest those who are kindred, and who bear the family name. Good examples among our forefathers must have an excellent influence among thoughtful descendants. He would not have spent the time and labor he has, if he did not think his work would be welcomed by large numbers, and be the means of much good in the widening circle of a numerous kindred.

His authorities are the New England Genealogical Dictionary, town records, church records, wills and deeds, admirable papers by the late Prof. Johnson T. Platt, of the Yale Law School ; also letters with full details from Prof. North, of Hamilton College ; from Frank H. Platt, Esq., of New York ; from Dr. T. Hull Platt, of Lakewood, N. J.; from Jonah H. Platt, Esq., and the Hon. Henry C. Platt, of New York ; from Dr. Walter B. Platt, of Baltimore ; also from Messrs. Joseph C. Platt, of Waterford; J. Cheney Platt, of New York ; James Augustus Platt, of Bucks County, Pa.; Jesse Platt, of Montclair; Cyrus Platt, of Delaware, O.; Lewis C. Platt, of White Plains ; C. H. Platt, of New York ; and H. C. Platt and N. G. Pond, of Milford. Many data have been received from Mrs. C. P. Underwood, of Auburn ; from Mrs. L. J. Atwood, of Waterbury ; from Mrs. Mary P. Parmele, of Greenwich, Ct.; from Mrs. J. G. Mitchell, of Columbus, O.; from Miss Anna Platt, of Washington, D. C.; and from Miss A. E. Platt, of Marcellus, N. Y., beside valuable details from many other correspondents who have kindly aided in these researches. Indeed there is a large number of others whose names might be given, who have sent important data to aid in filling out this extended family record ; to all whom the writer thus wishes to acknowledge his indebtedness and convey his thanks. Many correspondents have expressed great pleasure that the work has been undertaken, and they have spared no pains in helping to make it full and accurate.

Mrs. A. C. Maltbie, of Syracuse, N. Y., has kindly sent her "Rescript," entitled, "Down Seven Generations," treating of the genealogy of the Platt and Treadwell families, and giving valuable details, specially in the line of Judge Charles Platt, of Plattsburg. It has materially helped the writer, aided by valuable communications from Mrs. S. H. Bailey, of Plattsburg, and Mrs. Diell, of Hamilton, N. Y. Mrs. Maltbie's work is very creditable, and he is glad to say that she is among the first who have sought to put in order and preserve in print the records of the family. She is a grand-daughter of Judge Charles Platt.

"The Platt Chart," by the late Mrs. A. M. Redfield, of Syracuse, a cousin of Mrs. Maltby, kindly sent to the writer by Mrs. M. T. Smith, her daughter, is the first extended effort to preserve the family records. It was photographed, and it has been widely circulated. By the aid of a magnifying glass it opens to the view many interesting details. It has been a help in these researches.

Respecting the correctness of the details, it should here be remarked, that this will depend largely upon the accuracy of those who have kindly contributed many of the names, dates and events. Discrepancies, sometimes observed, have been carefully examined, and if possible, reconciled or corrected. The tracing of the ancestral lines has chiefly been by the aid of some public or legal record. Mr. Charles W. Platt, of Montclair, N. J., a student in the Lehigh University, Bethlehem, Pa., has given me many valuable extracts from rare books in the college library, respecting the English branches of the family, for which I feel greatly indebted. They will aid those who wish to trace the ancestral lines in the mother country.

III.

THE TWILIGHT OUT-LOOK.

Sir Hugh Platt, who lived in the days of Shakspeare and Bacon, was a noted agriculturist in England. He wrote several treatises on subjects suited to his taste and growing out of his engagements. He was very successful in the culture of fruits. There is an interesting sketch of him in Donald G. Mitchell's "Wet Days at Edgewood." He has left on record this eloquent passage: "That rare and peerless plant the grape." The writer of these memorials has often, in humorous moments, regarded himself as a lineal descendant of Sir Hugh, for the special reason that he has in his grounds more than eight hundred grapevines, most of which he has propagated and planted himself. The old chronicles have not been consulted, and their testimony cannot be brought in to decide this family question! It doubtless will remain among the undetermined problems of the past. Moreover, we are conscious that the age of fable precedes the age of fact. Therefore we look for remarkable naratives in the dim twilight period. Herodotus and

Livy tell many a classic story before they get into
the realities of history. It is generally conceded, too,
that Plutarch had great inventive powers. This inspiriting fancy respecting lineage, may hence not be
out of place in a record like this. Indeed, were all
facts known, it might prove, in the fatherland, that
the family there, more fully than in this country,
could trace their origin to a single individual. In
this connection it is well to say that there are several traditions. One, that the first ancestor came
from Poland, another, that one branch originated in
Germany. True, our forefathers were Britons,
supplemented by the Saxons, and these reënforced
by the Normans under William the Conquerer.
The Teutonic element, hence, is there in any view.
But history pushed too far back often runs into
myth or story. We propose to speak mainly in the
line of authenticated fact.

The name was sometimes written with one " t," an
economy which has not been followed in our extrav-
agant day, by the later descendants. Those who
claim a German origin, say that it was first spelled
Platz, which then became Plats, and Platts, then
fully anglicized Platte, and finally as we now have
it. In the Norman French it was Pradt, then Pratt.
In each instance it means an open, level piece of
land, showing a unity of origin.* Thus from the start
it seems to have an agricultural outlook. This is
primitive. By a slight change it might come from
the German " Blatt," a leaf. Leaves and flowers
have much to do with the fruit of the circling years.

* Lozelle J. Platts, Deep River, Ct.

In the old English records the name is written
"Playter." The termination "er," is German, in-
dicating activity, as we have in the Saxon, helper,
maker, doer. The Greek word, plasso or platto, to
do, might suggest a Helenic origin to our family
name. It is an honor to be ranked among the
world's workers.

IV.

THE CLEAR DAY.

Richard First.

COAT OF ARMS.

It is well known that our family name is quite frequently found in various parts of England. There is good evidence that coats of arms have been granted to six or seven of the family from the time of Edward III., 1326, to the twenty-first year of Queen Elizabeth's reign. In the records of the Heraldry Office in London, it is called " the ancient and honorable family of Platt." The first ancestor of by far the most of those who bear the name in the United States, was Richard Platt, who came from the very heart of the old country. We have reason to think that he was born in the same year that Queen Elizabeth died, if the following statement really applies to him: " Richard Platt, son of Joseph Platt, was baptized Sept. 28, 1603." This is claimed as an extract from the parish records of Bovingdon, a village near

Hertford, Eng. There are more Richards than one. Some have thought that Richard 1st, as we shall call him, came from Huntingdon or Norfolk, Eng., but the meagre evidence does not establish either of these statements as a certainty. Indeed, the research in England has been quite limited. The late Prof. Platt, of the Yale Law School, wrote a few weeks before his death, that "a certain Richard Platt founded a free Grammar School between Oldenham and Elstow, in Hertfordshire, during the last decade of the sixteenth century, and it is now in successful operation, or was so quite lately, on the original foundation. This is shown in Cansick's History of Hertfordshire. There is also a description of the school in Cluterbuch's History of Hertfordshire." The precise locality of our ancestors whence hence may be a question that needs more thorough research.

But our progenitor, Richard Platt, came to this country in 1638. and landed at New Haven. In the records of the colony of New Haven we read that Richard Platt had eighty-four acres of land in and around New Haven. In the Milford records we read that he was enrolled among its first settlers, Nov. 20, 1639, having four in his family. "He had probably brought with him from England his children, Mary, John, Isaac and Sarah; for his first child baptized in Milford, by the record, was Epenetus, July 12, 1640. Subsequently were baptized, Hannah, October 1, 1643 ; Josiah, 1645, and Joseph in 1649." After his arrival in New Haven, Richard Platt acquired possession, among others, of

several acres of land in what is now the best part of
the Elm City ; (it was on the south side of Chapel
street, near College street, adjoining the ground of
Peter Prudden,) in what was called the " Hertfordshire quarter." But the project of founding the
township of Milford, nine miles west of the city, was
soon after matured, and he threw in his lot among
the sixty-six who formed themselves into a church
organization, August 22, 1639, before they departed
from New Haven, and proceeded to carry out the enterprise of settling that flourishing township. Richard
Platt is on the records as a landowner. His name is
on the list of free-planters made out in 1646 ; he was
chosen a deacon in the first church in Milford in 1669.
It is recorded that his wife, Mary, died in January,
1676. His daughters, Mary and Sarah, too, probably
died before the father made his will, in 1683, for in
it he makes bequests to their children instead of to
them. He leaves something to each of his five sons
in addition to what he had given them before. It is
quite noteworthy that he left to one of his heirs a
legacy "towards bringing up his son to be a scholar."
This thought and this expression betray a profound
interest in the best things in life. The fact, too,
that he left by will a Bible to each of his nineteen
grand-children, shows in rough pioneer days how
sincere and earnest he was in his Christian profession and life, and that he regarded the divine word
as a precious legacy to his descendants. He appears
on the records as one of the witnesses to the will
of Peter Prudden. Richard Platt's estate was estimated at about 600 pounds sterling. He died in

1684. The place where he was buried is not known, as no stone has been found to mark his grave. It was probably in his orchard.

In August, 1889, at the late interesting and noteworthy commemoration of the settlement of Milford 250 years ago, his name was mentioned with honor, and among the coping stones of the beautiful memorial bridge erected over the Wapawaug, to perpetuate the memory of the early settlers, a stone was placed with this inscription :

"DEACON

RICHARD PLATT,

Obit 1684.

MARY, HIS WIFE."

This among the cap-stones in the bridge was placed there by the liberality and thoughtfulness of one of his descendants, the late Prof. Johnson T. Platt, of New Haven.

The sons and daughters of Richard as nearly in the order of their precedence as we are able to determine, were Mary, John, Isaac and Sarah, then those who were baptized in Milford, Epenetus, Hannah, Josiah and Joseph. It should be stated that Richard and his sons John and Josiah are recorded among the original purchasers and proprietors of New Milford. But John finally went to Norwalk, Isaac and Epenetus to Huntington, L. I.; only Josiah and Joseph remained in Milford, the first home of the family.

MEMORIAL BRIDGE OVER THE WAPAWAUG.

V.

HIS DAUGHTERS.

———

No record is full, and we may say just, that does not embody some memorials of the daughters as well as the sons. We give the first place to those of Richard 1st in this record. It is a privilege to honor the "mothers in Israel." His oldest daughter Mary married Luke Atkinson, of New Haven, May 1, 1651. A second marriage was to Thomas Wetmore, January 3, 1667. His daughter, Sarah, was also twice married, first to Thomas Beach and afterward to Miles Merwin. It was recorded many years ago in the New England Genealogical Dictionary, that "six Merwins had graduated from Yale College." His third daughter, Hannah, married and resided in Norwalk. The records give us but a few details of the descendants of Mary. There are more traces of those of Sarah and Hannah.

Martha, daughter of Miles Merwin and Sarah Platt (widow Beach) born January 23, 1666, married James Prime, son of James, Sept. 20, 1685; Mary, twin sister of Martha, married Mr. Hull. Hannah, third daughter, born Nov. 6, 1667, married Abel Holbrook, Dec. 20, 1683. Deborah, fourth daughter of Miles and Sarah Merwin, born April, 1670, married Samuel, son of Samuel Burwell. Sarah Platt Merwin, the mother, died in 1670. N. G. Pond, Esq., of Milford, says " that the late Samuel Irenæus Prime. is a descendant from the Sarah Platt Merwin marriage by Martha Merwin who married James Prime."

Hannah, daughter of Richard 1st, baptized October 1, 1643, married Christopher Comstock, October 6, 1663. Their children were: Daniel, born July 21, 1664; Hannah, born July 15, 1666; Abigail, born July 27, 1669, who died in her 20th year. Mary, born February 19, 1671; Elizabeth, October 7, 1674; Mercy born November 12, 1676, and Samuel, February 6, 1679. Norwalk was his residence. At a town meeting in 1673, "Christopher Comstock was chosen and approved of to kepe an ordinary for the entertayning of strangers." The excellent custom of appointing some "reputable householder to entertayne ye stranger," shows how wisely our fathers managed in their day.

—Daniel, son of Christopher Comstock, married Elizabeth Wheeler, daughter of John, of Fairfield, at Blackrock, June, 13, 1692.

—Samuel, youngest son of Christopher Comstock, married Sarah, daughter of Rev. Thomas Hanford, December 27, 1705. Their children were: Sarah, born March 25, 1707; Samuel, born November 12, 1708, and Mary, born August 5, 1710.

We hence see that the collateral branches of some of our first ancestors were the Atkinsons, the Wetmores, the Beaches, the Merwins, the Primes, the Hulls, the Holbrooks and the Comstocks.

From the sons and daughters of Richard Platt, the family branches have extended far and wide throughout our country, touching the Gulf, the Pacific Coast, and spreading in many of the intermediate States, as will appear by the record.

VI.

NORWALK BRANCH.

JOHN PLATT was probably the oldest son of Richard 1st, of Milford, as he is first mentioned in his father's will. He married Hannah Clark, of Milford, June 6, 1660, the ceremony being by the magistrate, Mr. Treat. He returned to Norwalk, Ct., his name appearing on the records soon after 1660. His children were: John, born June, 1664; Josiah, born December 28, 1667; Samuel, born January 26, 1670; Joseph, born February 17, 1672; Hannah, born December 15, 1674; and Sarah, born May 20, 1678. John Platt, according to the record in the first book of grants and deeds, had a lot of four acres, two roods. The date is 1663. He bought of Thomas Lupton four acres in 1665. It is recorded that he drew a lot for winter wheat. In the early days of the town history an estimate was placed upon each one's possessions. John Platt's estate was rated about £170 sterling. In 1675, in the Indian troubles, it was determined that the meeting-house should be fortified and garrisoned for the security of the town. John Platt was on the committee " for carrying on this work."

John, son of John 1st, married Sarah, daughter of Ephraim Lockwood, May, 1695. They had children : Sarah, born March 30, 1697 ; Elizabeth, born June 11, 1699 ; John, born April 2, 1702 ; and Abigail, born February 12, 1708.

Samuel, third son of John 1st, (deacon) married Rebecca, daughter of Samuel Benedict, of Danbury, June 18, 1712. He had one daughter, Rebecca, born April 9, 1713. He died December 4, 1713.

Sarah Platt, daughter of John Platt 1st, married Samuel Kellogg, September 6, 1704. The children were : Sarah K., born September 26, 1705 ; Samuel, born December 23, 1706 ; Mary, born January 29, 1708 ; Martin, born March 23, 1711 ; Abigail, born January 19, 1712 ; Lidiah, born October 30, 1713 ; Gideon, born December 5, 1717 ; and Epenetus, born June 26, 1719.

Joseph, fourth son of John the first, married, November 6, 1700, Elizabeth, daughter of Matthew Merwin, 2nd. Had issue : Elizabeth, born December 2nd, 1701. His wife died April 9th, 1703 ; January 26th, 1704, he married Hannah, daughter of Rev. Thomas Hanford. He had : Hannah, born October 29th, 1704 ; and Joseph, born September 9th, 1716, if there be not a suspected mistake of ten years.

This, the youngest son of John Platt 1st, seemed to be highly esteemed among his fellow citizens. A grant to Joseph Platt is recorded January 11, 1699, " of sixteen acres lying at West Rocks, west side of highway leading up to said Rocks." In the Indian troubles that annoyed the early settlers in New England, he, as a soldier, bore himself admirably well. He was too young to be in the " dismal swamp fight," which was a fearful struggle; 300 Indians were slain, and nearly as many taken prisoners. It was a dearly bought victory, for six captains and eighty men were killed or mortally wounded. One hundred and fifty afterwards recovered from their wounds. But the savage enemy were fully overcome. This was in King Philip's war. Some years after this fight, we find this in the town record, dated February 21, 1698: "Granted unto Joseph Platt, as he was a soldier out in the common service against the enemy, the town as a gratification for his good service, do give and grant unto him ten acres of land, to take it up a mile from the town, and where it lies free, not yet pitcht upon by any other persons." We find him called Captain Joseph in 1713. "Ye worshipful Joseph Platt, Esq.," was one of a committee to fix the limits of an upper village. After a visiting clergyman was at Norwalk, he was appointed to "attend ye Rev. Mr. Dickinson home into ye Jersies." He was a Justice of the Peace in 1726–7. These positions show the estimation in which he was held.

Abigail Platt, daughter of John Platt 2nd, born February 12, 1708, married Jabez Sanders, August 1, 1753. Children: Samuel, born February 22, 1754; Platt, December 14, 1756; Thomas, December 28, 1758; Aaron, December 23, 1760: Polly, born March 30, 1762; Esther, June 14, 1764; and Samuel, born May 16, 1767.

John Platt, son of John Platt 2nd, married Charity Morehouse, September 13, 1758. Their children were: Sarah, born September 4, 1759; Hannah, born

April 30, 1761; Anna, born February 12, 1764; Sukey, June 17, 1770; Esther, born November 12, 1772; and Jonathan, born April 14, 1775.

Samuel Platt married Ann Raymond, March 2, 1757. Children: Justus, born December 4, 1757, (died under seven years); Jabez, born November 22, 1761; Esther, born August 11, 1763; Joseph, born June 25, 1765; Justus 2nd, born September 10, 1768; Hannah, born May 24, 1771; Betty, born November 27, 1773; John, born December 17, 1777; and Ann, born February 6, 1781; Ann, wife of Samuel Platt, died February 20, 1781.

The Rev. C. M. Selleck, in a foot-note to his Centenary Address in 1886, at St. Pauls, Norwalk, remarks "that John Platt was the owner in 1792, of pew No. 12, in the old St. Paul's Church, Norwalk," which is believed to be the first church consecrated by Bishop Seabury.

John H. Platt, of Norwalk, whose grand-father was named Joseph, gives the following data: "My grand-father had five sons and four daughters, their names were: Alfred M., Jonathan (who was my father), Joseph, Charles, and Chauncey C. and daughters, Laura, Susan, Emily, and Minerva. Alfred M. was born October 6, 1800, died March 6, 1876. He had three sons, Giles, Cornelius and Frederick M., and five daughters; one son was drowned. Jonathan had three sons: David M., Augustus, and John H., and three daughters. Joseph had two sons, George M., and Edward, and two daughters. Charles had no sons; Chauncey C., had one son, Chauncey, and one daughter.

VII

OLDER HUNTINGTON BRANCH.

Isaac Platt.

His name is mentioned second in his father Richard's will. He and his younger brother Epenetus are enrolled among the fifty-seven landowners of Huntington, L. I., in 1666. They were doubtless residents there some years before this date. In 1646 Gov. Theophilus Eaton, of the New Haven Colony, purchased of the Indians a tract of land on Navy Island, now called Eaton's Neck, and within the present limit of the town of Huntington. In 1653 conveyances were made by the Indians to actual settlers who founded the town. Connecticut claimed the jurisdiction of Long Island, under the charter of 1662, and did not relinquish it until the decision of the commissioners appointed to determine the bounds of the Duke of Yule's patent, in the fall of 1664. At a general assembly held at Hartford, May 12, 1664, Isaac Platt, Epenetus Platt, and many others residing on Long Island, were made free planters, " with liberty to act in the choice of public officers, for the carrying on of public affairs in that plantation." The inhabitants of Huntington were yet obliged to take out a patent of confirmation from Gov. Nicoll, November

30, 1666, in which the names of both Isaac and Epenetus Platt appear as patentees. In 1688, also, a new patent was taken out, the names of the brothers appearing among the patentees. Here it is well to say, that a very interesting history of this old township is found in the Centennial Address of the Hon. Henry C. Platt of New York, entitled "Old Times in Huntington." Many of the details of this branch I find in its rich pages so full of names, dates, events, and manners and customs of a past century. Isaac with his brother Epenetus and others was imprisoned in New York by Gov. Andrews in 1681, for attending a meeting of delegates of the several towns to devise means to obtain "a redress of grievances under his arbitrary rule." After their release, at a town meeting a vote was passed to cover their expenses. He and his brother were among the sterling patriots of their time, fully recognizing and claiming their civil and religious rights. Their descendants showed themselves worthy of their parentage in the Revolutionary struggle which separated the colonies from the mother country in 1776 and 1783.

In the town records of Huntington we read that "Isaac Platt, September 2, 1679, received a deed of land from John Green;" also "a deed of land from Jonathan Hamet, May 15, 1683." We also read that "Isaac Platt was Recorder of Huntington in 1687."

In the census records of Huntington, in 1755, Isaac Platt appears as a holder of slaves; as also, Epenetus 1st, Dr. Zophar and Mary Platt.

In the records of Milford, Ct., we find that "Isaac

Platt and Phebe Smith were married March 12, 1640." He made a second marriage according to the records of Huntington, to Elizabeth, daughter of Jonas Wood, twenty odd years afterward. We find no record of children by his earlier marriage. This doubtless, is one of the gaps which often come in to puzzle the antiquary in his researches into the distant past.

Isaac Platt was a captain of militia, and it is said of him that " he held every office of consequence in the gift of his townsmen." He lived in Huntington till his death, July 31, 1691.

By the town records his children were : Elizabeth, born September 15, 1665 ; Jonas, born August 10, 1667 ; John, born June 29, 1669 ; Mary, born October 26, 1674 ; Joseph, born September 8, 1677 ; and Jacob, born September 29, 1682. We know little of John, Joseph and Jacob.

Jonas Platt, eldest son of Isaac, married Sarah Scudder; they had four sons: Obadiah, Timothy, Jesse and Isaac. Obadiah and Timothy went over and settled at Fairfield, Ct., (See Fairfield Branch). Jesse and Isaac 2d, remained in Huntington. Jesse, son of Jonas Platt 1st, had three children : Jesse 2d, Isaac 3d and Zophar.

Isaac Platt 3d, son of Jesse Platt 1st, married Esther Ketcham February 27, 1744-5, died December, 1772. Children : Obadiah, baptized March 23, 1745-6, died 1829 ; Elizabeth ; Mary and Sarah twins ; Jesse, baptized August 30, 1761, married Deborah Titus, died May 25, 1827 ; and Isaac 4th, born June 14, 1754, died August 8, 1849.

Obadiah Platt, son of Isaac Platt 3d, married Mary Platt, daughter of Epenetus Platt, in 1769. He died December 7, 1829, aged 84. She died June 7, 1825, aged 85. Seven children: Elkanah, 1770, Philetus, Daniel, Esther, Rebecca, Phebe and Sarah, the latter born 1783. This Obadiah Platt lived in the period of the Revolution, after which he made his home on his farm at West Hills.

Isaac Platt 4th, son of Isaac Platt 3d, married Eunice Platt, who died in Huntington in 1862, at the age of 97, leaving no issue. She was a daughter of Obadiah Platt, of Fairfield, Ct.

Jesse Platt 3d, son of Isaac 3d, had children: Lewis, David, Ira, Jesse 4th, Ansel, Sarah, Isaac 5th, and Joel. Elkanah, son of Obadiah, of Huntington, married "Deucy" Wood, daughter of Jeremiah, 1795, and had children: Elizabeth, born February 19, 1796; George W., late of New York city, born August 2, 1798; David, born May 4, 1801; Brewster W. and Daniel, twins, born July 1, 1804; Nathan C. (late Chamberlain of New York city), born December 20, 1806; Debora W., born February 4, 1809, and Hannah C., born February 2, 1812. Of these, Elizabeth married Mr. Mortimer; George Wood married Eliza Roshore, July 7th, 1821; David married Sarah Gould; Brewster died unmarried; Nathan married Jane Plumber—he died May 23, 1863; Debora married Curtis Merritt, and Hannah married Clark Merritt. The following details in this line are given by Charles Slason Platt, from the family Bible: George Wood Platt, the oldest son of Elkanah, born August 2, 1798, and his wife Eliza, left five children: Henry Mortimer, born July 7, 1822; Maria R., born April 20, 1825; George Washington, born August 27, 1833; Mary N., born November 19, 1835, and Eliza A., born June 15, 1838. George Wood Platt came from Huntington, L. I., to New York about 1810 or 1812. He was a jeweler, and established Platt's Gold and Silver Smelting Works, which are still in operation. He was associated with his brothers, Nathan and David.

Henry Mortimer Platt, married Caroline A. Weed, July 7, 1843. Their children were: Ella Louisa, born May 10, 1844; Charles Slason, born December 7, 1846; Grace A., born June 18, 1850; Frank Henry, born April 15, 1852. Caroline A. Platt died August 3, 1864. Charles Slason Platt, oldest son, married Florence Wemple Bissell, June 2, 1887.

—Grace A., second daughter, married Frederick Stallknect, October 22, 1872. Their children are four daughters: Caroline A., Laura, Alice, and Ella Platt.

—Frank Henry, second son, married Sarah E. Wiley, April 18, 1877. Their children are: Emelie Louise, Estelle Cooper, Frank Wood, Charles Henry and Sidney, who was born December 11, 1889.

Maria R. Platt, eldest daughter of George Wood Platt, married Isaac C. Withington, September 18, 1844. Their children are: Charles Sumner, born April 13, 1848; Laura E., Annie Louise, Irving Platt, Isaac Chandler, Maria R., who married Mr. Bellman, and Eliza Platt.

George Washington Platt, second son of George Wood Platt, married Mary Coles, September 18,

1857. They have one daughter, Mary Eliza, who married T. G. Aller. Their children are—Georgette and T. Gusten Aller. The son was born in 1885.

Mary N. Platt, second daughter of George Wood Platt, married James W. Todd, September 5, 1860. Their children : William Platt, born June 4, 1861; (he married Margaret Chrystal, but died without issue in July, 1886) ; Henry Hartman, born October 14, 1863; Walter Herbert, born 1865; George D., born February 13, 1869 ; and Irving Todd, born October 13, 1872.

—Henry Hartman Todd married Ella Grinzeback, April 27, 1889. They have a son, Clinton, born February 1, 1890.

—Walter Herbert Todd has a son, Harold, and a daughter. His wife's Christian name is Clara. They were married July 1, 1886.

The descendants of the late David Platt, second son of Elkanah Platt, live mostly in Huntington, L. I. He himself was a jeweler in New York many years. His son, Henry C. Platt, lives in New York where he was born in 1840. He graduated from Princeton in the class of '58. He married Jenny Dusenberry, daughter of Isaac A., of Glenville, Ct.; had one son, who died in '87, in the 21st year of his age. He is now in the full practice of law in his native city. He is United States Assistant Attorney for the Southern District of the State of New York. He has his summer home in Huntington. He has kindly contributed important data for this record. In his family Bible it is recorded that Clarissa Platt, born August 29, 1788, married David Munson, (born December 3, 1776) October 29, 1808.

Isaac Platt 5th, son of Jesse 3d, married Sarah Matthews, and afterwards Elizabeth Doty, of Cold Spring Harbor, L. I. He was born 1785 at Huntington, and died at Geneva, N. Y., 1880. His second marriage was at Oyster Bay. His wife died at Geneva, 1875, aged 83 years. They had five children: Stephen H., Ananias D., Sarah E., Mary F., and Isabella E. 1. Stephen Hendrickson Platt married Phebe Rudman, of Penn Yan; their only child, now Mrs. Carll, resides at Cincinnati, O. He died about 1850. 2. Ananias Doty Platt married Parmelia Hall, of Geneva. He died in New York, 1885. Their children are: Sandford Hall, Wilbur Fisk (who died 1887), Mary Belle, Lillie E., and Adelaide Platt. 3. Sarah E. Platt married William Rudman, of Penn Yan. She died 1844. They have a son living there, John J.; a second son, Isaac P., died aged 19. 4. Mary Fowler Platt married James M. Soverhill, of Geneva, N. Y., where she now resides. 5. Isabella E. married Charles D. Morris, of Phelps, N. Y. He died 1867. A son, Charles L. Morris, resides at Rochester. A daughter prettily writes: "My father and my brothers were respected in the circles of church and business in which they moved, and of each it might be said,

1198605

"He bore without abuse
The grand old name of gentleman."

Joel Platt, son of Jesse 3d, married Miss Suydam of Centreport, L. I.

Jesse Platt 4th, son of Jesse 3d, married Maria McChesney, of New York City.

Sarah Platt, daughter of Jesse 3d, was very beautiful; she had three husbands : Thomas Steele, John Scudder, of Vernon Valley, L. I., and Joshua B. Smith.

Philetus, son of Obadiah, of L. I., married Content Sammis, of Huntington, and had children : Obadiah, Zophar, Stephen, Oliver, Watts, Polly, Amelia, Sarah, Phebe and Nancy Platt.

Daniel Platt, son of Obadiah, of L. I., married Miss Smith, of New York city, and had children.

Esther Platt, daughter of Obadiah, of L. I., married Stephen Fleet, of Huntington, and had children : Platt, Ruth, and Mary Esther Fleet.

Rebecca Platt, daughter of Obadiah, of L. I., married a Mr. Duryea, and had one son, John Duryea ; she then married Jonas Sammis, of West Neck, L. I., and had four children : Nelson Sammis, of Huntington ; Daniel P. Sammis, of New York City ; Mary Sammis, deceased, and Sarah Sammis, wife of Jonah Denton, of Lloyd's Neck, L. I.

Phebe Platt, daughter of Obadiah, of L. I., married Nathaniel Chichester, of West Hills, L. I., and had children : Nathaniel, Eliphalet, Platt, and Mary Ann Chichester.

Sarah Platt, daughter of same Obadiah, married Jesse Rogers, of Huntington, and had one daughter, Elizabeth Rogers.

Zophar Platt, son of Jonas 1st, son of Isaac first, was born near 1734. He married Esther Platt of Huntington (Platt was her name before marriage) ; they had four children. Phebe, married Nathaniel Smith ; Richard, (his second wife was Harriet E.

Kirk); Anna Rogers, and Medad Platt. Anna Rogers Platt, born at Huntington November 26, 1793, died at Poughkeepsie October 31, 1861. She married Amos Platt Ketcham of Huntington, September 9, 1811; a second marriage was to Warren Skinner of Poughkeepsie, February 7, 1832. Medad Platt married Ann Eliza Gantz; a second marriage was to Mary Baker.

—Phebe Platt and Nathaniel Smith had four children: Phebe Smith, who married George Smith. The other three died in youth or infancy.

—Richard Platt and his wife Harriet had children: Richard and William now deceased; Harriet, who married George W. Wright, of Morristown, N. J.; Augusta, deceased, and John Platt and Fred Platt, both in Mexico

—Anna Rogers Platt, who married Amos Platt Ketcham, had five children: Esther Emily, Alonzo R., Zophar Platt, Andrew J., and Rebecca Ketcham. The children, two, by her marriage to Mr. Skinner, died in infancy. Esther E. Ketcham, born July 27, 1812, at Huntington, married John F. Parker, of Poughkeepsie, May 16, 1837; died February 7, 1839. They had eight children: Ann Augusta, Mary Vassar (married M. O. Dutton), George Parker (married Louisa Beach), Alonzo R., Elizabeth, Emily Platt Parker (married William B. Fox), Louise S. Parker and Matthew V. Parker, who married Eliza Augusta Wines. George Parker has one surviving child, George Parker. Emily Platt Parker had four children: William Fox, Harry (not living), Bessie and Esther Fox Parker.

Medad Platt (son of Zophar), who married Eliza Gantz, had six children who reached maturity; others died in infancy. No issue by the second marriage. They were: Caroline, deceased; Elizabeth, Emily Platt, now Mrs. T. J. Owen of New York; Maria and Charlotte, both deceased, and Annie Platt, now Mrs. Peter Moller, Jr., of New York.

—Alonzo R. Ketcham, son of Amos Platt, born August 6, 1814, died January 15, 1890, married Catherine Bogardus, March 19, 1831. A second marriage was to Sarah Hinsdale; a third to Anna M. Davis. No issue by first. The children of Sarah H. were four: Amos Platt (1842), lost at sea; Edward, who married Elizabeth Ramsdell; Alonzo C. and Sarah Ketcham, who married George Gatchell. There were five by the third marriage: William P., deceased; Emily, Anna F., Albert and Samuel Ketcham.

Zophar Platt Ketcham, born April 30, 1817, died June, 1822.

Andrew J. Ketcham, fourth child of A. P. Ketcham and his wife Anna Rogers Platt, born March 18, 1819, married Sarah Anderson October 25, 1842. Three children: Andrew Golding, born July 7, 1844, died May 24, 1854; Richard Platt and Annie Ketcham. A record marriage was to Frances Cowles. Issue: One son, Charles. Mr. A. J. Ketcham is a banker in Poughkeepsie, N. Y.

Rebecca Ketcham, fifth child, married Samuel B. Johnston, May 18, 1841. They had one child, Mary, who in 1867 married Edward Elsworth. They had four children : Grace Varick, Mary Johnston, Ethel Hinton and Edward W. Elsworth.

Robert Platt, U. S. N., (son of William Platt, of North Carolina, formerly of New York), was born in 1836. His father moved South in 1832. His mother was Margaret Ann Potter, daughter of Robert Potter, of North Carolina. He was true to the old flag in the war, and was in the South Atlantic Blockading Squadron ; piloted the fleet into Charleston harbor, South Carolina, and was wounded in the fight. He was many years on the Coast Survey, and is now in command of the steamer Fish Hawk, in connection with the United States Commission on Fish and Fisheries. His family reside in Washington, D. C. His grandfather was William, of New York, who had three brothers, George, Samuel and Abraham. Robert Platt had a brother Samuel, deceased : his brother Henry is living in North Carolina. Robert Platt gives these data.

Oliver Platt, (son of Philetus, son of Obadiah, son of Jonas, son of Isaac 1st), married Hulda Hand. Their children were : George, Edward and John, all deceased ; Timothy and Sarah, who died in childhood ; and Mary, also deceased ; Charles S., Oliver 2d, Ezra and Isabella. The father died in Brookhaven, July 2, '83, aged 81.

—Chas. S., second son, born January 1, 1826. married Urania M. Gerard. Their home is in Bellfort, L. I. Their children—two daughters—Kate G., who married H. W. Post, and Frances A., who married H. M. Goldthwait.

—Oliver Platt 2d, left five children, the oldest of whom is Frederick W. Platt. The father died fifteen years ago, leaving the family to the care of his oldest son, who married Emily L. Rodman, August 7, 1882, and has two children : Warren Nelson, born in 1886, and Irving Voorhis, born September, 1888. Their home is in Brooklyn, L. I.

Other details of the descendants of Isaac Platt, of the Older Huntington Branch, will be found in the Fairfield, Meriden, Washington, New Haven, and New Jersey Branches.

VIII.

YOUNGER HUNTINGTON BRANCH.

Epenetus Platt.

He removed from Milford with his older brother Isaac, and was recorded as one of the land-holders of Huntington in 1666. With him, he was imprisoned by the tyrannical Andros. In 1667, he married Phebe Wood. He died 1693. He has numerous descendants. His children were: Phebe, born March 19, 1669; Mary, born January 11, 1672; Epenetus, born April 4, 1674; Hannah, born August 23, 1679; Elizabeth, born March 1, 1682; Jonas, born April 24, 1684; Jeremiah, born November 25, 1686; Ruth, born June 13, 1688; and Sarah, born February 4, 1692. Phebe Platt married John Treadwell; Elizabeth married Jonathan Smith; and Mary Platt married Timothy Treadwell. The Huntington records say that Epenetus Platt received a deed of land from Gabriel Finch, February 24, 1666, and a deed of land from Thomas Skidmore January 22, 1672. Epenetus Platt filled many public positions with ability and credit. He was called Captain, and sometimes Lieutenant. His son Epenetus 2d was Major Platt.

Jeremiah Platt, the third son of Epenetus 1st, born 1686, married Hannah———, and had a son Jeremiah

2d, born December 12, 1747, who married Mary, a daughter of Miles Merwin, of New Milford. He, Jeremiah 2d, was buried in Bridgewater, 1805. His wife, Mary, died February 17, 1825, and was buried there. They left a daughter, Hannah, who married Colby Chamberlain, and a son, Newton Platt, born October 18, 1779, eighteen months after the sister. Newton married Elvira Canfield, daughter of Philo. Their children were James N. and Evelina C. Platt. In the grave-yard at Bridgewater, there is a stone in memory of Jeremiah Platt 3d of the name, buried 1839, aged 67. There is also a stone to "the memory of widow Sarah Merwin, late of Milford. She was the mother of Samuel and Capt. Epenetus Platt, and grandmother of Jeremiah Platt of Bridgewater." Newton Platt lived in New York and died there April 28, 1861.

James N. Platt above, born February 3, 1817, is a lawyer in New York. He traces to Newton, son of Jeremiah 2d, son of Jeremiah 1st, son of Epenetus 1st, son of Richard 1st of Milford, Ct. His only sister, Evelina C. Platt, born December 15, 1822, married December 26, 1845, Justin A. Bliss. They have two children, Justine Adele, who married William Frederick Stofford, and Ida C. Bliss. All reside in New York.

Jeremiah Platt, whose wife was named Abigail, was one of the founders of the Tontine Coffee House in New York in 1792. Of the 203 shares he owned two, and had them placed, one in the name of his son Sydney, born April 19, 1781, and the other in the name of his daughter Amelia, born July 20, 1782. Jeremiah Platt was a merchant in New York.

Epenetus 2d, son of Epenetus 1st, generally called Major Epenetus Platt, born April 4, 1674, was distinguished as a member of the Colonial Assembly from 1723 to 1737. He died in 1744, at the age of 70. His children were: Epenetus 3d, Zophar, Uriah, and Solomon, and Elizabeth and Phebe. Elizabeth married M. Townsend, Phebe married Col. Benjamin Treadwell. Their daughter, Phebe Treadwell (1730–1801), married Hendrick Onderdonk, and was the grandmother of the distinguished Bishops of that name.

The repetition of the same names is almost confusing. Some make out that he also had a daughter Mary, who married Timothy Treadwell. But this Mary, was the daughter of Epenetus 1st, was she not?

—Epenetus 3d, was a captain of militia, owned a large landed estate, but nothing has been learned of his sons, if his line be not extinct.

Jonas Platt, second son of Epenetus 1st, purchased the farm of Sunk Meadow, L. I., in 1717, (which in 1843 was owned by Jeremiah, one of his descendants,) it is now in the family. He spent his last days there, and left his estate to Zephaniah, of L. I., an only son. This one married Hannah Saxton, at Huntington, in 1730. His children were: Jonas, Zephaniah, of N. Y.; Nathaniel, Charles, Hannah and Elizabeth. A second marriage was to Anna Smith, widow of Richard Smith and daughter of Job Smith. He had children: Jeremiah, Daniel, Sarah and Dorothea.

"When Zephaniah was 74 years old, during the occupation of Long Island by the British, he, with many of his neighbors, was taken prisoner and driven into New York and confined in the old prison ship. His daughter Dorothea (Brush) hearing that he was ill with small-pox, drove, with a colored woman, into the city, and asked Sir Henry Clinton to allow her to take him home, as he could not live. 'He is an arrant rebel,' said Sir Henry. She answered him with tears in her eyes: 'He is an old man and can never more injure your cause.' Her tearful beauty and filial affection prevailed. The old gentleman lived only four days after his release; he is buried in the family plot at Sunk Meadow." (This is related by Mrs. Hugh McCulloch, of Washington D. C.)

The "Old Platt Homestead," of Sunk Meadow, now at King's Park, L. I., is the home of the family of the late Elias Smith Platt, who died December 27, 1890, at Lakewood, N. J. In this historic home six generations of Platts have been born. The widow's maiden name was Caroline Child, born in Brooklyn, May 11, 1848. She was married October 24, 1867. The children are: Lucien A., born September 27, 1869; Milton L., born February 20, 1872; Ellis S., born November 17, 1873; and Caroline Child Platt, born March 15, 1885, the first daughter born on the place since 1754. The Old Homestead is very interesting in memorials. In the spacious hall there hangs a portrait of Col. Richard Platt, the Aide of General Montgomery at Quebec. The grandfather of the present children was Jeremiah C., son of Jeremiah. Their uncles were: Lucien, died aged three ; Herman, who was ill at Princeton College, and died soon after he was brought home; Eugene J., the second son, is still living. The searcher for old historic lore will find much to interest him in the Old Homestead.

During the occupation of Long Island by the British in the Revolution, many young men crossed over to the Connecticut shore to enlist in the patriot army. Their hardships were severe. Mrs. McCulloch gives this narrative of some of the young men from the aforesaid meadow home. They came over from the mainland for food : "The mother left the window facing the Sound open a very little. They rowed over at high tide, and took the provisions from the pantry placed there for them. They asked her 'Is all well?' she answered 'all's well,' but did not see them, for when the sentinel came in the morning to inquire if any rebel had been seen, she could say 'no' without uttering a falsehood. Once, Jerry, the youngest of the four sons who were in the war, came over to see his mother and his young wife. An officer found him there, he ran for his boat, and the officer fired. Jerry fell, his wife fainted, and his mother thought him killed, but in the night he returned to let them know he was safe, that his foot was caught in the long grass, and he fell without the shot touching him. The officer supposed him dead, and did not take the trouble to wade into the salt marsh to see. The young man remained hidden until after dark, so as to free them at home from sorrow." How this lets in light upon the trials of our patriot fathers.

Jonas, oldest son of Jonas Platt 1st, married Temperance, daughter of Ebenezer Smith, settled in New York city, and died in 1775, aged 44. His children of whom we have record were : Richard, Elizabeth and Ebenezer. Richard married Sarah Aspinwall, and left two sons, Alexander Hamilton and Richard (who died young), and a daughter, Sarah Matilda, who died in infancy. Alexander Hamilton married and left one son. Richard Platt, the father of these, was a colonel and an aide-de-camp to General Montgomery at the storming of Quebec, December 31, 1775. There is a tradition that Montgomery died in his arms. He was the venerable marshal of the day when the General's remains were received in New York and re-interred in front of St. Paul's church in Broadway, July 8, 1818 ; and he was for a number of years Commissary General of the State of New York. Ebenezer was taken prisoner in the Revolutionary war and, it is said, carried to London. Regaining his liberty, it is related that he married the sister of the wife of Sir Benjamin West.

—Jeremiah, fifth son of Jonas 1st in this branch, occupied the family estate at what is now called King's Park, L. I. His wife's name was Hedges, of Easthampton. He left a son Zephaniah, of L. I. For a continuance of this history, the Plattsburg Branch gives interesting details of his four sons : Zephaniah, of N. Y., Nathaniel, Charles and Daniel, and their numerous descendants.

—Dr. Zophar Platt, second son of Epenetus 2d, heads the Zophar Branch, following this.

—Uriah Platt, third son of Epenetus 2d, was born

January 5, 1734, and died July 21, 1803. He settled in Queen's County, L. I., married Mary Smith, and had five children: Margaret, Epenetus 4th, Philip Smith, Uriah 2d, and Catharine Platt. Their home was at Hempstead. So far as names and dates can . be reconciled, it seems a second marriage was to Sarah Treadwell in 1761. She was born January 1, 1740, and died December 24, 1788. Benjamin Platt was their son, born July 11, 1762.

—Philip Smith Platt, (1732-1801) married Phœbe or Elizabeth Mott, (1733-1776) at Hempstead, L. I., June 29, 1766. Their children were: Phœbe. Mary, and Margaret Kissam Platt. Phœbe, (1768-1855,) married Daniel Kissam, (1770-1846); Margaret married Benjamin Treadwell Kissam. Phœbe and Daniel Kissam had eight children: Daniel, Philip, Elizabeth, (these died in childhood); Daniel 2d, Margaret, Benjamin T., and Philip S. Platt Kissam.

The will of Philip S. Platt, dated December 13, 1747-8, mentions his wife Phœbe, and children, Phœbe, Mary, John, Elizabeth, Selah, and Obadiah.

—Margaret Platt, the first born of Uriah 1st, married Isaac Smith at Hempstead. Long Island, January 2, 1744. There were children: Mary, Jacob, Uriah, Freelove, Platt, Phœbe, Elizabeth, Catharine, Philip, Isaac and Margaret. Catharine married Jacob Bockée, the father of Judge Bockée of Duchess County, N. Y., who married Martha Oakley. Their daughter Catherine J. married Augustus Flint, the father of Miss Margaret Bockée Flint, of New York.

—Epenetus 4th, M. D., is said to have been a surgeon in the Continental Army. After the war he lived at White Plains, Westchester County. He died of yellow fever in New York in 1796. His children were: Epenetus 5th, who removed to New York, and Sarah, who married Josiah Man, of New York.

—Benjamin Platt, son of Uriah 1st, born 1762, married September 7, 1783, Hannah Woolley, born October 5, 1763. Their children were: Sarah, Uriah, Eliza Treadwell, and Henry Woolley Platt born August 2, 1791. Sarah Platt, born October 20, 1784, married Charles Hewlett. Their children were: Eliza Ann, born March 28, 1808; Benjamin Platt, born September 17, 1809, died the next day; and Benjamin Platt, born August 4, 1811, died August 11, 1815. Charles Hewlett died January 31, 1829. Sarah, his wife, died 1817. Uriah Platt, oldest son of Benjamin, married Eliza Ann Peters. Their children were: Hannah Ann, born October, 1816, died 1886; Sarah Elizabeth, who married Benjamin Wiggins; Mariam Frances, born September 29, 1820, who married Joseph Williams, she died August 24, 1873; Jane Louisa Platt, born April 24, 1824, who married James Valentine; and Benjamin T. Platt, born March 24, 1826. died July 4, 1857. Eliza Treadwell Platt, daughter of Benjamin, born March 20, 1788, married Philip Allen, October 14, 1817. Their children were: Benjamin Platt Allen, December 24, 1818; Sarah Elizabeth, January 1, 1822; Emeline, April 2, 1824; Margaretta, born October 25, 1825. Emeline Allen married Bloodgood H. Cutter at Flushing, November 12, 1840; Sarah E. Allen married John Woolley, December 22, 1842; Margaretta married

Benjamin Woolley, January 29, 1845 ; Benjamin Platt Allen married Catharine Bergau. The old Platt homestead at Little Neck, north of Hempstead, is now occupied by Bloodgood H. Cutter, "the Long Island Farmer Poet," who married a descendant of Uriah Platt 1st. His wife departed this life March 24, 1881. He has at the homestead many of the old books in the Platt library. He gave some of these data:

Frederic Augustus Platt, of Brooklyn, L. I., traces back to Epenetus 1st, of Huntington. His father, Epenetus 5th, a merchant in New York, died there, 1843, leaving: William Epenetus, who died 1888 ; Maria E., who married Thomas Rodman Appleby, still surviving her husband; Caroline W., who died in 1888, and Frederick A. Platt, as above. He was born in 1817 ; married 1852, Mary Augusta Hull, of Derby, Ct. His children were: Frederick A., who died in infancy, Isaac Hull, and Mary Augusta, who died 1884, aged 26.

—Isaac Hull Platt, M. D., of Lakewood, N. J., born May 18, 1853, was named after his mother's paternal uncle, Captain Isaac Hull, of Constitution and Guerierre memory. He was admitted to the bar as a lawyer, but finally graduated in medicine from the Long Island College Hospital, 1882 ; married September 2, 1886, Emma, daughter of Aaron G. Haviland, of Brooklyn. His children are: Frederick Epenetus, born October 17, 1887, and Haviland Hull, born April 6, 1889. He is well established in his profession. His mother died January, 1890. His son Epenetus is the seventh of this name in the ancestral line.

IX

DR. ZOPHAR BRANCH.

———

Dr. Zophar Platt, second son of Major Epenetus 2d, heads this branch; born 1705, married November 19, 1738, Rebecca, daughter of Joseph Wood, of Huntington. He was quite eminent in his profession, and distinguished as a man of enterprise and influence in his day. He died 1792. His children were seven: Jeremiah, David, Ebenezer, Elizabeth, Phebe, Sarah and Hannah. Jeremiah died in New Haven; David was born 1754; Elizabeth married D. Phœnix; Phebe married Samuel Broome; Sarah and Hannah successively married Robert Ogden, of Elizabeth, N. J. The late Cornelius DuBois, of New York, was his grandson. Mrs. Nichol Floyd, of Mystic, L. I., is a daughter of Mr. DuBois.

—Mrs. T. C. Doremus, *née* Sarah Haines, mother of Professor Doremus, of Columbia College, New York, is gladly accorded a place in this ancestral line. She was a great-grand-daughter of Dr. Zophar Platt, of the younger Huntington Branch. Her grandmother was his daughter Sarah, who married Robert Ogden, of New Jersey, whose daughter Mary was the wife of Elias Haines, a prominent New York merchant. He was the father of Mrs. Doremus, who was the sister of Daniel Haines, Governor of New Jersey, and a sister of Henrietta, who established "the Miss Haines school," so well known in Gramercy Park, New York. Mrs. Doremus was the founder, in 1860, of the first distinctive Woman's Missionary Society in our country, the parent of all the others, which have already contributed over ten millions of dollars for foreign missions, and which unitedly have at this time an annual income of one million dollars to aid in lifting up the less-favored of their sex in heathen lands. These facts are derived from Dr. A. T. Pierson's "Crisis of Missions." He says : "The Woman's Union Missionary Society, organized in New York in 1860–61, under the leadership of the lamented Mrs. T. C. Doremus, and with the *Missionary Link* as its organ, is the pioneer in this country. This undenominational society led the way, and was the parent of the various boards now found in connection with all the great Christian bodies." The "Missionary Year Book" calls this the "mother society" of all the Woman's Missionary organizations in America. These are sterling facts.

—Ebenezer, third son of Dr. Zophar Platt, born in Huntington, 1754, married Abigail, daughter of Joseph Lewis. She was born in 1761 and lived to the age of 67. He was elected to the Legislature in 1784-85. In 1794 he was appointed first Judge of Suffolk

County, which place he held five years.   In 1799 he removed to New York, and was in the Custom House many years. He was able, courteous and hospitable. He died June 26, 1839, at the age of 85. His children were : Isaac Watts Platt, many years settled as a clergyman in Bath, N. Y.; Ebenezer, bank cashier, New York ; Elizabeth, who married James Rogers ; and Rebecca, who married Edmund, a brother of James, of New York.   The children of the latter were : The late Rev. E. P. Rogers, D.D., of New York ; John N., Sarah Platt, Julia and Harriet Rogers.

Isaac Watts Platt, (1788-1858) son of Ebenezer 1st, married Anna McClure, of Philadelphia.   He was a pastor of a church in Bath, N. Y.   He died 1869. They had five children : Ebenezer, born 1823 ; Joseph Sloan, deceased ; James McClure Platt, Archibald A. Platt, deceased ; and Elizabeth Platt.

—Ebenezer 3d, the oldest, married Anna, daughter of Dr. Charles Davis, of Elizabeth, N. J.   Their children were Charles D. Platt, Anna McClure Platt, William Clifford, and Luther D. Platt.   Charles D. Platt, A. M., graduated at Williams College in the class of '77. He is principal of Morris Academy, Morristown, N. J., where he has taught the last seven years.   He married Mary Jane West, August, 1883.   Their children are : Eleanor W., Dorothy, and a son, Richard Huntington, born 1890.

—James McClure Platt, D. D., son of Isaac Watts, born 1826, married Frances E. Upson, of New York. Issue : William Alexander and Alice McClure Platt. William A. married Julia Hawkinson ; two children,

William Wallis and James McClure Platt. William Alexander, the father, is on the editorial staff of the *Evening Mail and Express*. The grandfather, the Rev. Dr. Platt, was a successor to his own father in the Church of Bath, N. Y., but after an interval of nearly twenty years. He died in 1884.

—Mary Gildersleeve Platt, daughter of Ebenezer Platt 2d, married Rev. John G. Johnson, of Upper Red Hook, Duchess County, N. Y. She died November 15, 1854, leaving two children, E. Platt, and Ellen G. Johnson. The father, whom the writer of this knew very well, was an able minister of the gospel, and his memory is gratefully cherished by many in his church neighborhood. He died July 3, 1870. His daughter Ellen Gray, married Henry L. Underwood. She died in Newark, N. J., July 3, 1880. Mr. Underwood lives in Birmingham, Alabama.

—E. Platt Johnson, the oldest son of John G., is a graduate of Williams College, in 1869. He is a lawyer of twenty years' practice in New York City.

—Amarintha N. Platt, daughter of Ebenzer 2d, married Rev. George R. Williamson, late of Amity, N. Y. He died in his 30th year, September 6, 1852, from injuries received in the explosion of the steamer "Reindeer" on the Hudson, near Tivoli, N. Y., on that day. His wife and his oldest son were fatally injured, too, the former dying September 15, and Norman, the five-year-old son, in a few hours after the explosion. An only son remains, Edwin B., born April 5, 1852. He graduated from Rutgers College, New Brunswick, N. J., in 1871, and from the Columbia Law School, New York, 1873, and he was admitted to the bar the same year. He is in the practice of law in Newark, N. J.

—Sarah Platt, daughter of Dr. Zophar Platt, born September 27, 1750, married May 19, 1772, Robert Ogden 3d, son of Robert and Phebe (Hatfield), of Elizabeth, N. J. Their children were five : Elizabeth Platt, who married Col. Joseph Jackson, of Rockaway, N. J.; Robert Ogden 4th, who removed to New Orleans, was Justice of Supreme Court of Louisiana, and ancestor of the Ogdens of that State ; Mary, who married Elias Haines, of New York City, grandfather of Rev. Alanson A. Haines, of Hamburg, N. J.; Jeremiah, who was drowned in boyhood; and Sarah Platt, who married Cornelius DuBois, of New York City. She is the mother of Henry A. DuBois, of New Haven, Cornelius DuBois of Staten Island, and George W. DuBois, D. D., rector of a church in Essex, N. Y.

Robert Ogden 3d lost his wife Sarah Platt, 1781 soon after the birth of his daughter Sarah. He was obliged in 1776 to remove his family to Morristown, and a year later to Turkey, (now New Providence,) to escape the raids of the British from Staten Island. He resided here until near the close of the war.

—Hannah Platt, sister of Sarah, was the second wife of Robert Ogden 3d. They were married at Huntington on Sunday, just after service, at the parsonage, by Rev. Nathan Woodhull, Dr. Platt's family not being aware of the marriage, until the parties walked home and announced it. Their children were: Rebecca Wood Platt, who married Dr. Samuel Fowler, of Franklin Furnace ; Hannah Amelia Jarvis, who married Judge Thomas C. Ryerson, of Hamburg, N.

J.; Phebe Henrietta Maria, who was Judge Ryerson's second wife; Zophar Platt, William Henry Augustus, and John Adams Ogden. In 1786, Robert Ogden 3d, and his wife Hannah removed to Sparta, N. J., where she died. He afterwards went to Franklin Furnace. He died at Hamburg, February 14, 1826.

X

THE JOSIAH BRANCH.

THE fourth son of Richard 1st, Josiah, is the founder of this line. There were many of his name, and numerous descendants. He remained in his native town ; he was baptized in 1645, the probable year of his birth. The town records say that "Josiah Platt and Sarah Camfield, both of Milford, were married December 2, 1669, by Mr. John Clark, Commissioner." It is stated, too, in the church records that " Josiah Platt and Sarah, his wife, were admitted to membership October 22, 1672." Their family were four sons and four daughters. His eldest, Josiah Platt, was born June 29, 1671. He probably died in infancy or early youth, as within eight years another son bears his name. Sarah, the oldest daughter was born September 17, 1673 ; Mary was born November 13, 1675 ; John, a favorite name in most of the branches, was born September 5, 1677 ; a second Josiah was born January 12, 1679 ; Richard Platt was born August 9, 1682 ; Hannah Platt was baptized November 29, 1685 ; Abigail was baptized March 4, 1688 ; and Joseph, January 15, 1693.

Richard Platt 2d, son of Josiah 1st, married Ester Buckingham, November 7, 1706 ; Ester Platt, his oldest daughter, was born April 18, 1708 ; Ann Platt was born November 14, 1710; Mary, September 4, 1713, and Richard Platt 3d, was born February 2, 1715. This Richard married Mehetable Fisk, daughter of Ebenezer, March 1, 1737. The first Fisk Platt was a son of Richard 4th and Sarah Camp, born 1768. "Richard Platt," it is recorded, "son of Richard Platt, jr., was born March 30, 1742." This was the fourth in the ancestral line, the father of Fisk. "Mehetable, daughter of Richard and Mehetable Platt, was baptized August 30, 1741." Richard Platt had a son Joseph, "who was baptized September 5, 1784." So much for the Buckinghams and the Richards in the old time before us.

Sarah Platt, daughter of Josiah 1st, married Richard Bryan. Their children were: Sarah, who married a Nettleton; Richard, who married Mehetable Clark, daughter of Samuel, afterwards, in 1721, Sarah Treat, daughter of Joseph; Frances married, 1725, Jeremiah Gillett, afterwards, Stephen Miles; Augustus, born January, 1707; Alexander, October, 1709; Hannah, born January, 1712, married a Baldwin; and Nathan, born December, 1714, married Elizabeth Whitman, daughter of Zechariah, June 27, 1739.

Mary Platt, daughter of Josiah 1st, married Joseph Clark, son of Thomas. Their children were: Mary, born March, 1704, married Joseph Sanford, afterwards Thomas Baldwin; Hannah, born January, 1706, married Jonathan Fowler, son of William, January 9, 1729; Joseph, born October, 1708, married Mary Sanford, daughter of Andrew; and Daniel, baptized April 8, 1716, married Abigail, daughter of

Samuel and Silence Buckingham. Prof. J. T. Platt wrote that the town records of Newtown, Ct., give these data following: "Josiah Platt, of the town and county of New Haven, in consideration of love and affection to his son Josiah Platt, of Newtown, willed him half his land on Gelding Hill in Newtown, October 18, 1758. (Vol. 7, p. 157.) Josiah Platt, of Milford, Ct., in consideration of love and good will which I have and do bear unto my grandson Josiah Platt 3d, now of Newtown, October 18, 1758," willed him land in Newtown. (Large vol. 7, p. 155.) Josiah Platt, sr., of Milford, to his son Josiah Platt, jr., of New Haven, willed "108 acres on Gelding Hill in Newtown." Id, 1–49.

The will of a Josiah Platt, dated October 26, 1758, is on record in the Probate Court of New Haven. The testator mentions his wife, Sarah, and sons Josiah, Nathan, Isaac, Jonas, and daughter Frances, (Peck) and grand-daughters, Sarah, Abigail and Mary. He gave lands in Newtown to his sons Josiah and Jonas, and to his grand-son Josiah. He gave lands in Waterbury to his sons Nathan and Isaac.

"Nathan Platt and Amos Platt conveyed to Mary Platt, wife of Isaac Platt, lands in Zoar, descended to them from their mother, Sarah Platt."

John Platt was an early settler in Newtown. On February 7, 1721–2, he conveyed to his brother Josiah Platt, of Milford, the one-fourth part of a whole right of commonage in undivided land throughout the whole township, (Bk. 1. fol. 26). John Platt, of Newtown, conveyed land to his brother Richard Platt, of Milford, April 20, 1725, (Vol. 3 and 4, page 462).

John Platt, of Newtown, conveyed land in that town to his sons, Ebenezer, John and Moses, in 1741.

In Newtown it is recorded, March 11, 1766, that Josiah Platt was aged 91; January 3, 1769, his widow was about 91 years of age.

In the Newtown Records (Vol. 8th) this is found: "Josiah Platt and Sarah Sanford were joined in marriage covenant, November 13, 1758. Children: Hannah, born October 3, 1759; Nathan, born March 3, 1761; Isaac, born December 24, 1762; Louisa, born May 28, 1765; Amos, born January 12, 1768; Jonas, born January 11, 1770."

It is on record in Newtown that Nathan Platt, of Waterbury, Amos Platt, of Southbury, Isaac Platt, Josiah Platt, Hannah Platt and Lois Mallery, of Newtown, obtained from Lidia Platt, of Newtown, widow of Josiah Platt, late of Newtown, a release of her dower interest in his estate, February 10, 1804, (Vol. 23, page 38). This shows a second marriage by Josiah Platt. "Woodmont," the house his grandfather built about 1700, is still standing; in architecture, a fine specimen of the American antique, with its long retreating roof.

Nathan Platt, eldest son of Josiah Platt and Sarah, (Sanford) tracing back to the Milford Josiah stock, was born in Newtown, March 3, 1761; he married Ruby Smith of same place. He lived many years in Waterbury, Ct. He was "a soldier of the Revolution." A second marriage was to Charlotte Dickerman. He died in Wallingford, 1845, in his 84th year. His children by his first marriage were: Levi Smith, Alfred, Ely, Almon, Anner, Leonard, Sarah and Martha. He was buried in Waterbury. His wife, Ruby, died 1829.

—Levi Smith, his eldest son, born 1787, married Patty Hawley, of Danbury. He spent his closing days on his farm there. He died, aged 58. His children were: Emmon, Mary Ann, William, Lorin, and Elizabeth. His son William, born 1814, married Fanny Sherman, of Danbury, (born 1817). He resides in Newtown, Ct. William's children were: Francis, Emily, Charles, Fanny and Roger. Of these none survive but Charles S. Platt, born May 1, 1846; he married March 31, 1879, Ella E. Ingraham, of Bridgeport, and has three children: Charles R., born January, 1880; Arthur P., born February 22, 1882; and Agnes E. Lorin, the next son of Levi S. Platt, was born in 1817; married Jane Sherman, of Danbury, 1844; he died in Springfield, Mass., May 16, 1875, leaving two children living, Annetta and Joseph. He had a farm in Pennsylvania.

—Elizabeth, Smith Platt's youngest daughter, married Harrison Weed, of New Haven. They are residing there now. They have four children: DeWitt, Lorin (deceased), Harry, and Libbie.

—Alfred Platt, second son of Nathan Platt, and Leonard Platt, his youngest son, give rise to the Waterbury Branch.

—Ely Platt, third son, heads the Norwich Branch.

—Almon Platt, fourth son, married Alvina Allen, of Waterbury, March 6, 1817. She died 1837, aged 41, leaving five children: Albert, Martha S., who died in her 18th year; Mary Jane, Elizabeth S., and Ely Platt. A second marriage was to Volutia Hall, of Wallingford ; she died aged 62, leaving children: Ruby Alvina, died aged 11; Harvey Almon, died in infancy; Harvey Almon 2d, born in 1842, died in his 15th year; and Emily Hall Platt. Almon Platt died December 29, 1882, aged 86. His oldest son Albert, born December 24, 1818, married Jerusha Ives about 1840. They had two daughters, Martha and Sarah A. Albert married in succession, Lucy B. Barrows, of Pawtucket, Rhode Island, then Paulina Pickett, of Litchfield, and Mary Tuttle, of Southington. His daughter Martha married Charles Braithwaite ; two children, Albert and Wesley. They live in Shabbona, Ills. His daughter, Sarah A., married Fay Tiffany, of Berkhamstead. They have children, Mary and Arthur. The family now live in Albion, Nebraska.

Mary Jane, second daughter of Almore Platt, born June 25, 1824, married Junius Brown, of Waterville. He died without children.

Elizabeth S., born August 23, 1827, married Lewis J. Atwood, of Waterbury, January 12, 1852. Three children : Lizzie Alvina, born July 22, 1853, died May 12, 1856; Fannie Finette, born March 25, 1856; and Irving L., born May 17, 1861. The second daughter, Fannie, married Albert I. Blakesley, December 11, 1879 ; she died October 10, 1884, not long after the birth of a daughter, Beth Margaret, who died in infancy. Irving L. married Jennie M. Ford, December 28, 1882. Their children are : Lewis Irving Atwood, born November 14, 1884, and Carlton F. Atwood, born October 3, 1886. The Atwood home is in Waterbury, Ct.

Ely Platt, second son of Almon Platt, born March 4, 1830, married Frances Harrison, of Wallingford, Ct., September, 1851. They have children, Harry and Alice, and others ; residing at Carbondale, Kansas.

Emily Hall, youngest daughter of Almon Platt, born July 3, 1844 ; married Jerome Wedge. They have Alice M. and Minnie. The family reside at Morris, Ct.

—Of the daughters of Nathan Platt, Anner, unmarried, lived to the age of 79. Sarah married Daniel Tuttle ; she lived to her 89th year ; died at Kenosha, Wis., 1889, leaving children : Edward, Rebecca Ann, Ruby Smith, Aaron, Elizabeth, Sarah Irene, and Eliza Grace. Of these Rebecca Ann married David Hull of Newtown, Ct. They have five children ; they are living in Dunlap, Iowa. The second daughter, Ruby Smith. married Alanson Craw ; they live in Waterbury. (A son, Edwin Craw, is married.) Aaron, son of Daniel and Sarah Tuttle, born in 1823, died in youth. Elizabeth M., third daughter, born 1824, married John A. Smith, of Dunlap, Iowa ; both deceased. Sarah Irene, born 1826, married Horace Osborne, 1852 ; both deceased. Eliza Grace, fifth daughter, married Hiram Smith ; she died 1857. The family removed to Dunlap. The youngest son, Edward Tuttle, born 1835, married Hannah Curtiss, 1858; they have three children living ; their oldest daughter, Lizzie, married W. H. Fuller ; living in Passaic, N. J. Edward Tuttle, his wife, and Josiah and Louise. His children, are living in Kenosha, Wis.

—Martha, daughter of Nathan Platt, married Asahel

Judd. Their children are: Franklin, Calvin, Leonard, and one daughter, deceased. Calvin, born 1824, is living in Iowa. Franklin resides at Plattville, where his mother died, August 22, 1886, in her 89th year.

George Fowler Platt, born 1841, deacon of the First Church, Milford, traces from Richard 1st, through Josiah 1st, Joseph, then deacon Joseph, and Captain Joseph, to Nathan, his grand-father, and Nathan his father; his farm has come down to him through five generations. He married Elizabeth Addis; has one son, William F., born 1867. His brother, Norman S., resides in Cheshire, Ct., who married Estelle Beers, of that place. Has no surviving children. A third brother is N. Dwight Platt, of Milford, who married Elizabeth Manville, October 13, 1869. Frank N. Platt, their only child, was born December 14, 1875. E. B. Platt and Richard Platt are ex-deacons of the First Church in Milford; G. F. Platt and H. N. Platt are now the acting deacons. This honorable distinction in the First Church in Milford, has continued among those of our name from the time of Richard 1st.

Other descendants of Josiah 1st, now resident in Milford are:

Richard Platt, son of Richard, born December 29, 1821; he married Angelina Bedell, of Elizabeth, N. J.

David Baldwin Platt, also son of Richard, born 1823, married Mary Camp, daughter of Elias.

Henry Newton Platt, son of Newton, born November 25, 1830, married Susan Tomlinson, daughter of Nathan (widow Isbell). His brother Jonah C. Platt resides in Ansonia, Ct.

George Fisk Platt, son of Nathan, born April 10, 1835, married Mary Montague, of Northampton, Mass.

Elliot Baldwin Platt, son of Joseph and Elizabeth, was born April 2, 1833.

Joseph E. Platt is the son of Richard Willis Platt and Abigail (Clark).

William Platt, son of William, born November 17, 1823, married Sarah Oviatt, daughter of Curtis; afterwards, Almira A. Hand, of Watertown.

Phineas Platt, son of William, born, February, 1833, married Jane Elmira Clark, daughter of Rogers. He has a brother Richard in New Haven.

———

Willis Platt, son of David, 1795, and grandson of Benjamin, says that his father left Milford about 1812, and located at Skaneateles, N. Y. His mother's maiden name was Betsey Higby. The children were : Charles, Harvey, Hannah, Eliza, Daniel, Martha (Reed), Abigail (Avery), Elizabeth, Isaac R., and Willis. Daniel, Elizabeth, Isaac and Willis only are living. Their home is in Skaneateles.

———

Rev. William H. Platt, D.D., of Petersburg, Va., is a son of Henry Jarvis Platt, who, born at New Bedford, Ct., married Sarah Dakin at Amenia, N. Y. They had six children. The son above, and his brother George Fisk Platt, of Crawford, Ga., are the only ones living. The former married Cornelia Cuthbert, of Mobile, Ala., but formerly of Georgia. Three children : Charles W., Horace G. and Edward C. Platt. A second marriage was to Emily Beverly Meade, of Petersburg, Va. Two children: Cornelia G. Kent, of New York, and John Meade of Anacortes, Washington. His present wife is Indiana Meade of Petersburg. One daughter, Mary Meade Platt. He received his degrees of D.D., and LL.D. from William and Mary College, Va. He was rector some years in San Francisco, Cal., a professor of legal ethics in Hastings Law College, Cal. He was rector of a church in Rochester, N. Y., for several years. He has written "Hand Book of Art Culture," "Influence of Religion in the Development of Jurisprudence," "Legal Ethics," "God Out and Man In," a reply to R. G. Ingersoll; "Is Religion Dying?" and the "Philosophy of the Supernatural," the Paddock Lectures in '86, before the General Theological Seminary, New York.

—George Fisk Platt, of Crawford, Ga., born in 1812, married Mary A. E. Smith of Georgia, November 1, 1836. He has one son only living, R. H. Platt, who makes his home in Atlanta, Ga.

The family of Henry Jarvis Platt, in full, is as follows: George Fisk, Ephraim Hamlin, Elizabeth H., William Henry, Edward, and Edwin. The grandfather of these was Ephraim Hamlin Platt, sen., of New Bedford, Ct. The ancestral line is not fully traced. "Fisk" is a name for the most part belonging to the Josiah stock, whilst the name "Jarvis" comes in the Fairfield branch from the older Huntington line of Isaac 1st, son of Richard 1st. The true line it is difficult to determine; the marriage in Sharon Branch may be a clue.

XI

YOUNGER MILFORD BRANCH.

JOSEPH.

HE is often called Lieut. Platt. Richard 1st left the homestead to Joseph, his youngest son, with a share of the arable and pasture lands to Josiah, next older. Joseph, baptized 1649, married Mary Kellog, of Norwalk, May 5, 1680; Joseph 2d, his son, born February 4, 1683, married Elizabeth Woodbury, January 19, 1702; (Sarah Platt, daughter of Joseph 2d, was born March 28, 1703); Epenetus Platt, 2d, son of Joseph 1st, was born May 7, 1696; Mary, daughter of Joseph 1st, was born May 6, 1704; Samuel Platt 1st, son of Joseph Platt 1st, was baptized September 7, 1690; "Samuel, son of Samuel Platt, was baptized March 17, 1723."

—Samuel Platt, jr., son of Samuel 1st, married Hannah Prudden, May 13, 1742. Issue: Hannah, born May 24, 1743; Samuel 3d, born October 22, 1744; Hester, born May 17, 1747; Mary, born January 29, 1749, and Gracie, born August 12, 1750. Samuel, it seems, was of the house and lineage of Joseph.

In the Milford records we read that "Joseph Platt, jr., and Mehetable Fenn were married June 16, 1720;" if this is Joseph 2d it is a second marriage. Their children were: Sarah, born September 4, 1721; and Joseph, born November 13, 1724. This is another record : " Joseph, son of Joseph Platt, was baptized May 13, 1711." This Joseph it is difficult to place ; it may be Joseph 3d ; possibly dying young he may have left his place and name to Joseph 3d, just mentioned, the son of Mehetable Platt.

The descendants of Joseph 1st, now resident in Milford, Ct., are : Nathan C. Platt, son of Clark, born April, 1828, married Virginia Brown, daughter of Horace ; also, Luke Platt, son of Clark, born 1833, married Ellen Cadwell, of Rome, N. Y.; Theodore, also son of Clark Platt, born November, 1837, married Marrietta Newton Driver, June 12, 1861.

Also, George E. Platt, son of William and Mary, born 1837, married Miss Wakely, then Nellie Merwin, daughter of Miles Merwin.

Henry C. Platt, of Milford, descends from Lieut. Joseph, the youngest of Richard's sons. This Joseph had a son Joseph, and his son Ebenezer, late in life married Hannah Green. These had, among others, a son Jonah who left eight children : Clark, William, Jonah, Charles, Maria, Aurelia, Eliza, and Mary ; of these there are now living only Jonah, in his 82d year, (who resides with his only son, Henry C. Platt,) and Mary, who married Jared Merwin, she surviving her husband. Her sister, Maria, married Isaac Treat, of Orange, who has eight children. Aurelia married Charles Merwin. Eliza married Abram Marks. Of the brothers Charles Platt left one son only, Howard B.; William Platt left two sons, George and Albert ; Clark, the eldest, left three sons, Nathan C., Luke, and Theodore Platt. These are still living. William Platt left two daughters : Catharine, deceased, and Laura, wife of Isaac C. Smith ; Clark left one daughter, Esther, who married William H. Cox.

H. C. Platt, above named, married Emma Treat, a direct descendant of Robert Treat, the celebrated Colonial Governor of Connecticut. His oldest son, Harrison Gray Platt, graduated from Yale in the class of '88. He taught a year in the Bishop Scott Academy at Portland, Oregon. He is now in the Yale Law School. The youngest son, Robert Treat Platt, graduated from Yale in the class of '89. He is now teaching in the Betts Academy, Stamford, Ct. Mr. H. C. Platt has a law office in New Haven, Ct. His residence is at Milford. He delivered an address at the 250th anniversary of the settlement of Milford, August 20, 1889.

Joseph 1st continues his line of descendants through the Gideon Branch, and through a portion of the Vermont record.

XII.

FAIRFIELD BRANCH.

—

This is an offshoot from the older Huntington stock. Obadiah Platt and his brother Timothy, sons of Jonas, the oldest son of Isaac 1st, crossed the sound and located at Fairfield, Ct. The name of Obadiah is mentioned in its records, about the year 1724, and he is described as from Huntington. According to the book of marriages (p. 109), Obadiah Platt and Mary Smith were joined in marriage August 10, 1722. Their children were: Abel Platt, born August 2, 1723; Sarah, born June 25, 1725; Jonas, born October 9, 1727, ancestor of Hon. O. H. Platt; Obadiah, born August 8, 1729, ancestor of Prof. Johnson T. Platt; Ann, born November 5, 1731; David, born September 15, 1734; Mary, born January 7, 1736, and Elizabeth, born May 10, 1737. Mary, wife of Obadiah 1st, died at Ridgefield, November 16, 1771. Abel lived in the parish of Redding, in the northerly part of Fairfield, and in Ridgefield, to which he removed about 1756. Tradition says he was taken prisoner during the Danbury raid, and carried to New York city, where he died.

Obadiah Platt, son of Obadiah and Mary, was born August 8, 1729, and died November 25, 1784. He resided in the parish of North Fairfield, and the house in which he lived is still standing, although somewhat altered. He first married Miss Treadwell but he had no issue; a second marriage was to Thankful Scudder, of Huntington, who was baptized there May 18, 1735. Miss Scudder's mother died when she was a year old and Thomas and Abigail Jarvis, of Huntington, brought her up. She died at Danbury 1816, in her 82d year. She was buried at Starr's Plain cemetery. Their children were: Jarvis, born 1759; Jesse, Obadiah, Alexander Smith, Sarah, who died in infancy, Eunice, Polly, and Abby. There is great probability that all who bear the name of Jarvis will be able to trace their ancestry in this line.

Jarvis Platt, son of Obadiah, of Fairfield, was born September, 1759, and died at Fayetteville, Va., in 1841; His wife was Annie Nichols, of Newtown, Ct. He lived for a time in St. Lawrence Co., N. Y., also in Newtown, Ct., and in Virginia. They had children: David, 1782-1814; Philo N., 1795-1871; Alexander Smith 1800-1826, unmarried. Sallie married E. Sanford, then A. Wilcox, (she was born 1780); Charlotte, who married Lemuel Sanford; and Abigail, who married Norman Tyler. David had two children: Philo Toussey and Alesia or Elosia.

Philo N. Platt, son of Jarvis, born January 11, 1795, married Paulina Edwards, November 30, 1811. Children: Eunice, 1818-1834; Albert G., 1820, married Jane Ross, May, 1856: Nicholas, born May 23, 1823, married Rhoda N., 1855; Paulina, born July 5, 1826, married J. C. McDaniels, May, 1853; and Eunice M., born March 31, 1832, married Flemming Huddleston, 1848, (the latter name not very legible)

Jesse Platt 1st, son of Jonas, lived at Huntington. His children were : Jesse 2d, who lived at Hempstead and died in 1769, (two children, Hannah and Mary); Isaac, who died 1772, and Zophar, born 1734, died March 27, 1811.

Isaac Platt, son of Jesse, married Esther Ketcham, Feb. 27, 1744–5. Their children were: Obadiah, Elizabeth, and Mary and Sarah (twins), Jesse and Isaac. The last was baptized June 14, 1754. He died Aug. 8, 1849.

—Obadiah Platt, son of Isaac above, married Mary Platt, daughter of Epenetus, 1769. He died Dec. 7, 1829, aged 84. She died June 7, 1825, in her 85th year.

—Jesse Platt, born 1762, second son of Obadiah, of Fairfield, and Thankful Scudder Platt, married Hannah Raymond, of Norwalk, Ct., settled at Weston, Ct., and left one child, Clarissa Platt, born Aug. 29, 1788, who married Judge David Munson, of Danbury, whose daughter, Caroline A. Munson, was the wife of Isaac A. Dusenberry, of Port Chester, N. Y.

—Obadiah Platt, third son of Obadiah of Fairfield, married Elizabeth Hawley, of Newtown, Ct. He lived at Ogdensburg, N. Y., and had children : Eunice, Mary, Elizabeth, Catharine, Samuel, Jesse, Jarvis, Obadiah, Smith and David M. Sherman Platt, of the Treasury Department, Washington, D. C., and Miss Bessie Platt, of Chicago, are descendants of this Obadiah Platt.

—Smith Platt, fourth son of Obadiah of Fairfield, settled at Galway, eight miles from Ballston, N. Y.; married Annie Wakeman, of Greenfield, Ct., and had children: Polly, Abby, Eliza, Wakeman, Jarvis and Obadiah H. Platt. The last two, dec., were ministers. Obadiah H., a lawyer, was some time in government service at Washington, D. C.

—Abigail Platt, youngest daughter of Obadiah, of Fairfield, married Peter Williams, of Weston, Ct., and removed to Ballston, N. Y. Her children were: Smith, Jonathan, Moses, Platt, Abby, Eunice and Clarissa Williams.

—Eunice, born July 9, 1767, married Isaac Platt, of Huntington, Oct. 18, 1787. She died without issue, Aug. 22, 1862, in her 96th year.

—Polly Platt, second daughter of Obadiah, of Fairfield, married Denny Hull, of Greens Farms, Conn., April, 1786, and had children Isaac P., Eunice, Denny and Polly Hull. She died October 9, 1850, in her 81st year.

It is stated that of the children of Obadiah Platt of Fairfield, David, Amos, and Jonas, died during the revolution. Amos and Jonas were taken prisoners by the British army, and confined in the old "Sugar House" prison, in consequence of which both died. David left a large farm at Ridgefield. He had one daughter and four sons, who all died just before or soon after their father's death, Sept. 19, 1776. The tradition is, that he visited the American camp at New York, where he contracted the "Camp distemper," so called. Returning home, the disease proved fatal to him and his children. Their names were John, David, Sarah and Nathan.

Timothy Platt, son of Jonas Platt, of Huntington, L. I., who came over with his brother Obadiah about 1723 or 4, settled in Fairfield, in the parish of Redding. In the book of marriages and births, in the town clerk's office, at Fairfield, this record appears (page 143): "Timothy Platt, son of Jonas Platt, and Margery Smith, daughter of John Smith, were married August 22, 1728." Timothy Platt, son of foregoing, was born June 26, 1729. Also, Hezekiah, born April 22, 1732; Abigail, born April 14, 1736; Anne, born August 26, 1739; Jesse, born July 4, 1741; and Zebulon, born Feb. 28, 1743. His will was dated Sept. 22, 1784, and in it he mentions his wife Rebekah (a second marriage, it seems), also his children Timothy, Hezekiah, Jesse, Zebulon, Abigail and Anne. Abigail married Nathaniel Hull, and Anne married Hezekiah Whitlock. Jesse and Zebulon were executors. Jonas, son of Isaac 1st and father of Timothy, was born August 10, 1667, Huntington, L. I.

Six persons of the name of Platt signed the Redding Association, Conn. (to uphold the Continental Congress), viz.: Abel, Joseph and Josiah, of Fairfield Co.; Obadiah, of Fairfield, and Isaac, Hezekiah, and Timothy, of Redding.

Zebulon Platt died July 23, 1816, aged 72. Phebe, his wife, died Jan. 30, 1790, in the 39th year of her age. Elizabeth, his second wife, died March 14, 1811, aged 59.

In the Fairfield land records there are nearly thirty transfers of land to and from those of the name of Platt—Obadiah, Timothy, Abel, Hezekiah, Jonah, and several others.

Charles H. Platt, son of Allen, born at Stepney, Ct., May 30, 1850, is a descendant of Timothy, the brother of Obadiah. His grandfather was James, of Redding, Ct. His great-grandfather was also a James, the son of Zebulon Platt, son of Timothy 2d. The family after the burning of Danbury removed to New Fairfield, Ct. Zebulon Platt lived at one time at Lonetown, west of Danbury and Bridgeport turnpike. James 1st had two sisters, Margaret and Martha. His children were eight: Joseph, 1794; James 2d, born 1800; David Montgomery, 1808; and Abel, 1814; Hulda, 1812; Betsey, 1801; and Deborah, 1803. Joseph, the oldest, died in 1841, David died at Buffalo, Montgomery at New Fairfield. James 2d, died at Bethel, Ct. C. H. Platt, grandson of James, has been a railroad manager many years. He is now General Manager at the Grand Central Station, New York. He married Emma J. Burritt, of Southington, Ct., in 1870. He has a son Allen Hemingway, who was born at Fishkill, N. Y., Feb. 11, 1885. He gives the following data:

The children of James 1st were all born at New Fairfield, Ct., he having removed to that place with his father Zebulon in 1791. The house the family occupied is still standing.

Joseph Platt 1st, eldest son of James 1st, married Lydia Mirick, at New Lisbon, N. Y., March 21, 1824. She died September 14, the following year. A second marriage was to Olive Earl, May 10, 1826. She died November 24, 1881. Joseph died at Hamburg, N. Y., May 11, 1841. Their children were

Charles M. Platt, son of Lydia, born March 4, 1825, died January 23, 1875 ; Lydia M., daughter of Olive, born March 9, 1827 ; William C., son of same, born at Vernon, N. Y., September 21, 1828 ; Horace J., born January 14, 1830, died March 28, 1832 ; Francis M., October 30, 1831, died March 11, 1832 ; Horace J., born at Hamburg, N. Y., March 1, 1833 ; David W., 1835, died 1837 ; Sarah A., born December 11, 1836 ; and Francis H., born January 3, 1840, died August 17, 1865.

—Charley M., oldest son of Joseph, born 1825, married Asenath A. Dayton, at Eden, Nov. 9, 1847. Their children were : John D., born March 30, 1851; Frank L., 1852 ; M. Louise, Nov. 13, 1854; Nettie D., Feb. 18, 1856 ; and Lewis D., May 29, 1859. Of these John D. died Sep. 4, 1852 ; M. Louise married Frank L. Barnet, attorney at Hamburg, N. Y., Sept. 8, 1881 ; Lewis D. married Anne A. Hawthorne, at Alden, N. Y., Oct. 18, 1887.

—Wm. C. Platt, second son, married Julia E. Dart, July 3, 1852. Their children were : Ward D., born April 21, 1853 ; Ida M., April 19, 1855; Carrie F., April 9, 1859. Of these Ward married Mary J. Barnard, of Buffalo, July 9, '78 ; (one child, Mary born May 1, 1888, died 12th of same month.) Ida M. married Adelbert Robert, of Evans, April 29, 1875, and Carrie F. married Oct. 26, 1887, G. C. Hardesty, President of Bank of Angelica, N. Y. Ward D. Platt is a clergyman at Hornellsville, N. Y.

Ida M. and Adelbert Roberts have two children : Olive Daisy and Grace Henrietta.

—Horace J., third son, married Pamelia F. Church

Oct. 10, 1867. Their children are : Clarence W., born May 16, 1870; Eva M., Oct. 5, 1878 ; and George Asa, Feb. 6, 1881.

—Lydia M., oldest daughter of Joseph Platt, married Dr. L. R. Leach, Hamburg, September 5, 1858. Their children are : Willis R., Frank P., Frederic, and Joseph E. Frank P. is a clergyman.

—Sarah A., second daughter, married Myron Walker, at Hamburg, December 10, 1885.

James 2d, second son of James Platt 1st, married Mary Jacobs. November 25, 1818. Their children were : Orrin, born October 27, 1819 ; Silas B., born April 22, 1821; Allen, January 15, 1823 ; Sarah, August 12, 1825 ; Hulda J., June 7, 1831 ; Lorintha, May 12, 1833 ; William H. and Sylvester, born March 27, 1840. Of these Orrin married Betsey Purdy; they had one daughter, Lydia, who married Henry Fairchild. Betsey P. died at Stepney depot, 1863. Her husband married again, and he is living at Stepney. Silas B. died at Macedon, leaving one unmarried son, James, who was born February, 1845. Allen married Harriet Hemingway, October 9, 1844. He died at Stepney August 30, 1863. She died at Shelton, Ct., April 7, 1890. Their children born at Stepney were : Theodore F., born January 4, 1846 ; Charles H., born May 30, 1850 ; Mary E., born July 3, 1855 ; and Ella J., May 1, 1862. Of these, Theodore married H. Augusta Bristol, November 15, 1866; Charles H., married E. J. Burritt, of Southington, June 8, 1870—one son, Allen H. Mary married J. C. Fields, September, 26, 1876 ;

two children, Hattie and Julia; the mother died December 20, 1889. Ella married Dr. J. D. Patterson, of Brooklyn, L. I., January 20, 1885; one son, Theodore.

Sarah Platt, oldest daughter of James 2d, married Charles Fowler, now living at Mill Plain, Ct.; two children, Frank and Emma. Hulda married Rev. W. H. Stebbins; she survives her husband. Lorintha, her sister, married Edwin Whaley, now living at Danbury; two children, Chester and Alice. Of the youngest sons of James 2d, Sylvester died when a soldier in the Union army, unmarried. His brother William Henry married Mary J. Taylor, of Redding, now living at Bethel, Ct.; one son, George, born July 4, 1866, who has one daughter, Grace, born January 6, 1889.

Betsey, Deborah and Montgomery, children of James Platt, 1st, remained permanently at New Fairfield, Conn. The first married Ethal Wheeler: Debora, married Nelson Porter; and Montgomery, married Lucy Whaley, Dec. 19, 1832. The latter has three sons: Lorenzo D., Edward C., and Lafayette W.

Hulda, the youngest daughter of James 1st, married Leander Beers. She is now a widow, living at Danbury, Conn. Two children living: Clark and Emma.

Abel, the youngest son of James 1st, married Phebe Porter, of Buffalo, N. Y., in 1835. He died at Dixon, Ill., Jan. 13, 1877. Their children were: Julius A., born May 28, 1836; Homer, Dec. 4, 1837; Charlotte, Dec. 1, 1838; Jerome, May 2, 1847; and

Imogene, born Feb. 9, 1858. Of these Julius married Hannah S. McDonald, Jan. 9, 1868. Their children were: Albert D., born Feb. 24, 1869 ; Ada May and Charles J., born April 20, 1872. Homer died Aug. 17, 1839. Charlotte M. married Elias A. Miller, at Dixon, Ill., Dec. 28, 1864. They have one child Anna, born in 1866. Jerome married Carrie L. Hutchings, at Chicago, Ill., Dec. 18, 1872.

Miss Bessie Platt, of Chicago, Ill., gives these data: Her grandfather, Obadiah H. Platt, married Elizabeth Hawley. Jesse Platt, his oldest son, was her father. Her uncle is Jarvis E. Platt, living in Manitowoc, Wis. Her brother, Jarvis H. Platt, is of Lisbon, N. Y. A cousin, O. H. Platt, a lawyer, lives in Hyde Park, Ill. A part of the year he resides in Tampa, Florida. His brother was the Rev. Wakeman Platt, formerly of New York city. The latter has several daughters. One is a teacher in the musical conservatory in Dubuque, Iowa; one married a Mr. Boardman, a lumber merchant, who has an island near Mackinaw, stocked with blooded horses. Miss Bessie Platt says: A short time ago thirteen cousins visited me. They were from Trumansburg, St. Louis and New York City. At a wedding in Chicago I met a Mr. Henry Platt, of St. Louis. My father's cousin Philo moved to Virginia. I have an Aunt Eunice living in Lisbon, N. Y., quite aged, who at one time lived on Long Island with her uncle Isaac Platt, whose wife was named Eunice. My father's brother, O. H. Platt, died in Lisbon nearly a year since. I have a cousin, Sherman Platt, living in Washington, D. C.; he has been in the Treasury Department ever since the war. He married Miss Emma Carpenter, who was a daughter of my father's sister Catherine. I have also a cousin in Manitowoc, Mrs. Joseph Vilas, daughter of my father's brother, M. S. Platt. Our family originally settled in Fairfield Co., Ct. I have a sister, Mrs. Dr. J. P. Webb, who lives in Oakland, Cal.; another, Mrs. Dr. MacRae, living in San Francisco. I have a nephew, L. C. Collins, in Collins, Tex. I have always understood that the name of Jarvis became a family name in this way : "My great-great-grandmother was Thankful Scudder. She was left an orphan very young, and went and lived with a relative whose name was Jarvis. She not liking her Puritan name, took the name of Fannie Jarvis."—From a letter to Prof. J. T. Platt, of New-Haven.

Philo R. Platt, son of Albert J., was born in Fayetteville, W. Va., in 1856. He lived there nearly thirty years. In 1885 he removed to Moundsville, W. Va., and in 1887 married Jennie Israel, of the latter place, where he now resides.

XIII.

REDDING BRANCH.

THIS is not fully traced. The first name is that of Isaac Platt, located in the northern part of the town. The Redding town records give these data : Isaac Platt's children : Philip Picket Platt, born February 13, 1766 ; Sally, May 19, 1767 ; Huldah, November 12, 1769 ; Rhoda, June 8, 1772 ; Mary, June 5, 1775 ; David, born April 3. 1784, died November 27, 1784. The burial place of this family is Starr's Plain in the southern part of Danbury. The following inscriptions were copied from the stones in the cemetery there : "Issac Platt died March 5, 1830 in his 88th year." "Mercy, wife of Isaac Platt, died May 5, 1827, aged 84." "Philip P. Platt died July 25, 1840, 74 years." "Elizabeth, wife of Philip P. Platt, died July 1, 1847, aged 81." "David Platt, died July 1, 1855, aged 63 years and 5 months." "Elizabeth, wife of David Platt, died March 28, 1876, aged 82 years and 14 days." David was a son of Philip P. Platt. The present representative of the family is Henry Burr Platt, as singularly one male member only has perpetuated the name. He told Prof. J. T. Platt that they were related to a Mr. Samuel Platt. The Redding records show that Samuel Platt and Abigail Hall were married October 17, 1770. The will of the above Isaac Platt, dated August 23, 1814, proved at Danbury March 22, 1830, mentions his wife Mercy, his children : Philip Pickett Platt, Sally Rusco, Huldah, widow of Ezra Bates ; Rhoda, wife of Solomon Warren ; and Mercy, wife of Cornelius Hull. On page 241 of Vol. II, Fairfield land records, is recorded a deed from Samuel Gold to Josiah Platt, of land in the Parish of Redding, north of Starr's Ridge, dated April 8, 1754. It is quite possible that this Josiah Platt was the ancestor of Isaac Platt above, and if Josiah died before 1782, his estate would have been settled at Fairfield. These facts were sent to the writer by the late Prof. J. T. Platt.

XIV.

PLATTSBURG BRANCH.

This traces its origin to the younger Huntington branch of Epenetus 1st, Long Island. Zephaniah, Charles, Nathaniel and Daniel, sons of Zephaniah, of Long Island, were the first settlers and proprietors at Plattsburg, N. Y. Having purchased, soon after the Revolutionary war, a number of military land warrants, they located them on Cumberland Bay, on the northwestern shores of Lake Champlain, Clinton Co., N. Y. They in person surveyed and marked out the patent in 1784. To induce a rapid settlement a hundred acres were offered to each of the first ten settlers who should come on, bringing their families with them, and a hundred acres also as a donation to the first male child born on the patent. It is now a large and flourishing township, with a population of nearly 10,000.

1. Zephaniah Platt, the oldest of the brothers who settled Plattsburg, was born in Huntington, L. I., May 27, 1735. He purchased a farm at Po'keepsie about the year 1764. There is an incident occurring near 1775, which marks his love of right and his sterling patriotism. When the first open revolt against the English rule began to manifest itself, at an inn east of Po'keepsie just beyond

the turnpike, the people had erected "a liberty pole." The Sheriff, who represented the King's authority, with his deputies and constables came and cut it down. A sharp altercation took place between the Sheriff and Zephaniah Platt, one of the leaders, during which the Sheriff accused him of treason and threatened to arrest him. Mr. Platt seized a club and said he would defend himself if he touched him. The Sheriff drew his sword, but was persuaded to withdraw and leave the patriots unmolested. The incident created much excitement. After the Revolution was in full progress Zephaniah Platt became an active and prominent man in Duchess County. He at once reached the position of a trusted leader. He was a delegate to the Provincial Congress, also to the Congress under the old confederation. He was elected a member of the New York Convention of 1776, for framing a Constitution for the State. In 1777 he was one of the Committee of Safety, with John Jay as a colleague, for Duchess County. In 1778 he was elected a State Senator. He was one of the seven delegates from Duchess County to deliberate respecting the acceptance of the Constitution of the United States. He with De Witt, Gilbert Livingston and Melancthon Smith voted for its adoption. There were thirty votes in favor and twenty-seven against it. Their votes thus secured its ratification. He was made first Judge of the Court in Duchess County soon after the court was organized, which position he held till 1795. He was also a Regent of the University of the State.

Thus his positions and honors show that he ranked as an able and efficient leader in his day. He married Hannah Davis, and had a son Zephaniah and a daughter Hannah, who married Peter Comstock. She left five children: Zephaniah, Platt, Hannah, Daniel and Sarah Comstock. Zephaniah Platt 2d, in this branch 2d, married Bertha Ward, and left six children: Mary, Elizabeth, Anne, Jeremiah, Daniel and Harvey Platt. A second marriage of Zephaniah, (1st in this branch) was to Mary, a daughter of Theodorus Van Wyke, of Fishkill-on-Hudson. Their children, all born in Po'keepsie, were twelve in number: Theodorus, Elizabeth, Mary, Jonas, William Pitt, Charles, Nathaniel, Robert, Mary 2d, Levi, David and James. Among the closing works of an active life was the founding of Plattsburg. Here he died September 12, 1807. His wife, Mary Van Wyke, died 1809, at the age of 66. She may well be regarded as "a mother in Israel." Her remains are in the family tomb at Plattsburg.

—Theodorus Platt, the eldest, was born March 23, 1763. He married Charity, daughter of Henry Peltze. Issue: Elizabeth, who married Thomas Green, of Plattsburg; Henry, who married Charlotte Elmon; Mary, who married Heman Cady; and Charles T., who married Eliza Walworth. There were four other children, who died in infancy or under 20 years of age. A second marriage was to Julia Sailley; issue, a daughter, who married George Marsh, of Plattsburg. Theodorus Platt was the first Surrogate of Clinton County, 1788.

Charles T. Platt, son of Theodorus Platt, was appointed a midshipman in the United States Navy, June 18, 1812. In 1817 he was ordered to the "Hornet." .He was promoted to lieutenant, March 28. 1820. He was on the " Guerierre " and then on the "Shark." He was on duty with Commodore Porter on the "Beagle"; then on the "Java," and afterward on the "St. Louis." In 1838, he was on the lighthouse service. September 8, 1841, he was promoted to commander. From October 15, 1850, he was two years in command of the "Albany." His last service was in charge of the navy yard at Memphis, on the Mississippi. He died at Newburg, N. Y., December 13, 1860.

The record given above is from the Navy Department in Washington, D. C. He married Eliza Walworth, sister of the Chancellor. They had three children : Charles Henry, Sarah Walworth and Eliza Platt. Charles Henry Platt, his only son, graduated from Hobart College in the class of '39. He delivered the Master's oration at the Hobart commencement in 1842. He was rector of the Episcopal Church in Lockport for some years, then at Binghampton, N. Y., five years. He was chaplain of the 28th New York Vols., from July 4, 1861, to September 13, 1862, resigning on account of failing health. He died in Binghampton, February 24, 1869. He ranked as a fine scholar in college and showed decided ability in his pulpit and parish duties. He was a member of the Alpha Delta Phi fraternity. He married Mary Louisa Jackson, of Lockport, N. Y. One daughter, Mary Walworth, who married C. N. Webster, of Binghampton, N. Y. She is now Mrs. F. S. Peabody, and is residing in Chicago, Ill. By her father's second marriage there were three daughters. The eldest is Mrs. W. B. McLaughlin, of Austin; her husband is a physician. The youngest is the wife of James V. Campbell, son of Judge Campbell, of Detroit, Mich. The second daughter is not married. The widow, Mrs. Emma T. Platt, resides in Lyons, N. Y.

The writer of this was in college with Charles Henry Platt, and he is very glad to speak good words in remembrance of his faithful fellow-student.

—Elizabeth Platt, oldest daughter of Zephaniah Platt 1st, married Gen. John Smith, of Mastic, L. I. No issue.

—Mary Platt, second daughter, married Abraham Brinkerhoff, of New York. She died in 1812. James Augustus Platt, her nephew, has a well-preserved oil portrait of her at his daughter's, Mrs. J. Morton Brown, of Norristown, Pa. Her children were: Abraham, who died aged 32; Mary; Peter, who married Maria Lawrence, of New York; Dorothea and Charles Brinkerhoff.

—Jonas Platt, the second son of Judge Zephaniah, heads the Judge Jonas Branch.

—William Pitt Platt, third son, a large landowner on Lake Champlain, born April 30, 1771; married Hannah, daughter of Moss Kent, and a sister of Chancellor Kent. They had six children: James Kent, Zephaniah, Mary, William, Elizabeth, and Moss Kent Platt. 1. James Kent Platt was a graduate of Middlebury College, Vt.; studied medicine, and was a Professor in the medical department of Burlington College, Vt. He died April 4, 1824. His two children died young. His wife died in Philadelphia, 1883, aged 82. 2. Zephaniah Platt, second son, born August 12, 1794, married Lucretia, daughter of Thomas Miller. Two children : Elizabeth, who died young, and Mary, who married James Westcott, then Edmund Hathaway. No issue. 3. Mary Platt, born July 15, 1796, married Benjamin J. Movers, December 30, 1813. A lady of marked ability and cultured taste. She died April 8, 1869. They left ten children : Eliza, Susan, Hannah Maria, Wm. Platt, Mary, John Henry, Moss Kent, Benjamin, Sophia, and Robert Platt Movers. 4. William, born February 25, 1799, died aged 30. 5. Elizabeth Platt, born May 15, 1806, married May 29, 1824, Henry Ketchum Averill. She died aged 35. Chancellor Kent says of her in writing to his mother (his sister) : "She was a woman of strong mind, and of strong feelings, and of great energy and decision of character." They had three children : James Kent, Henry Ketchum, and Mary Elizabeth Averill. 6. Moss Kent Platt, born May 3, 1809, was a State Senator, a Republican Presidential Elector, 1868 ; in '72, Inspector of State Prisons, an elder in the Presbyterian Church. He married, October 14, 1830, Elizabeth Freligh ; a second marriage was to her half sister, Margaret Freligh. He had five children : Hannah K., Lucy, John F., Sarah E., and Margaret F. 1. Hannah Kent, born October 27, 1832, married September 26, 1853, Joseph M. Myers. They had one child, Elizabeth. 2. Lucy M., born May 15,

1835, married Lemuel Stetson, a lawyer in Plattsburg, November 27, 1856. He was killed in the battle of Antietam, while in command as Lieutenant-Colonel. 3. John F. Platt, died a senior in college, 1858, in his 21st year. 4. Sarah E. born October 6, 1839, married William A. Fuller. Three children survive: Margaret Platt, Moss Kent Platt, and Elizabeth. 5. Margaret F. Platt, born November 30, '43, married 1866, Michael P. Myers, now living in Plattsburg. No issue.

—Charles Z. Platt, fourth son of Judge Zephaniah, born July 22, 1773, married Sarah, daughter of James Bleeker, of Albany. Their children were: Hetty, Bleeker, Van Zant, Mary Platt, Charles Edward, Joseph, Robert, and Rachel. Hetty Platt married Dr. Peter Staats, of Albany. Nine children: Sarah, Elizabeth, Charles, Edward D., Bleeker, Mary, Platt, Ettie, and Edward. Bleeker Platt married Ellen Jerolomon. Three children: Charles Platt, Lansing, and Bleeker. Mary Platt, daughter of Charles Z., married James Wilder. Three children: Bleeker, Hettie and Josephine Wilder.

—Nathaniel Z., fifth son of Zephaniah, of Po'keepsie, born December 16, 1775, died 1820. He was a member of the State Assembly for Clinton County, 1807. He married Sarah Keyes, 1802. Six children: Elizabeth, Mary Van Wyck, Theodorus, Stephen, Samuel Keyes, and William Platt. Of these Elizabeth married Captain Samuel Russell, U. S. A. A second marriage was to Frederick C. Sailly. Mary Van Wyck married General C. A. Waite, U. S. A. Theodorus married Marietta Nichols. Stephen and William died young. Samuel married Sarah J. Cady first, then Lydia Mount. He is living in Plattsburg,—the only one surviving of his father's family.

William Nichols Platt, M.D., a son of the late Theodorus and Marietta Platt, of Plattsburg, married November 23, 1880, Elizabeth L. Jones, of Shoreham, Vt. This is the place of his residence.

Henry Russell Platt, M.D., of Rutland, Vt., is also son of Theodorus. He was born March 4, 1866. He is unmarried.

—Robert Platt, sixth son of Zephaniah, owned nearly a thousand acres of land on Cumberland Head, near Plattsburg. He gave about 200 acres to his brother, Judge Jonas Platt, on condition that he should reside there after retiring from the practice of law. He was a member of Assembly for 1814-15. He married Mary, daughter of Nathaniel Dagget, of New Haven. No children.

—Levi Platt, seventh son of Zephaniah, born in Po'keepsie, April 17, 1782, died March 31, 1849. He married Eliza H. Miller, January 1, 1834. They had twelve children : David, who died young ; Margaret, Mary, John M., Robert, who died in infancy; Helen, Levi, Jonas, Susan H., James, Peter M., and William Pitt, twins. Margaret married Cyrus Cady; Mary married James B. Campbell, then John Morgan. Helen married J. Douglas Woodward. Jonas married Isabella Morris, then Mary Eames. Susan H. married James Bailey ; Mrs. Bailey resides in Plattsburg. Peter M. married Charlotte Morgan. William Pitt married Jane McNiel, then Mrs. Mary Hammond. The father, Levi Platt, was many years

Judge of Clinton County. He was eight years postmaster of Plattsburg. His son, Levi 2d, following his father, was postmaster nearly twenty years.

—David Platt, next to the youngest, was born June 6, 1784; died May 30, 1805.

—James Platt, the youngest son of Judge Zephaniah Platt, of Po'keepsie, heads the Oswego branch.

---

2. Nathaniel Platt, the second of the brothers of Plattsburg, a son of Zephaniah, of Long Island, was born in 1741. He married Phebe, daughter of Richard Smith, of Smithtown, L. I., November 10, 1766. At the breaking out of the Revolution, he, Nathaniel Platt, is credited with having raised the first company of troops on the island. He was attached to General Woodhull's brigade in the battle of Long Island. He was very active as a partisan officer in preventing Tory risings in Suffolk County, until finally the garrisoning of Setauket and other places, and the arrival of the British fleet in Lloyd's harbor, obliged him and many others to cross the sound into Connecticut. He was afterwards transferred to the commissary department, and was quite efficient in getting both supplies and recruits for Washington's army on the line of the Hudson River. His sword, bearing the name of "Nathaniel Platt, 1776," is in the possession of his grandson, N. P. Bailey, Esq., of New York. Captain Platt died at Plattsburg, 1816. His children were: George W., Isaac S., Hannah, Phebe, and Maria Platt.

—Isaac S., second son of Nathaniel Platt, married Dorothy daughter of Richard Smith, and had issue:

Sarah A. Platt, who married Rear Admiral Theodorus Bailey.

—Hannah Platt, oldest daughter of Nathaniel, married Gen. Benjamin Movers, distinguished in the Revolution as major and adjutant of General Haven's brigade, and in the war of 1812, as general commanding the militia forces at the battle of Plattsburg, September 11, 1814. Their children were: Benjamin, Charles, Charlotte and Ann Movers.

—Phebe Platt, second daughter of Nathaniel, married Judge Wm. Bailey, and had issue Phebe A. Theodorus, John W., Nathaniel P., James Q., Henry and Mary Bailey.

—Maria Platt, youngest child of Nathaniel, married Albon Man, M.D., having issue Albon P., Susan Maria (two by this name), Hannah Maria and Phebe Alida. A second marriage was to Rev. Theodoric Halsey, leaving one daughter, Letitia. A third marriage was to Isaac B. Platt, of Plattsburg.

Phebe A. Bailey, eldest daughter of Phebe Platt and the Judge, born 1799, married Capt. Sidney Smith, U. S. Navy. Issue, William Sidney, Margaret and Catherine. A second marriage was to Asa Mascall, of Malone. Bailey and Theodorus B. are his children.

Admiral Theodorus Bailey, son of Phebe Platt and Judge B., born at Chatauugay, N. Y., April 12, 1805, entered the navy as midshipman, Jan. 1, 1818; became captain 1855, commander 1865, and rear-admiral 1866. He was engaged in the capture of slaves on the African coast, 1820–1; twice sailed around the world on the Vincennes in 1833-36 ; and again on the Constellation. He served on the west coast of Mexico in the Mexican War; in 1861-2, commanded the Colorado in the gulf-blockading squadron. He commanded the van division of Farragut's fleet, having left his own frigate—the Colorado, which was unable to cross the Mississippi bar—and hoisted his flag on the Cayuga, April 24, 1862; he "led up the river past Forts Jackson and St. Phillip, brushing away and destroying the enemy's fleet, capturing with his flag-gunboat three of the rebels' steamers as well as the Chalmette regiment of infantry, and the next day, the 25th, was sent by Farragut to land and pass through a hostile population, to demand the surrender of New Orleans, which he did successfully." He afterwards commanded the East Gulf blockading squadron, capturing 156 prizes, large and small vessels, entirely stopping the rebel commerce on the station guarded by his squadron. He afterwards served in command of Portsmouth naval station, N. H. He married Sarah A., daughter of Isaac S. Platt, June, 1831. Issue: Annie B. (who married Walter R. T. Jones), Theodora, Sarah R., Margaret S. and Edmund S. The admiral died Dec. 10, 1877, leaving an honorable name in the annals of his country.

—John W. Bailey, born 1807, son of Phebe Platt and William Bailey, married Emily Thurber. Issue: Thurber, William, Robert and Phebe (who married C. J. Ames.) Nathaniel P., son of William and Phebe Bailey, married Eliza M., daughter of Jacob Lorillard, of New York. Issue : Mary, James M. and Lorillard. Of the children of Marie Platt by her first husband, Dr. Albon Man, Albon Platt Man, a lawyer in New York, married Mary Louise Brower, of Wilkes Barre, Pa. Issue: William, Frederick Halsey, Albon Platt, Jr., and Laura Gardiner, deceased. A second marriage was to Mary Elizabeth, daughter of Alrick Hubbell, of Utica; he had issue Mary, Alrick Hubbell, Edward, Mary, Gertrude and Arthur Man. Alrick H. Man is a lawyer in Wall Street, New York.

Susan Marie Man, daughter of Albon Man, M.D., of Plattsburg, married March 21, 1838, the Hon. Hugh McCulloch, secretary of the treasury under Presidents Lincoln and Johnson. They celebrated their golden wedding in 1888 at their home in Washington, D. C. Her grandfather on her mother's side was Nathaniel Platt, of the Army of the Revolution. Her grandfather on her father's side was Dr. Ebenezer Man, brigade surgeon at the battles of Monmouth and Yorktown; both holding commissions from Washington. Her children are Charles Hawkins, born September 3, 1840; Fred. Halsey, born May 22, 1842; Louise, born January 18, 1856; and Marie Stewart, born January 19, 1867. Charles H. McCulloch married Sadie Ross, of Vincennes, Ind., May, 1865. Their children are John Ross, born November 15, 1869 (a banker at Fort Wayne), and Fred. Halsey, born July, 1885. Fred. H. McCulloch married Carrie Riddle, of Cincinnati, April, 1867. Children: Hugh McCulloch, born March 9, 1869 (at Harvard in the class of '91); Charles, born June 7, 1873, and Lilly, 1879. Louise McCulloch married J. B. Yale, June 3, 1884. Mrs. McCulloch has an excellent portrait of her grandmother, Phebe Platt, at her home in Washington.

———

3. Charles Platt, the third of the Plattsburg brothers, was appointed a Judge on the organization of Clinton County, and he held the first court in 1780. He held office till he was sixty, the constitutional limit. He had been educated as a physician in Paris. He practiced medicine in Plattsburg for many years, gratuitously among the poor. He was upwards of a year in the army under Washington. He was born in 1744, and lived to the venerable age of 87. He married in 1772 Caroline Adriance, of Fishkill. Their children were three daughters and five sons : Margaret, Letitia, Hannah, Zephaniah, Isaac C., Charles C., Nathaniel, and Nathaniel 2d. Margaret, born 1793, married N. H. Treadwell, in 1813 ; she died April 8, 1859. Letitia married Rev. Frederic Halsey in 1798. Hannah married Eliezer Miller.

—Isaac C. Platt, second son, born April 11, 1781, died aged 91. He was offered his father's judgeship but declined. He married Anne Treadwell, January 13, 1802. She died 19 years after. He married Nancy Bristol, January 20, 1823. A third marriage was to Mrs. Maria Platt Halsey, October, 1848. His children by his first wife were : Anne Treadwell, born November 10, 1803 ; Zephaniah C., born July 30, 1805 ; and Caroline Adriance, born July 1, 1807. Anne Treadwell Platt married Dr. Lyman Foote, U. S. A. They had seven children. Zephaniah C. Platt married Anna Eliza Miller, January 14, 1829. Their children reaching mature years, were : Ann Elizabeth, Caroline, John Diell, and Mary Platt. Caroline A. Platt, daughter of Isaac C., married Rev. John Diell, eight years Seaman's Chaplain at Honolulu, Sandwich Islands. He died at sea, homeward bound, January 19, 1841. They had four children : Anna M., Eliza G., Mary (now Mrs. Spear), and Caroline Platt Diell. Mrs. John Diell's home is in Hamilton, N. Y., with her son-in-law, Rev. P. B. Spear, D.D.

Caroline Platt Diell married James M. Armistead, of Richmond, Va.; both deceased. Their children were : Maria Terese, Caroline A., Annie D., and William Johnson Armistead. Her sister Anna married Charles Rathbun, of Buffalo. Eliza G. Diell, married F. R. Blanton, of Farmville, Va. The Armisteads reside in Richmond, Va.

Mrs. Carrie Platt Thompson, widow of the late Judge John Thompson, of Po'keepsie, is a granddaughter of Rev. Frederic Halsey, whose wife was Letitia, daughter of Judge Charles Platt, of Plattsburg.

—Zephaniah C., oldest son of Judge Charles Platt, died of yellow fever in 1805, at St. Thomas, W. I.

—Charles C., second son, married Eliza Ross. He died in 1809, leaving two daughters, Caroline and Elizabeth. The latter was Mrs. B. Shumway. She had six children.

—Nathaniel, youngest son of Judge Charles Platt, married Maria Nase, 1814. One son. A second marriage was to Pamela Grant. Four children. He died 1854.

Samuel, son of Nathaniel, and grandson of Judge Charles Platt, is now living in Plattsburg.

Zephaniah C. Platt, son of Isaac C., had a son John Diell Platt, who married Susan D. Phelps, October 1, 1867. Their children were: Anna Mary, Zephaniah C., William Phelps, and James P. Platt.

---

4. Daniel, the fourth of the Plattsburg brothers married Charlotte Graham, of New York. They had four children: Maria, Daniel, Jeremiah, and Charlotte Platt. Maria married Jovette Thompson, of Troy, N. Y. Daniel and Jeremiah died at Plattsburg, unmarried. Charlotte married Wells Cliff, of New York. She died a few years since. Neither of the daughters had children.

XV

JUDGE JONAS BRANCH.

JONAS PLATT, second son of Judge Zephaniah Platt, and Mary Van Wyke, was born in Po'keepsie, N. Y., June 30, 1769. After he had finished his preparatory studies at a French academy in Montreal, he entered the law office of Richard Varick, in New York, and under his able guidance prosecuted his legal studies. He was admitted to the bar in 1790. The same year he married Helen, the youngest daughter of Henry Livingston, of Po'keepsie, a sister of Dr. John H. Livingston, President of Rutgers College, N. J. Soon afterwards he was made clerk of Herkimer County. He made his home in Whitesboro', near Utica, in 1791. Oneida was set off as a county in 1798, and he was made the first county clerk. He had previously, in 1796, represented this district and Onondaga in the Legislature at Albany. He was General of Cavalry in the State militia. He was two years a member of Congress, from 1799. He was four years in the State Senate, from 1809. In 1814 he was made Judge of the Supreme Court, with Judges Kent and Spencer as associates. He filled this high office with distinguished ability upwards of eight years. He was a member of the Convention which framed the State Constitution of 1821. Under its amended provisions he lost his judicial position. He returned to the practice of his profession, and opened a law office with his oldest son, Zephaniah, at Utica. In three or four years he removed to New York, where he prosecuted his profession with assiduity and success. But warned by coming infirmity, he retired in 1829, to his farm, seven miles from Plattsburg, on the shores of Lake Champlain. It should be recorded that in 1810, he was the popular candidate of his party for the governorship of the State, and though beaten by his opponent, Daniel D. Tompkins, he made a well-contested canvass. It should be stated, too, that he was the earliest of the promoters of the Erie Canal enterprise. When Thomas Eddy applied to him as a leader in his party, for his influence to authorize the building of a canal from Oneida Lake to the Seneca River, he said: No; a canal should be constructed from Lake Erie to the Hudson. The Senator persuaded him that this was the true plan. At Mr. Platt's suggestion they invited to their counsels De Witt Clinton, a prominent leader of the democracy. He approved the project. Senator Platt then moved the first resolution, preparatory to building it, which was seconded in the Senate by Clinton; and this was finally passed by both houses of the legislature. Renwick, the biographer of De Witt Clinton, says of Judge Platt, " he was well entitled to the merit of having made the

first efficacious step towards the attainment of the
great object of uniting the lakes with the Atlantic."
His honors and his public positions show how he
was appreciated, as a man, a jurist and a statesman.
He had a well-trained intellect, a well-stored mind
and a well-balanced character. A strict regard for
what was just, eminently distinguished him. His
life, public and private, is without spot, and his distinguished career still sheds honor upon those who
bear his name, and those who are numbered among
his kindred. He died at his home near Plattsburg,
February 22, 1834, in his 65th year. Helen Livingston his wife, died at the residence of her son Zephaniah, at Yonkers, N. Y., April 8, 1859, aged 93.
Most of these facts are derived from Dr. M. M.
Bagg's "Pioneers of Utica."

It is with reference to Judge Jonas Platt and
his father's family that the N. Y. Genealogical Record justly says: "Few families have furnished so
many distinguished names, and all in close proximi-
ty to each other, to the civil service of the State."
Every one of the nine sons of Judge Zephaniah
Platt and Mary Van Wyck, with one exception, held
prominent positions in public life.

Mrs. Bayard Boyd, née Manetta Lansing, has very
valuable portraits of Judge Jonas Platt, and his
wife Helen Livingston, painted shortly after their
marriage. Another one of the Judge, painted later
by Trumbull, is in the possession of her sister,
Mrs. Judge Willard. These paintings are at the
residences of the grand-daughters in Washington, D.
C. There is an interesting incident about the last

portrait. Trumbull's wife was an English lady, and he petitioned the New York Legislature to allow her to own property in this country. On the final vote, (it was in the midst of the excitement just before the war of 1812), Senator Platt stood alone in favor of granting the petition. He deemed it just, and though it periled his popularity when he was in nomination for the governorship of the state, yet he strenuously defended his position. Trumbull put on the back of his portrait of the Judge the date of this vote, and this motto—"*Justum et tenacem propositi virum, non civium ardor prava jubentium mente quatit solida.*" A just man and tenacious of the right, no popular passion shakes him from his firm purpose. This is an admirable estimate of his character. Trumbull, who had been an aid to Washington, was indignant at the refusal, and highly appreciated his friend's wisdom, justice and courage.

Judge Jonas Platt left two sons and six daughters: Mary, Susanna, Zephaniah, Cornelia, Mary 2d, Elizabeth, Helen, and Henry Livingston Platt.

—Susanna, his second daughter, married Richard R. Lansing, of Utica. They had thirteen children: Edward, Jonas Platt, and Gerrit, all deceased; two named Richard and Francis Tappan, also deceased; Manette, Helen and Charlotte; Cornelia Platt, Melancthon Wolsey, and Phillipina, deceased; and Susan Lansing. Manette Lansing, the oldest daughter married Bayard Boyd, surviving her husband, and residing in Washington, D. C. Charlotte married Willard Smith, and resides in Washington also.

Helen, (deceased) married Judge Sylvester Larned, of Detroit. None of the sons are living. The father, R. R. Lansing, at one time resided in New York. His place of business was burnt out in the great fire of 1835, and his insurance company was ruined. He removed to Detroit, Michigan, and became interested in the growth of that young State. Lansing, which later became the capital, was named after him. He died in Detroit, September 29, 1855. The children of Edward R. Lansing, his oldest son were: Marie, Mauette, wife of Judge Reilly, of Detroit; Richard R., a physician living in Detroit; and Philip lately residing in Boston, Mass. The children of Manette Lansing Boyd are: Anna M., wife of Rev. Thomas Nichols, of Milford, Pa.; Helen Livingston, wife of Wells Isbell, of Chicago; Charlotte L., wife of George C. Webb, of Fulton, N. Y.; Elizabeth L., and Susan Platt, wife of James T. Sweetman, M. D. The children of Helen Lansing Larned, of Detroit, are: Helen Livingston, wife of Frank Bowen, living in London, Eng., and Jennie, wife of Wm. Fitch, of Louisville, Ky. The children of Charlotte Lansing Smith, are: Margaret Norvell, widow of Forrest Norvell, of Detroit; Helen Livingston, wife of Wm. N. P. Parker, of Va.; Mauetta L., wife of John McKinney, of Washington, D. C.; Eliza Belle, wife of Edwin McKeever, of Washington, D. C.; and Louise, wife of Rev. T. McB. Nichols. The children of Susan Lansing Reeve, are: Christopher, living in Chicago, and Manette, wife of Wm. Valk, of Washington, D. C.

The children of Anna M. Nichols, of Milford, Pa.,

are: T. McB., living in Nyack, N. Y.; Bayard Boyd, living in Chicago ; Manette L., wife of Joseph Carpenter, late of Chicago ; Samuel Hall, and Susan Baldwin.

The children of Richard L. Boyd, are : Caroline, Manette, Bayard and Louise.

The children of Charlotte L. Webb, of Fulton, are : Manette L., Harry, Chandler and Bayard Boyd.

Margaret Norvell's children are : Willard S., Emily, and Bayard Boyd.

Helen Parker's children are : Charlotte, Helen, Henry and Sarah

Eliza B. McKeever has one son Edwin.

Manette Valk's children are : Helen Livingston, Ralph and William.

The children of Jennie Fitch are : Julia and Edward.

Helen L. Bowen's children are : Florence, Frederic, Ethel, Arthur and Sylvia.

—Zephaniah Platt, oldest son of Judge Jonas, graduated from Hamilton College, in 1815. He practiced law in Utica with his father, then in Detroit and Jackson, Michigan. He was attorney general of the state. After the civil war, he removed to Aiken, S. C., and there was chosen U. S. Circuit Judge. He discharged his high duties with impartial ability, as witnessed in the estimate of him in the Charleston Courier. He married Cornelia Jenkins, of N. Y. They had seven children : Anna, now living in Washington, D. C. ; Cornelia ; John Howard, who died young; Helen : Mary Ann, who also

died young ; Mary Platt ; and Howard Jonas Platt.
Cornelia married J. Blackwell first, then A.
J. Willard, who after the war went to South Carolina,
and became Chief Justice of the Supreme Court of
that State. Mary married S. J. Agnew, son of Prof.
Agnew of the Michigan University. Two sons : How-
erd and Holmes. Afterwards, she married Theo-
dore W. Parmele, grandson of Judge Jonas Platt.
Howard Agnew married Marion Wester of New York.
He has a little girl named Myrtle. Helen Livingston Platt, grand-daughter of Judge Jonas, married
H. O. Weed, of Newburg, N. Y. Their children are :
Josephine, Isabel, Benedict, Nina, Lulu and Marcus.
Howard Jonas, the youngest son, entered Yale College, but ill-health compelled him to go to sea. He
entered the Coast Survey Service. He was on the
U. S. ship Arctic at Halifax to receive the first tel-
egraphic cable. He materially assisted Capt. Bar-
ryman in the preparation of his report on "deep sea
soundings." The following year, he was on the editorial staff of the N. Y. Evening Post, and he gave
promise of early excellence as a public journalist.
But he died suddenly at Yonkers in 1838, at the age
of 22. His father, Judge Zephaniah Platt, died at
Aiken, S. C., April 20, 1871. His mother died, at
the remarkable age of 96, in Washington, D. C., in
the autumn of 1890. She had rare and excellent
qualitles.

—Helen Platt, the youngest daughter of Judge
Jonas, married Truman Parmele, a prosperous mer-
chant of New York. They had seven children :
Theodore W., Howard, Alfred, Platt, Mary, Helen

and Frederic. Theodore W. married Mary Platt, grand-daughter of Judge Jonas in 1870. They had one only son, Henry Livingston, who died within his first year. Their daughter, Helen Livingston, is Mrs. J. Holmes Butler; their son, Charles R., who married Miss Alice Butler, has a son Charles and a daughter Alice. Mrs. Butler has a son Holmes. Howard Parmele, second son of Truman, married a neice of S. F. B. Morse. Their children are: Bessie, Mary, and Howard. Alfred, third son of Truman, married Miss Andarine. Their children are: Marie, Edward, Truman and Allie Parmele.

—Mary Platt, the oldest daughter of the Judge, died in her youth. Also, her sister Elizabeth.

—Henry Livingston Platt, the second son of Judge Jonas, born 1807, married Sarah M. Morey. They had two sons: Robert, who died in his youth, and Jonas H. Platt, of New York. Jonas H. married Sarah Gilman, of Plattsburg. They have two sons: John Bailey Platt, born 1863, and Arthur Livingston Platt, born 1871. John B. married Kitty Snyder, 1884. They have a son and a daughter, Jonas H. and Edith Platt. The grandfather, Henry Livingston Platt died in 1844. Jonas Platt's place of business is in Wall street, New York.

XVI.

OSWEGO BRANCH.

THIS is an offshoot from the Plattsburg stock.
James Platt was the youngest of the twelve children
of Zephaniah and Mary Van Wyck ; born in Pough-
keepsie, N. Y., January 2d, 1788; married Eliza,
daughter of Wm. and Joanna Floyd, of Western, N. Y.
His children were four : Wm. Floyd, James Augustus, Robert and Elizabeth. (The last died in infancy.) He subsequently was twice married, to
Susan Katharine Auchmuty, of New York, then to
Saran Breese, widow of Bleeker Lansing, of Utica,
N. Y. By these marriages there was no issue.
Utica was his residence for some years. He was
postmaster there under President J. Q. Adams.
He was also a director in the Ontario Branch Bank
at Utica. At length he went to Albany, and in
1836, he removed to Oswego on Lake Ontario, where
he was prospered. In this place he was made
Mayor under the new city charter ; and in 1852–3
he was State Senator from his district. He was
also President of the Lake Ontario National bank at
Oswego. He was of the Alexander Hamilton school

of politicians, a Henry Clay Whig, unostentatious in manners, and sociable in disposition. He has been justly described, as "earnest, affable, public-spirited and high-principled." His death was at Oswego, May 8, 1870, at the age of eighty-three.

—Wm. Floyd, oldest son of James Platt, born at Utica, N. Y., 1814; married, at Oswego, January 2, 1838, Catharine Amelia, daughter of Henry L. and Unice Woolsey, of Geneva, N. Y. Children : Wm. Floyd, Jr., died in infancy; James, died in 1889 in New York, (twice married.) Wm. Floyd Platt, 1st, died at Oswego, 1844.

—James Augustus Platt, second son, now of Pineville, Pa., was born at Utica, N. Y., July 25, 1816. He graduated at Hamilton College, Clinton, N. Y., in the class of '35, taking the first honor, the valedictory. He is a member of the Greek letter association of Alpha Delta Phi. He married April, 1852, Elizabeth, daughter of James Sellers, of Upper Darby, Pa. Their children are three : Isidor Elizabeth, Samuel Floyd, and Charles Sellers. They were born at Mineral Point, Wisconsin.

1. Isidora E., born October 7, 1855, married J. Morton Brown, of Philadelphia, now of Norristown, Pa; they have two daughters and a son living : Mary P., Isidora E. and Charles P.; Elizabeth and Evangeline died young.

2. Samuel Floyd Platt, born July 14, 1857 ; married Macre A. Cadwalader, of Upper Makefield, Pa.; they have a daughter and a son, Hannah C., and Floyd Sellers Platt.

3. Charles Sellers Platt, born June 3, 1859 ; mar-

ried March 12, 1883, Martha Eyre, daughter of Preston Eyre, of Upper Makefield, Pa.; two sons, Samuel Platt and Joseph E. Platt.

—Robert, third son of James Platt, born at Utica, September 20, 1818; graduated at Union College; a member of Kappa Alpha; died at Oswego in the spring of 1838.

XVII.

SHARON BRANCH.

THIS crosses the State line into Duchess County,
N. Y. It claims Stephen Platt as its head. He was
baptized at Huntington, L. I., March 20, 1731; and
Israel Platt (supposed to be his brother) was baptized 1740. They are descendants of Isaac 1st, or
Epenetus 1st. They moved from Huntington, in the
early part of the Revolution, settling, Stephen in
Sharon, Ct., and Israel in Pleasant Valley, an adjoining township in Duchess County, N. Y. There
were three brothers, Epenetus, Stephen, and Peleg,
baptized at Huntington, 1775, supposed to be sons of
Stephen Platt, and to have removed with their father
to Sharon, Ct. The father died there about 1798.

Israel Platt above, who lived sometime in Pleasant
Valley, or Amenia, Duchess County, N. Y., was a
captain in the militia in the Revolution. He married Elizabeth Scudder of Huntington, L. I. He died
of yellow fever in New York, 1796, aged 58. He had issue: Stephen born March 28, 1762, baptized at Huntington, July 26, 1762; Edwin, who died young;
Sarah, who married D. Cyrenius Crosby; Zilla,

born 1773, who married Egbert Barton; Ruth, born 1778, who married Samuel Reynolds; Betsy, (1781-1848,) who married Ariovistus Pardee; Harriet, born 1785, who married Walter Perlee; and Nancy, born 1768, who married Rufus Herrick. This Isreal Platt by deed dated Amenia Precinct, Duchess Co., N. Y., (in which he is designated, "Yeoman") conveys to his son Stephen, fifty acres of land, May 14, 1785, for 230 pounds sterling.

—Stephen Platt, eldest son of Israel Platt, above mentioned, removed to Freehold, Albany Co., (since Green), about 1788, and there he was drowned in a freshet, December 12, 1800. He was a lieutenant in the army of the Revolution at the age of 19; later was a justice of the peace, and a member of the legislature for Albany County 1793–5. He left among others, twin sons, born April 5, 1793, Isaac L. and Jacob L. The former lived in New York. He married Marion Erskine Ruthren. His children were; John R., Mary Jane R., Samuel Reynolds, Lydia and Isaac S. Platt. John R. lives in New York. Mary Jane R. Platt married John P. Adriance of Poughkeepsie. Their children are: Isaac Reynolds, born in N. H., January 1, 1851; John Erskine, born in New York, December 1853; James R. born 1856, died 1879; Marion R. born 1858, married Silas Wodell, January, 1887; Harris Ely; William Allen; and Francis Henry Adriance. The home of the family is in Poughkeepsie. The other twin son of Stephen Platt, namely, Jacob L., married Catherine Waldron; issue, a daughter, Mary Jane. Platt Street, New York, it is said, was named from Jacob L.

Platt. Samuel R. son of Issac L., had one son, Furman Nefis, born April 18, 1853. Lydia, daughter of Isaac L., married Geo. Ackerman, June, 1864.

We here remark, as a help to trace the line, that Treadwell, Stephen and Peleg, Elizabeth, Mary and Hannah, were children of one Epenetus Platt, of Hempstead, but what one, it is not determined. His wife's name was Hannah. An Epenetus Platt was baptized at Huntington, L. I., 1730. The line is probably the younger Huntington Branch of Epenetus first.

—Henry, second son of Israel Platt, of Amenia, born 1764, removed to Stephentown, Rensselaer Co., N. Y. He was a member of the Legislature of New York. He died October 9, 1842, leaving three sons: Israel, Henry and Alonzo. Israel married Margy Schermerhorn; resided some time in Hudson, N. Y. Henry married a Graves, and had a son resident in Stephentown. Alonzo, M. D., married Lorilla Smith, and removed to Grand Rapids, Michigan, or Ann Arbor.

Stephen Platt above, son of Israel, married Dorcas Hopkins, daughter of Roswell. Besides his sons, Isaac L. and Jacob L., twins, he had other children: Fanny, who married Charles Griggs; Abigail or Abby, who married John House, of Waterford, N. Y.; Sarah, who died 1811, unmarried; and Dorcas who married Rev. Samuel Robertson. A second marriage was to Lydia Southerland. Their children were: Harriet, who married Bela Brewster; Eliza, who married Gerard Van Skaick; and Aramenta, 1801–1886, who became the second wife of Mr. Van Skaick. A second marriage was to Mr. L. Adams.

John House, who married Abbey Platt, daughter of Stephen, had two sons, Samuel R. and John C. House. Samuel R. House, M. D., of Waterford, N. Y., born 1817, married Harriet Pettit, (born 1820). He was a missionary in Siam from 1846 to 1876. His brother married first Lucy Gaylord, then Mrs. Jennie V. Lewis. Dr. S. R. House gives these interesting data: Dorcas Platt, daughter of Stephen, married Rev. Samuel Robertson. Their son was Rev. Wm. S. Robertson, missionary to the Creek Indians, whose wife translated the New Testament into the Creek language. Their son, Henry M., is a D.D. Julia, a daughter, was the wife of Gov. Pierrepont, of Virginia. Stephen Platt, born 1762, had a brother, Henry Platt, whose son Israel, of Hudson, N. Y., had a daughter Elizabeth, who married Rev. Abram Van Zandt, D.D., Professor in New Brunswick Theological Seminary. Henry's sister, Nancy Platt, married Rufus Herrick; and their son, Richard P. Herrick, of Greenbush, N. Y., was a member of Congress in 1846-7. Another sister, (Elizabeth Betsey), married Ariovistus Pardee, who died 1843, and their son, Ario Pardee, gave an endowment of $500,000 to found the scientific department of Lafayette College at Easton, Pa. This munificent gift to learning makes him a princely benefactor to our race and country. His oldest son is General Ario Pardee of Philadelphia, Pa. The father, who is the owner of extensive coal mines, residing at Hazelton, Penn., was born November 19, 1810. He

married Elizabeth Jacobs. A second marriage was
to Anna M. Robinson. His children number five
sons and five daughters: Ario, Calvin, both civil
engineers; Ellen E.; Israel Platt, of Stanhope,
N. J.; Anne; Barton, of Lockhaven, Mich.; Frank,
Bessie, Edith and Gertrude—the last six by his
second marriage. Bessie is Mrs. Augustus Van
Wickle. The two older sons graduated "C. E." at
the Rensselaer Polytechnic Institute, Troy, N. Y.

John Platt, born in Huntington, L. I., Jan. 2, 1735;
married Mary Blydenburg, born May 23, 1733. A
second marriage was to Phebe Husted, widow, whose
husband was taken prisoner in the Revolution, and
died in New York, December 15, 1777. John Platt
died at Alder Creek, Boonville, N. Y., July 30, 1810,
in his 76th year. He had ten children: William,
born 1759, Elizabeth, Richard, Mary, Samuel, May
3, 1766, Phebe, Abigail, Obadiah, John, jr., and the
last, Experience, born February 22, 1777. John Platt,
jr., was born in Duchess County, N. Y., April
3, 1774. His wife was Phebe Hoyt, of New Canaan,
Ct. They had eleven children: Sarah, William L.,
Louise, Mary, Abigail, Matthew H., Esther, Sarah
B., Chauncey, and Eliphalet, born at Trenton, N. Y.,
February, 1817. Most of these were born in Oneida
County, N. Y. William L. Platt, son of John, jr.,
was born in Steuben, N. Y., October 25, 1802; married Jane McElroy, October 28, 1824; lived in Boonville, N. Y. Their children were: Eliza, John Blydenburg, Mary, Abbia, Jane (Scott), James M., Chauncey A., and William A. Platt, who was born in Boon-

ville, N. Y., August 8, 1840.   Louise Platt, aged 86, and her sister Esther, aged 72, reside in Hamilton, N. Y.

John Blydenburg Platt married Elvira A. Shover, of Canandaigua, N. Y., September 30, 1851.   Three children, two only living: Eddie and Jennie.   The family reside in Delaware, O.

Wm. A. Platt has two children: Arthur McElroy, born 1871, and Mary Emily, not yet in her teens, living in Sherburne, N. Y.   He gives the above data respecting John Platt and his descendants.

XVIII.

RHINEBECK BRANCH.

———

THIS traces closely to Sharon, Ct., and then further on to the younger Huntington branch, L. I. John Platt, son of Eliphalet, of Pleasant Valley, made his home near by, in Clinton, Dutchess County. He was a deacon in the Presbyterian Church, Pleasant Valley. He served in the War of the Revolution. He married Catherine Barnes, and had three children: Dr. Eliphalet Platt, Wm. Barnes, and Isaac I. Pratt. A second marriage was to Jerusia Spencer: one son, Henry, who made his home in Philadelphia. The two brothers, Dr. Eliphalet Platt and Wm. Barnes Platt, a banker later in life, made Rhinebeck their home near 1835. The other brother, Isaac I., married Angeline Baldwin and lived in Poughkeepsie. They had no children. Dr. Eliphalet Platt took his degree of M. D., about the time of his coming to Rhinebeck. He was liberally educated, kind and courteous, a skillful physician and a worthy citizen. He married Mary Ann Dibble ; he has left two daughters, Julia and Cornelia, and a son. J. Warren, born in Rhinebeck. The son has removed to New Orleans. He writes me that his father, Dr. Eliphalet Platt, late of Rhinebeck, N. Y., was born in Pokeepsie, 1796. The son was born April 16, 1836. He went to Louisiana early in 1855; married, January 6, 1862, Halmaida Brèmond, of New Orleans, born there October 10, 1840. She died March 5, 1887. Eight children: Mary Julia, born August 10, 1866; John W., born in Bay St. Louis, October 17, 1868; Joseph Brèmond, December 16, 1872; Adèle, January 29, 1875; Ernest, born at Bay St. Louis, December 16, 1876; Alma, January 7, 1879; and Catherine, February 9, 1881. Most of these were born in New Orleans. The father is a merchant in his adopted city.

John Platt, the head of this branch, son of Eliphalet Platt 1st, died in 1851.

—William Barnes Platt, the brother of Dr. E. Platt, was born in Pleasant Valley, N. Y.; he married Miss Stautenberg, of Hyde Park. His children were John H. and Elizabeth. John H. Platt, born in Rhinebeck, removed to New York. He married Mary Cheney, May 27, 1858. His children are ; John Cheney, Charles Adams, Richard Goodman, Elizabeth and Wm. Barnes Platt, 2d. Charles A. Platt, on the 17th of March, 1886, married Annie C. Hoe, daughter of Richard M. Hoe, of New York. She died on the 18th of March, 1887. No issue. John H. Platt, the father, died in New York, May 21, 1886.

—Elizabeth Platt, the only daughter of William Barnes Platt 1st, married Charles H. Adams, of Cohoes, N. Y., a manufacturer, and at one time a member of Congress. Their children are William Platt Adams, and Mary Egbert Adams. Wm. Platt Adams married Katherine W. Elseffer, of Red Hook, N. Y., January 23, 1884, the daughter of J. W. Elseffer, Esq. They have two daughters, Elizabeth Platt Adams and Katherine Elseffer Adams. Wm. Platt Adams for a time took his father's business. He graduated from Union College in the Class of '79. He is a member of the Greek letter association of Alpha Delta Phi. His only sister, Mary Egbert Adams, born in Rhinebeck, married Robert Johnston of Cohoes in 1881 ; he was a graduate of Union College in the class of '77; he also was an Alpha Delta Phi. He died in 1883, leaving an only son, Robert Johnston, born August '82. Mrs. Johnston now occupies her pleasant home in her native village in Duchess County, N. Y.

———

Henry Platt, merchant, son of John Platt, of Clinton, by a second marriage ; born August 8, 1808, in Pleasant Valley, Duchess County, N. Y., resided in Philadelphia, Pa. ; married Abigail Hart Knowles of Titusville, N. J., April 11, 1833. He was killed by the falling of a tree as he was traveling near Thomaston, Ga., August 27, '49. His children, five : Edwin Knowles (died in his third year), Edward Augustus, William Henry, Eliza S. and Mary Knowles; all born in Philadelphia.

—Edward Augustus, born August 25, '38 ; married Annie E., daughter of John Scherzer of Annville, Pa. ; has a daughter, Effie Abigail.

—Eliza S., born April 15, '43 ; married Wm. H.

Chaffee, February 1, '71 ; residing in New York ; one child, Bertha Eliza.

—Mary Knowles, born February 2, '46 ; married Charles J. Carroll Taylor, November 25, '68, residing in New York ; one daughter, Mary Platt Taylor.

—Wm. Henry Platt, born June 18, 1841 ; married Hannah Jeffries, of Philadelphia, December 12, 1872. They have one daughter, Cornelia M. Early. They reside in Philadelphia.

XIX.

POUGHKEEPSIE BRANCH.

———

THIS traces closely to Sharon, Ct., and thence to the younger Huntington branch, L. I. Its head is Eliphalet Platt, who was born July 12, 1733. He married Miss Scudder, of Huntington, and made his home in Pleasant Valley, Duchess County, N. Y., near 1780. They had four children: Henry, John, Jemima and Betsey. A second marriage was to Hannah Cansten. Her father, Joseph, was one of the "nine partners," who owned a large track of land east of Poughkeepsie. She inherited one-fourth of her father's estate. Eliphalet's children by this marriage were four: Joseph, born September 25, 1771, died 1836; Isaac, born November 23, 1774; Israel, born February 6, 1777; and Sarah Franklin, who died June 30, 1779. Isaac died November 11, 1802. Eliphalet Platt 1st, married as a third wife, the widow Bunce, who had two daughters by her former marriage, Dibbie and Betsey. Dibbie married her step-father's oldest son Henry.

—Henry Platt, son of Eliphalet, had by this marriage with Miss Bunce, seven children: Eliphalet,

Fanny, Betsey, Nancy, Joseph, Jermima and Henry S. Their home was in Marcellus, N. Y. Fanny married E. Rice, Betsey a Mr. Hopkins; Nancy married Silas Crane; Joseph, Emma Dodge, afterward Ann Ocherman. Jermima married Henry Combs, afterwards, Joseph Rhodes. Henry S. married Miss Wood, afterwards, Mrs. Dickerson.

Henry S. Platt, of Marcellus, died October 21, 1829, aged 69 years. Debora, his second wife, died January 19, 1833, aged 69 years. Eliphalet, brother of Henry S., died May 21, 1809, in his 21st year. Betsey (or Frances) Platt, died April 20, 1816, aged 69. Jemima, daughter of Henry S. and Debora Platt, married Allen Cook; she died April 16, 1826, in her 23d year. Henry S. had a son Joseph, who died October 22, 1851, aged 57 years. Emma, Joseph's wife, died December 16, 1838. Dr. Henry Combs, grandson of Jemima Platt, and son of Henry Combs, resides in Rome, Mich. Mrs. Frances (Crane) Wright resides in Adrian, Mich. Also, Mrs. Ann Elizabeth (Hopkins) Van Brunt, resides in the same place.

—Jemima Platt, oldest daughter of Eliphalet 1st, married C. Ackerman. Their children were: Hannah, Caty and Eliphalet. The first two, were in succession, first and second wife of Samuel Thurston. Eliphalet married Ann Verplank, of Queenland's Patent.

—Betsey, the second daughter of Eliphalet 1st, did not marry.

—John Platt, the second son of Eliphalet 1st, heads the Rhinebeck Branch.

Eliphalet Platt (1st), was a ruling elder in the Presbyterian Church in Pleasant Valley, N. Y., in the year 1789. He died in that place in 1795.

—Joseph Platt, son of Eliphalet and Hannah Cansten, married Hannah Barnes, Jan. 4, 1800. They had two sons: Isaac Platt, born July 17, 1803; and Joseph Cansten Platt, born Sept. 25, 1805; and a daughter, Catharine, born 1801, who died 1836. Joseph Cansten Platt married Elizabeth Bowne, Aug. 30, 1836. Seven children: Mary Scofield, Catherine, Susan B., Cornelia B., Anna E., Cansten, and Susan E. A second marriage was to Almira Parsons, Sept. 9, 1854. Their children are: Isaac, Caroline, Almira, Adeline, and Frances. Cansten Platt was born Feb. 4, 1851; he died April. 7, 1874. Isaac Platt, son of Jos. Cansten, died in childhood. Elizabeth B. Platt, wife of Joseph C., was born July 25, 18—, died June 4, 1853; and his second wife Almira was born March 9, 1817, and died Jan. 10, 1890.

—Mary S., oldest daughter of Joseph Cansten Platt, married Harrison Bishop; they have two daughters, Josephine and Cornelia. Catherine, the second daughter, married James Chapman; they had three children, Lewis, Elizabeth and Gertrude; Lewis died aged 27. A second marriage was to Egbert Sherwood; they have one daughter Abbie Ann. Susan B., the third daughter of Joseph C. and Elizabeth Platt, died in her tenth year: Cornelia B. fourth daughter, married Theodore Alvord. Anna E. the fifth daughter has not married. Of the children by his second wife, Caroline died in infancy;

Almira married Joseph Tallcot, a descendant of the first Joseph Cansten. The home of the family is Marcellus, N. Y. Joseph Cansten Platt, died Jan. 24, 1890.

Isaac Platt, son of Joseph, was born at New Baltimore, N. Y., July 17, 1803. He learned printing. In 1828, he became the editor of the Duchess *Intelligencer*, which, in 1838, was changed to the Po'keepsie *Eagle*. He was editor and proprietor of this during the rest of his life. He was appointed postmaster of Po'keepsie under General Taylor's administration. He was on the commission to locate the boundary between New York and Connecticut, 1859 and '60, Provost Marshal of the 12th Congressional District of New York for 1863 and '64. He was an early advocate for the Hudson River Railroad. He was an editor 44 years. He married Harriet Bowne, September 19, 1837. Their children are: John Isaac, born June 29, 1839 ; James Bowne, born August 11, 1841 ; Edmund Pendleton, December 2, 1843 ; Henry Barnes, born January 12, 1847, and Harriet B. Platt, the youngest. The father died 1872. His widow is still living in Po'keepsie.

—John I. Platt, son of Isaac, married Susan F. Sherwood, June 3, 1862. Their children are : Edmund, Eliza Strong, Sarah Sherwood, Isaac, Francis Wheeler, and Edith May. One, Susan, died in babyhood.

—James Bowne, second son of Isaac, married Emma Bartlett, October 23, 1875. Their children are : Elizabeth Otis, Louise Bartlett, and Anna Margaret.

—Edmund P. Platt, married Mary E. Bartlett, June 22, 1870. Their children are : Emily Bartlett, Wm. Vedder, Howard, and Mary Alletta. Edmund P. is a merchant.

These four families reside in Po'keepsie. John I. and James B. Platt are the publishers of the Po'keepsie *Eagle* (daily and weekly). John I. was a member of the New York Legislature, 1886-7 and 8. He is President of the Po'keepsie Board of Trade.

—Henry Barnes Platt ; married Mary Estella Smith, of Pleasant Valley, N. Y., June 12, 1875. Their children are : Raymond, Mabel and Henrietta. He is a chemist at 36 Platt Street, New York.

XX.

WINCHESTER BRANCH.

———

John Boyd in his annals of Westchester, Ct., has these data: "Daniel Platt from Danbury, bought of Benjamin Benedict a lot of land on Waterbury River turnpike, a little south of the Potter place, in 1771, which he conveyed to Philip Priest in 1776. He and his wife Thankful had a son, Stephen, who was baptized March 13, 1774."

Joseph Platt, from Danbury, uncle to Levi Platt, lived on a lot north of the Ed. Rugg farm. He had a fulling mill on the brook a little south of the Potter tenement house. He sold in 1787, and moved to Ohio.

Levi Platt came from Danbury to Winchester when he was a boy. He was a school teacher in his early manhood. In 1790 he bought of Martin Hulbut land, it is now thought part of Henry Andrew's farm, where he lived four years ; then bought and occupied for the residue of life, the farm recently owned by his son Sylvester Platt, deceased. He was characterized as a puritan of the puritans, with intense convictions, and withal a man of humble and earnest piety. Religion with him was the dominant thought—72 years a member of church—a deacon, in many respects a model Christian. He was Town Clerk and Recorder. He was a member of the Convention of 1818, which formed the Connecticut State Constitution. He married, February 5, 1792, Esther Alvord, daughter of Eliphaz. She died March 28, 1840. He died August 14, 1856, in his 91st year, his mental and bodily forces unabated to the last. He is described "as gigantic in form, of stern stuff, a patriarch and a puritan." His children were: Abi, born July 25, 1793; Eliphaz Alvord, May 3, 1796, died in his 12th year; Ezra Hart, born September 18, 1798; Sylvester, born May 17, 1800; Levi, born April 11, 1802; Lucy, born October 31, 1804; Elizabeth, born September 19, 1806; Eliphaz Alvord, born February 6, 1809; and William born, December 16, 1816, died February 28, 1840. Abi married Hiram Royce, of Norfolk, widower, the husband of her late sister Lucy. Levi went to Collinsville, Ct., thence to Hartford. Sylvester filled the office of Justice of the Peace and that of Representative. He died at Winsted, September 18, 1870. He married Mary, daughter of Wilcox Phelps, at Norfolk, September 4, 1833. His children: Levi Wilcox and Helen Rebecca, both died in early youth; and Edwin Sylvester, born September 30, 1839, who married Elizabeth Brooks, February 12, 1863.

Levi Platt, 2d, married Pamelia R. Munger. Children: Helen Esther, born December 27, 1824; Ruthy Smith, born October 10, 1826; Elizabeth, born September 5, 1828; and Mary Jane, August 22, 1831.

Sarah Platt married Daniel Andrews; she died 1848, aged 72, leaving children: Platt, born March 6, 1799; Amos, Augustus, Hiram Lewis, Hulda, and Harriet, the last born November 4, 1819.

Joseph Platt's name is among those who took the oath of fidelity to the State in 1778, and Obadiah Platt was among the new electors. in Winchester in 1801.

XXI.

NEW HAVEN BRANCH.

———

THE late Prof. Johnson T. Platt, of the Yale Law School, heads this branch. He was a descendant of the older Huntington stock of Isaac 1st. The oldest son of Isaac, Jonas, had a son Obadiah, whose son Obadiah 2d, left a son Jarvis, born September 6, 1759, who married Ann Nichols. Their son David married Lucretia Tousey of Newtown. They had a son Philo Tousey Platt, who married Jeanette E. Tuttle, of Southbury, Ct. He was the father of Prof. Johnson Tuttle Platt; this one married Mary Jay Pettee, of Pittsfield, September 3, 1867. He left no children. His ancestral line from Richard of Milford is through Isaac, of Huntington, Jonas, Obadiah, Obadiah 2d, Jarvis, David and Philo Tousey Platt.

He was born at Newtown, Ct., January 12, 1844. He graduated from the Harvard Law School in 1865, and entered into the practice of his profession at Pittsfield, Mass. After a six months residence, he removed to New Haven, and soon became quite prominent in his profession. On the reorganization of the Yale Law School in 1869, Mr. Platt, and Profs. Robinson and Baldwin, were placed mainly in charge of the institution. In 1873, he received the degree of Master of Arts from Yale. He was a member of the Court of Common Council for several years, and in 1874, was made Corporation Counsel. He revised the city ordinances, and did a large amount of other valuable work for the city. He was Registrar in Bankruptcy, Master of Chancery of Connecticut for a number of years; and he was U. S. Commissioner up to the time of his death. He died suddenly January 23, 1890, of cerebral hemorrhage. He was just going to his class in the Law School when he was stricken, and soon becoming insensible, he died in a few hours after reaching his home. All testify that he was a man of fine intellectual abilities, and many noble qualities. As a lawyer he was able and ready. As an instructor, he was thorough, gentle, helpful and sympathetic. He won the hearts of all his students. His literary culture was extended and full. He was fond of history and poetry, and was often ready with an apt quotation. He was a good conversationalist, sincere and agreeable in his manner, and he had hosts of friends. In the Law School, his range was first equity and pleadings, then "torts," or criminal law, and finally general jurisprudence and the history of law. The New Haven County Bar, in a minute approved by them, January 24, 1890, used these fitting words: "He was not only well read in the ordinary literature of his profession, but long and loving study had made him familiar with the science of Jurisprudence in its widest range. His sympathies were warm, and his friendships true and deep-rooted. During nearly a quarter of a century at the Bar, and twenty years in the Yale Law School, he had been honorably known as a learned lawyer, an independent thinker, a public-spirited citizen, a kind-hearted and high-minded man."

His course of lectures on Jurisprudence, it is hoped, will soon be given to the press. He published two valuable essays, one on "The Assertion of Rights," and the other on "The Opportunity for the Development of Jurisprudence in the United States." This science was his favorite legal study. A brief, but admirable sketch of his life was written by Morris F. Tyler, Esq., a member of the New Haven Bar. It should be stated, that Professor Platt had been, during twenty years, gathering facts about the "Platt Lineage," and the writer of these memorials is exceedingly indebted to him for important and interesting contributions to the accurate history of the family. By the courtesy of his wife, he has had access to his manuscripts also. His age was 46. He was summoned in the maturity of his powers. His brief but energetic and successful life is an honor to the family name.

His only brother Theron Eugene Platt, lives on the old place at Newtown, where both were born. His brother, born May 16, 1848, married Mary Catherine Russell, of Southbury, November 26, 1873. He has one son, Philo T. Platt, born May 20, 1880. A son Clifford, born March 9, 1884, died May 13, 1889.

Their only aunt, Elosia, married Erastus Pierce, of Southbury. Two sons, Granville T., of South Britain, Ct., and David F., who married Eliza Bradley, of Southbury. They have two daughters and one son : Mary E., born December 20, 1875, Frederick E., March 11, 1878, and Anne H., born May 17, 1880.

———

Richard Platt, resident of New Haven, son of William, is of the Josiah Branch. His wife, now deceased, was the daughter of Richard Platt, of Milford. Her brother, in Milford, is also a Richard. There seem to be six Richards in the field. All honor to those who honor the first in the line. Richard Platt of New Haven has a son and a daughter. The latter is married and resides in New Haven.

XXII.

MERIDEN BRANCH.

THIS traces to Fairfield, then to the older Huntington Branch of Isaac 1st, the son of Richard 1st. Orville H. Platt, U. S. Senator from Ct., is its oldest living representative. The ancestral line comes from Obadiah, of Fairfield. This Obadiah was son of Jonas, oldest son of Isaac 1st, and Elizabeth Wood, of Huntington, L. I. In 1724, Obadiah Platt, of said town, purchased lands in Fairfield, and soon after removed thither. He married Mary Smith, August 10, 1722. They had eight children: Abel, born August 2, 1723; Sarah, born June 25, 1725; Jonas, born October 9, 1727; Obadiah, August 8, 1729, ancestor of the late Prof. Johnson T. Platt; Ann, born November 5, 1731; David, September 15, 1734; Mary, born January 7, 1736; and Elizabeth, born May 10, 1739. Mary, wife of Obadiah, died at Ridgefield, November 16, 1771. Abel purchased lands in Redding, and in 1756 at Ridgefield in company with his father. He is said to have died while a prisoner of war at New York. Jonas Platt settled at Redding, and on October 17,

1747, married Elizabeth Sanford, daughter of Ehpraim, of that place. Both were admitted church members at Redding, July 5, 1749. Their children born at Redding were: John, baptized February 5, 1752; Daniel, baptized August 11, 1754; Eunice, baptized May 30, 1756. The two following named are recorded as born at Ridgefield: Obadiah, May 17, 1758; and Isaac, born April 13, 1760. Jonas had other children, namely: Samuel, Jonas, William, Jehu, and a daughter Hulda. Jonas was taken prisoner during the Danbury raid, April 25 and 28, 1777, and is said to have been carried to New York. His name appears among those who marched to Fishkill to reinforce Gen. Putnam, during the Burgoyne campaign in October, 1777. John, son of Jonas above mentioned, was in the army, and was taken prisoner at Fort Lee, November 16, 1776. He settled at Washington, Ct. He married Elizabeth Parmle, July 7, 1775. Their children were: John, born February 21, 1776; David, born August 31, 1778; Ruth Ann, born March 30, 1782; Betsey, born May 8, 1790; and Daniel Gould, born July 25, 1797.

—John Platt 2d, son of John and Elizabeth, married Larenda Warner, November 24, 1800. Their children: Lavinia, born May 22, 1802; Robert S., born May 22, 1804; Eurotus, born December 29, 1806; Laurren R., born June 29, 1809; Fanny Janette, born September 27, 1814; and John Taylor, born July 8, 1820, residing in Washington, Ct.

—David Platt married Jerusha Lewis, November 19, 1806. His sister, Ruth Ann. married Leman

Canfield, November 8, 1802. The children of Ruth were : Daniel N.; Betsey A., born March 24, 1806 ; Lewis A., born March 31, 1809 ; Daniel N. 2d, born September 9, 1812 ; and Julia, born 1819.

—Betsey Platt, 2d daughter, married Harvey Smith, November 17, 1813. Issue : a son Henry, born January 4, 1815. A second marriage was to Elisha Garret.

—Daniel G., of Washington, Ct., youngest son of John Platt 1st, married Almyra Hitchcock, Jan 3, 1817. Their children are : Orville, born March 11, 1822, died 1826; Orville Hitchcock, born July 19, 1827 ; and Simeon D., born February 12, 1832. A second marriage was to Harriet Davis, Cold Spring, N. Y., September 26, 1857. She died December 18, 1885. He died October 26, 1871.

Orville H. Platt, Senator, married Ann Bull, of Towanda, Pa., May 15, 1850. Their children are : James Perry, born at Towanda, March 31, 1851, and Daniel Gould, born at Meriden, February 7, 1858, died January, 1864.

—James Perry Platt, his son, is a lawyer of Meriden. He married Hattie Ives, of that place, December, 1885. They have one daughter, Margery Platt.

The head of this branch, Orville H. Platt, U. S. Senator, was born at Washington, Ct., July 19, 1827. After a thorough academic course, he studied law at Litchfield, and was admitted to the bar in 1849. He has since practiced law at his present home, Meriden, Ct. He was Clerk of the State Senate in 1855 and 1856 ; was Secretary of State of Connecticut in 1857 ; a member of the State House of Representatives in 1864 and 1869, serving the last year as speaker. He was elected to the U. S. Senate, a Republican member, and took his seat March 18, 1879. He was re-elected in 1885. His steady advancement in public life is a creditable recognition of his ability and efficiency, and his twelve years in the Senate show a long, faithful and honorable service in our highest legislative body. He is justly ranked among our rising statesmen. In January 1891, he was re-elected for a third term of six years as United States Senator from Connecticut.

Simeon D. Platt, brother of Orville H., residing in Torrington, married Helen M. Logan, of Washington, December 10, 1855. They have one son, Wm. Logan Platt, born at Washington, April 20, 1859.

—Wm. Logan Platt married Rose Cook, of Washington, January 11, 1882. They have a son, Daniel Phillip, born March 29 1886, and one daughter. William L. is a physician in Torrington.

———

Isaac Platt, born April 3, 1760, son of Jonas and Elizabeth, had children: Mills Platt, born August 1, 1789; Hulda, Lydia, and Aaron. This last lived at Westport, but at length went West. Mills Platt married Lucy Frost, December 1, 1814. He died March 2, 1865. Hulda died single. Lydia married Isaac Bertram, of Redding, Ct.

—Mills Platt and Lucy Frost had seven children: Jerome M. Platt, born December 3, 1815, died March 1, 1816; Curtis F. Platt, born June 25, 1817, of New Haven; Hulda E., born July 22, 1819; Daniel M.

born December 29, 1823, died February 22, 1888 ;
John D., living in Sharon Valley, N. Y., born May
12, 1827 ; Mary S., born March 4, 1830, married Wm.
Wheeler, living at Litchfield, Ct., and Charles E.
Platt, born December 20, 1833.   Isaac Platt above,
died in 1797.

XXIII.

WASHINGTON BRANCH.

Benjamin S. Platt, Clerk of the U. S. Senate, Washington, D. C., son of Lauren R. Platt, of Washington, Ct., was born in 1839, at Albany, N. Y.; married there 1865, Julia H. Feltham, from England. He was thirteen years in the Government Printing Office; in 1879 he went into the publication office of the War Records; in 1885 he was made Engrossing Clerk of the U. S. Senate, his present official position. He was treasurer of the Washington Topograph. Association, also a delegate to the National Topograph. Convention in Baltimore, 1872. He has three children : Gertrude, (born in Albany, N. Y.), Mabel and Harry. The latter two born in Washington.

—His brother Amos R., born in Ct., 1842, married Mrs. Kate Reynolds, (née Cochran) of Washington, D. C., now deceased, leaving one son. He is in the Government service.

—His sister, Lavinia E., born in Albany, married James M. Christian in 1864. She is still living there.

—His second sister Fannie E. is living in Albany, N. Y.

John Taylor Platt, an uncle of Benjamin S. Platt

resides in Washington, Ct.   He has two daughters living. He is a son of John Platt 2d, in the Meriden line.

The Hon. Orville H. Platt, Senator from Connecticut, is a resident of Washington, D. C., most of the year.   There are others of our lineage who make their home at the Capital—several from the Plattsburg and Judge Jonas Branches, also one or more from the Tioga and the Lake Shore Branches.

XXIV.

GIDEON BRANCH.

———

This starts from Joseph Platt, of Milford, the youngest son of Richard 1st. Joseph Platt, often called Lieut. Platt, baptized April 1, 1649, married Mary Kellogg, daughter of Daniel Kellogg, of Norwalk; May 5, 1680. Gideon Platt, son of Lieut. Joseph Platt, we read in the Church records, was baptized September 29, 1700. This Gideon Platt married Mary Buckingham, February 28, 1726. Their oldest son Gideon Platt was baptized March 24, 1734. This name has been kept in a number of the families to the present time, 1890. Gideon 1st and Mary made Middlebury, Ct., their home. Their children were: Gideon, Asa and Mabel.

Gideon 2d who married Hannah Clark, had three sons, Gideon 3d, Merrit, and Joseph.

—Gideon 3d married Lydia Sperry, of Waterbury, November 8, 1807. They had children: Joseph, Anson, Gideon Lucian, Merrit, Maria and Luther S. Gideon 3d, died October 22, 1846.

—Joseph Platt, son of Gideon 3d, resides in Southington.

—Luther S. Platt, of Naugatuck, married Dianthe Thompson, still living. They have one son, Fred.

Gideon, who married Thankful F. Lee, in August, 1879. He had a son Howard Luther, and a daughter Bertha D. A second marriage in March, 1885, was to Lilian Rockwell. They have two children by this marriage, Lula F., and Helen R. Platt.

—Anson, second son, died in California, 1849.

—Gideon Lucian, third son of Gideon 3d, was born in Middlebury, Ct., July 20, 1813; graduated from the Yale Medical College, 1838; established himself in practice in Waterbury, held a high rank in his profession; he was in succession President of the County and State Medical Associations. He married Caroline Tudor, of Windsor, Ct., December 18, 1844; he died November 11, 1889. She is still living. Their children are Dr. Lucian Tudor, Medora Caroline, Dr. Walter Brewster, and the youngest, Charles Easton. Charles Easton, born October, 1856, resides in Detroit, Mich. Dr. Walter Brewster Platt, born December 20, 1853, married Mary Perine, daughter of E. G. Perine, Esq., of Baltimore, December 4, 1889. He has one son, Washington Platt, born October 6, 1890. He took the scientific degree of Ph.B., from Yale College in 1874, his M.D. from Harvard in 1879, and his F.R. C.S. in London in 1883. He resides in Baltimore in the full practice of his profession. His sister Medora C., married Dr. W. Hamlin Holmes, of Calais, Me., April 6, 1881, a nephew of the Hon. Hannibal Hamlin, late Vice-President. Their home is in Waterbury, Ct. Dr. Lucian Tudor Platt, born in 1845, graduated from Yale College in 1864, took his M.D. in 1869, from the University of Pennsylvania, Philadelphia. He married September 15, 1871, Rebecca Hurlbut, of Winchester, Ct. One daughter, Theodora H. Platt. His home is Vineland, N. J., where he is practicing medicine.

—Merritt Platt, fourth son of Gideon 3d, married Mary Bronson, of Middlebury, November 25, 1838. Have had two children, Edward Bronson and Mary Eliza. Residence, Waterbury, Ct.

—Maria H., second daughter, of Gideon 3d, married Elan P. Osborn, of Camden, N. J., both deceased; their children are: Lydia M., who married Isaac P. Treat, of Orange, and Platt D. Osborn, of New Britain, Ct.

XXV

WATERBURY BRANCH.

ALFRED PLATT, second son of Nathan Platt, of Newtown, Ct., was born April 2, 1789. He founded the manufacturing hamlet of Plattsville, near Waterbury. He married Irene Blackman, of Brookfield, in 1816. He died December 29, 1873. She died November 2, 1863, aged 72. Their children were: Nirom B., Charles Sanford, William Smith, Clark Murray, Alfred Legrand and Seabury B. Platt.

—Nirom, eldest son, born September 1, 1818, married Eliza Kirtland, Waterbury, September 17, 1810. Children: Fanny, Margaret, Ida and William. Fanny married Charles Russell, who died Christmas, 1889, at Los Angeles, Cal. Margaret married W. N. Osborn; they reside in Waterbury. Ida K. married Lewis Perkins, of same place. William's home is in California. The father died October 14, 1863.

—Charles S. Platt, second son of Alfred, was born in Waterbury, July 30, 1820; he removed to West Stockbridge, Mass., 1848, and built the "Rockdale Mills." He was a member of the State Legislature in 1841. He married Mary M. Tobey, of West Stockbridge, September 4, 1861. Their children are: Mary J., born November 17, 1862; Frederick T., born October 15, 1864, residing in Troy, N. Y.; Charles E., born October 31, 1866, and Jeannette E. His public life is marked by his opposition to saloon politics and saloon influences. His home is in Stockbridge, Mass.

—William S. Platt, third son of Alfred, born in Waterbury, January 27, 1822, married Caroline Orton, daughter of William, October 1, 1844, born the same year as her husband. He was a manufacturer, and he showed a very remarkable aptitude in the adaptation of new means to desirable ends. He invented many admirable appliances of great practical value, as his very handsome estate proves. In brief, he was an "inventive genius." His factories employed over 200 workmen, and his industries have greatly enlarged Plattsville. The business of his firm is now one of the largest in Waterbury. He died March 27, 1886, in his 64th year. His children are: Orton William, died in infancy; Helen Irene W.; Caroline Amelia; William Hubert, died in his 7th year, and Irving Gibbs, born June 18, 1860. Helen Irene Wilhelmina, born March 4, 1849, married Wallace H. Camp, October 17, 1878; their home is in Waterbury. Mrs. William S. Platt survives her husband, and lives at the homestead with her daughter and son.

—Clark Murray, fourth son of Alfred Platt, born January 1, 1824, has long been in business in company with his brother William S. He married, May 20, 1846, Amelia M. Lewis, born January 3, 1826, of Naugatuck, Ct. His children are: Bertha

Louise born May 10, 1851, and Lewis Alfred, born May 31, 1854. Edward Legrand, the youngest, died 1862, in his 6th year. Lewis A. Platt married Ellen Brainard, June 20, 1882. Bertha Louise Platt married Jay H. Hart, May 20, 1873. Their children are: Amy Louise Hart, born October 4, 1874; Bertha Murray, born October 10, 1876; Lewis Jay, born August 21, 1878; Alfred Lucius, December 10, 1880; Ruth Spencer, born September 22, 1882; and Dorothy Nettleton Hart, born February 27, 1889. Lewis A. Platt is a graduate of Yale.

—Alfred L., fifth son of Alfred Platt, born January 1, 1825, married Sarah A. Sherman, of Danbury, July 28, 1847. Their children are: Alfred S., born November 12, 1854, and a daughter, Sarah Jane, older, born January 8, 1849. She married, May 10, 1870, Jared P. King. Two children: a daughter, Lillie, born June 10, 1872, died same year, and a son, Rupert Vivian, born October 17, 1877. The son Alfred S. Platt, married Eugenie A. Nettleton, December 18, 1876. They have a daughter, Alice E., born October 7, 1879. They reside in Waterbury.

—Seabury B., sixth son, born October 8, 1828, is a lawyer, living lately in Birmingham, Ct. He was three years at Yale College. Ill health prevented his graduation. He was chosen a judge of the District Court, but has recently returned to the practice of his profession. He is now resident in Lakeville, Florida.

———

Leonard Platt, youngest son of Nathan, born in March, 1804, married Clarissa Hosmer, of Vermont.

He was senior warden of the Episcopal Church in Waterbury for several years; and chairman of the building committee to build a new stone church. His children are: Henry, Maria, Richard, George L. and Clara. They live in Waterbury. He was very much interested in the ancestry of the family. While in Europe, he sought facts, and made a valuble record, which, indeed, suggested the compilation of these memoranda. He invented several valuable machines. He died suddenly at Shrewsbury, N. J., July 4, 1858, in his 55th year. His remains were brought to Waterbury for burial.

———

There are several of the family from other branches residing at Waterbury. Some of the descendants of the late Dr. Gideon L. Platt are there, also, his brother Merrit and family of the Gideon Branch. Mrs. Lewis J. Atwood, residing in Waterbury, is Elizabeth, daughter of Almon Platt, of the Josiah Branch.

XXVI.

WESTCHESTER BRANCH.

———

In this the name of Benoni Platt comes first. He resided in Northcastle, Westchester Co., N. Y., as early as 1730, since he is then registered in the records as a town officer. His Christian name seems to be a new one in the family. He died in Northcastle in 1763, leaving his widow Hannah Platt, two sons, Jonathan and Benoni 2d, and one daughter Abigail. His will is recorded in the Surrogate's office in New York (lib. 6, p. 31,) dated May 20, 1761, proved May 14, 1763; in which he mentions his wife, two sons, his daughter Abigail's children, his grand-daughter Abigail daughter of his son Benoni 2d, and his son Jonathan's oldest daughter, also his grand-daughter Hannah, then under 16. The will of his widow, Hannah Platt, is also on record, (lib. 25, p. 427,) dated March 8, 1764, proved February 25, 1767, in which she mentions her sons as above and her daughter Abigail, and her grand-daughter Hannah, the daughter of Abigail. There is also on record the will of Benoni Platt 2d, of Northcastle, recorded liber K, p. 271, dated May 26, 1824.

There is no Benoni Platt among the family records in Huntington, L. I., or in Milford, Ct., that the compiler of these memorials has discovered. There is a Jonathan in the Norwalk Branch, but it was after Benoni Platt's oldest son was so named. There was a Jonathan Platt an early settler in Rowley, Mass. Jonathan Platt 2d in this line, went eastward to Greenwich, Ct., to find his bride. This slight clue is the only one we have. Judge Platt, of White Plains, is of the opinion that Benoni was a grandson of Isaac 1st, of Huntington.

Col. Jonathan Platt 1st, of Bedford, N. Y., removed in 1793 with his son Jonathan 2d to Tioga Co., N. Y., where he died in 1795, the founder of an important branch of the family. Consult the Tioga records. Benoni Platt 2d, remained on the homestead place at Northcastle. He died November 3, 1796, in the 63d year of his age. His children were: Stephen, Cynthia, Hannah, Abigail, Debora, and Benoni Platt 3d, who was born August 8, 1764. Of these, Stephen married Miss Green, both dying young, leaving no issue. Debora never married.

—Cynthia Platt, daughter of Benoni, 2d, married Charles Rundle. They lived in Greenwich, Ct. Their children were: Hannah, Jarvis, William and Benoni.

—Hannah Platt married Mr. Dibble, who left a daughter, who married Mr. Hubbard. Their descendants live in New York City.

—Abigail Platt, third daughter, married Benjamin Tripp, of Northcastle. Four children: Isaac, Benjamin, Jr., Hannah (who married P. Hopkins,) and Debora, who married William Palmer. Of these, Hannah Hopkins lived and died in Northcastle. They left one child, Hannah, wife of John P. Tripp. Debora Palmer died in New York, leaving children now residing there.

—Of the grandchildren of Benoni Platt 2d, Benoni Rundle had a son Charles, and a daughter, Elizabeth of Northcastle. James Rundle resides in Brooklyn, L. I. Charles Rundle died leaving a daughter Mary. Isaac Tripp, of Northcastle, left a son John Platt Tripp, lately of Bedford. Benjamin Tripp, jr., left David, and Sarah, now residing in Middletown, N. Y.

—Benoni Platt 3d, who died May 13, 1824, married Charity Reynolds. His children were: Orsomus, born July 4, 1785, dying without issue, April 19, 1831; Rachel, born October 15, 1787, who married Mr. O. Marvin, but died without issue in her 24th year; Cynthia, born July 9, 1790, died in her 18th year; Horton, born August 9, 1792, died December 18, 1867; Stephen, born June 24, 1794; Charity, born April 10, 1796; Reynolds, born October 15, 1798; William, born December 1, 1801; and Jane Ann, born Feb. 4, 1804. These were by his first wife. A second marriage was to Betsey Brush. His children were: Edward Brush, born October 9, 1811; Lewis C. Platt, born March, 7, 1818; and Jesse Holly, born December 31, 1820.

—Stephen Platt, the third son, married a Miss Underhill. He died July 11, 1861. His children: Wm. Platt, Edwin, and Emily (Keller), all of Po'keepsie; Rachel (Wealtheav), of Montrose, Fannie

(Mosher), and Ann Eliza (Van Anden), both of Amenia, N. Y.

Benoni Platt 4th, married Jennie E. Ham, of Pine Plains, N. Y. Their children were : Frank Platt, of Hartford, Ct., and Charles H. Platt, of New York. Benoni P., died in El Paso, Ill., 1860. Charles H. Platt, of New York, January 29, 1884, married Frarcis J. Jauriet.

The widow of Benoni Platt 4th, married C. M. Clute, of El Paso, where she now resides.

—Charity, born April 10, 1796, married Stephen Sands, (still living a widow residing at Aurora, N. Y.) Her children are : Alexander, (married), Marcus, Alanson, Rachel and Samuel, of Aurora.

—Reynolds, born October 15, 1798, died aged 73, leaving a son Ebenezer G. Platt, who married and is residing at Northcastle ; and a daughter Sarah E., (Mrs. W. H. Green.)

—Wm. Platt, born December 1, 1801, died in his 38th year, leaving Horton and Francis, both deceased.

—Jane Ann, married Augustus Cliff ; died without issue, April 24, 1825.

—Edward Brush Platt, died October 9, 1811, leaving Edward Lewis Platt, of Mt. Kisco, and Mary, deceased.

—Lewis C. Platt, married Laura S. Popham, May 1, 1853. His children are : Mary S., Eliza, Benoni, Wm. Popham, Jane H., Alethea Hill, Lewis C. jr., Julia Ward, and Theodora Platt. Judge Lewis C. Platt is a lawyer, residing in White Plains, N. Y. He sent me most of these data.

—Jesse Holly Platt, died July 8, 1884, leaving two children, Lewis Holly and Alice, who .married Rev. Wilberforce Wells.

Jonathan Platt 1st, when he removed to Tioga Co., left one son, Charles, at Bedford, N. Y.

Charles Platt, of Bedford, N. Y., son of Jonathan 1st, was born February 10, 1771. He married Hannah Leek, November 23, 1791. Their children were: Philip L. Platt, born in Bedford, July 22, 1795, died in California, April, 1852; Joseph S. Platt, February 6, 1798; Eleanor M., May 27, 1800, died November 16, 1851; Charles S., born July 9, 1802; Hannah L., born August 18, 1804, died July 9, 1841; Samuel H., born May 6, 1806; Jonathan and Mary A., born October 14, 1807, died in infancy; Erastus E., born October 10, 1809; Catherine M., March 1, 1813, died September 8, 1820; and Deborah R., born June 6, 1815. She (Mrs. Holly) only is living. She resides with her niece Mrs. Kate M. Smith, Middletown Ct. The father, Charles Platt died March 17, 1839.

—Joseph S., son of Charles, married Esther Mills, daughter of Jonathan, of Bedford, N. Y. Their children are: Rachel A., Joseph M., Kate M., and Mary E. The youngest died, leaving no children. Rachel married Wm. C. Merritt, living in New York. They have six children: Charles Anderson, born 1853; Wm. Platt, February 12, 1857; Edith Augusta, Caroline Warren, Anna Bertha, and Henry M., the last born September 12, 1867.

Joseph M. Platt, married and has one daughter, Flora, who married Albert Bendall; they are now

living in Brooklyn, L. I.   Kate M. Platt, married J.
Lincoln Smith, of Lanesboro, Westchester Co., N.
Y. One son, Howard M., who is residing in New
York. The father, Joseph S, Platt, died at his
daughter's home in Middletown, July 7, 1873.

Edward Erastus Platt, late of Albany, N. Y., son
of Charles Platt, of Bedford, N. Y., married Maria
Leek Knapp, near 1835. Their children were : Joseph Hall, Edward Erastus, May Elizabeth, Charles,
Hubert, Eleanor, E. Harvey, and Virginia. Two
others died quite young. Four of these only sur-
.vive : Edward E., Mary E., E. Harvey, and Virginia.
The youngest son and the two daughters reside with
their venerable mother in New York. The father
was in the service of his country in the late war,
and after its close, he was still retained in service in
the Freedmen's Bureau. He died, 1869. Edward
E., his son, was also in the war. He married Seraph
N., daughter of Marshall Newton, of Vt., May 5,
1865. Their children are : Mary Leek, James Newton, and Grace Platt, born in Springfield, Mass.
They reside in Worcester, Mass.

XXVII

TIOGA BRANCH.

THIS is an offshoot of the Westchester stock. Col. Jonathan Platt, of Bedford, N. Y., went with his son Jonathan, to Tioga County, N. Y., in 1793, and died there two years later. Both the father and the son, doubtless, served in Gen. Sullivan's army, which in 1779 crossed from Trenton, N. J., to the Susquehanna River, and drove the Indians out of the Wyoming Valley, and it was that expedition which in all probability led them later to move back into the Susquehanna Valley. Jonathan Platt, the father, was a prominent patriot in the Revolution. He was a member of the Provisional Congress of 1775, from New York. He is referred to in Lossing's Field Book of the Revolution, (vol. 1, p. 691,) as one of the " distinguished patriots " who constituted the Committee of Safety at White Plains, N. Y., 1776. His father was Benoni Platt, of Northcastle, Westchester Co., N. Y. The Colonel lived long enough to see his son well established in his Tioga home. Jonathan Platt, son of Jonathan 1st, was born April 20, 1764 ; he married Anna Brush, born October 8, 1766, of Greenwich, Ct. Their children were : Jonathan 3d, born 1783 ; Mary, born May 20, 1785 ; Benjamin, born June 5, 1787; Edward, August 19, 1789; William, October 29, 1791; Brush, born August 6, 1795; Nehemiah, July 25, 1797; Charlotte, born January 25, 1800: Benjamin, April 2, 1803; Deborah, born August 6, 1805; Charles, May 11, 1808; and Sarah, May 9, 1811, who is still living. Jonathan Platt 2d, was prominent and influential in his neighborhood, and he is well remembered by people still living. He acquired a fair property in his day. He died December, 1824.

Jonathan Platt 3d oldest son of Jonathan 2d, was born in Bedford, N. Y., October 13, 1783, ten years before the family removed to the Susquehanna Valley. He made his home in Nichols, Tioga Co., N. Y., and he became a leading man in his neighborhood. He married Betsey Goodrich. She died 1878. He died January 16, 1857, leaving seven children: Charlotte, Mary, Charles, and George, who died 1851, aged 27; and Frances Sarah, who died 1883, aged 52, and Elizabeth Caroline, and Edward Jonathan Platt.

—Charlotte Platt, the first, born August 7, 1817, married George Underwood, a lawyer of Auburn, N. Y. He was a graduate of Hamilton College, in the class of '38; a member of the Greek letter fraternity of Alpha Delta Phi. He established a successful practice in his profession; he was attorney of the N. Y. Central Railroad; a member of the N. Y. Legislature 1850–2; and Mayor of Auburn in 1854. He died May 25, 1859, in his 44th year. His wife survives; she is occupying the homestead in Auburn. Their children were: George Platt, Charlotte Platt, and William, who all died nearly two years of age ; and Jonathan Platt, George Underwood 2d, and Fanny Goodrich Underwood. Jonathan Platt Underwood, born September 14, 1849, is a graduate of Hamilton College in the class of '70. He is an Alpha Delta Phi. He married November 5, 1890, making his home in Chicago, Ill. His wife Caroline, is the daughter of George Trumbull, of that city.

--George Underwood 2d, born July 17, 1855, is a lawyer in Auburn, N. Y. He is a graduate of Yale, in the class of 1875. He married, October 20, 1880, Grace Kennard, of Boston, Mass., born July 27, 1858. The name and mantle of his father fall upon him in his native place. Their children are : Grace, born 1882, died in infancy ; George Underwood 3d, born September 29, 1883 ; Kennard, born August 16, 1886 ; and Rosamund Underwood, born October 8, 1887. Fanny Goodrich, the youngest of the children of George Underwood 1st, born July 12, 1857 ; married June 6, 1888, Joseph C. Anderson, a banker in Auburn, born March 25, 1853.

—Mary Platt, second daughter of Jonathan Platt 3d, born September 17, 1819, married September 3, 1845, Henry Morgan, of Aurora, N. Y., born August 22, 1810. He died, January 30, 1887. He left one daughter living, Kate Morgan ; Chas. Henry, born September, 1848, died May, 1851 ; and John Platt Morgan, born May, 1851, died September, 1852. Mrs. Morgan resides in New York. Her daughter Kate Morgan born January 5, 1847, married June 23, 1870, Wm. Brookfield, of New York, formerly of Brooklyn.

They have five sons: Henry Morgan, born October 17, 1871; Fritz James H., born April 25, 1874; Frank, November 18, 1875; Edwin Morgan, September 22, 1877; and Herbert Brookfield, born July 4, 1880. Harry, the oldest, is in the class of '93 in Columbia College, and is also a member of the fraternity of Alpha Delta Phi.

—Charles Platt, oldest son of Jonathan 3d, born March 19, 1822, married May 10, 1848, Nancy H. Ely, of Binghamton, N. Y. He died June 18, 1869, leaving one daughter living, Louise Tivers. His son William H., died 1873, aged 24; Charles Henry died 1870, aged 13; Fanny E., died May 3d, 1878, in her 18th year; and Frederick Platt, born 1868, died same year. Louise Tivers Platt, born April 16, 1851, married Aaron Putnam Storrs, of Owego, now residing there. They have children: Charles Platt Storrs, born September 25, 1874, and Fanny Platt Storrs, 1878.

—Elizabeth Platt, fourth daughter of Jonathan 3d, born June 6, 1833, married September, 1858, Silas Condit Hay, residing in New York. They have two children living, the youngest, Charles Cortland Hay, born May 7, 1876, in New York. Two, Elizabeth Platt and Fanny, died in infancy in 1865 and 1866. The oldest, Louis C. Hay, born November 29, 1859, married November 2, 1887, Jennie Burt, of Saginaw, Mich. They have one son, Wellington, born August 4, 1888.

—Edward Jonathan Platt, youngest son of Jonathan 3d, born September 3, 1838, married Emma Ketchum, of Owego, N. Y. They lived in San Francisco, Cal., nearly twenty years. They returned to their old home in Owego, in the fall of 1890.

Nehemiah, sixth son of Jonathan 2d, has a son, George Platt, living in Owego.

Charlotte Platt, second daughter of same, married Gurden Hewitt. Their children are: Gurden, Jr., Frederick, both living in Owego; and a daughter, who married Stephen Arnot, of Elmira, N. Y.

Debora, third daughter of Jonathan 2d, has a son, Edward Turner, living in Flint, Michigan. He is a banker.

William, fourth son of Jonathan 3d, born at Bedford, N. Y., October 19, 1791, two years before the removal to Tioga, married Lesbia Hinchman, of L. I., of the family of that name prominent in the Revolution and in the old French War. His home was at Owego. He was a lawyer. He died January 12, 1855. His children, still living, are: Frederick E. Platt, of Owego; Emily Platt, who married Mr. Skinner, of Owego; and the Hon. T. C. Platt, of New York.

Thomas Collier Piatt, youngest child of William, was born at Owego, July 15, 1833. His first studies were at the Academy in his native place. He entered the class of '53 at Yale. In his junior year he left on account of illness, which prevented him from graduating; but the college granted him an honorary degree in 1876. In 1852 he married Ellen Lucy Barstow, daughter of Hon. Chas. R. Barstow, of Owego. He entered into business, becoming interested in lumbering in Michigan. He became President of the Tioga Bank. He took an active part in politics. He was clerk of Tioga Co. three years. He was member of Congress from the 29th District, 1872 to 1876. In 1879 he became general manager of the U. S. Express Co. From 1880 he was several years quarantine commissioner of the port of New York. January 13, 1881, he was elected U. S. Senator from his native state. He resigned his seat in the Senate May 16, the same year. His prominent and responsible positions in public life indicate that he has marked ability in the conduct of affairs. He has been an influential leader in his party. His children are: Edward Truex, Frank Hinchman, and Henry Barstow. Edward resides in Washington, D. C.

—Frank H. Platt is a lawyer in New York. He married, November 1, 1881, Caroline Elizabeth Livingston, daughter of Alan Cameron Livingston. They have a son, Livingston Platt, born March 7, 1885, and a daughter, Ellen Barstow Platt.

—Henry B. Platt, the youngest son of the ex-Senator, married, November 9, 1887, Grace Lee Phelps, of Wilkesbarre, Penn.

XXVIII.

STEUBEN BRANCH.

NATHAN PLATT, of Hornellsville, N. Y., was born in Prospect, Ct., August 20, 1809. He was the son of Joseph born December 14, 1778, in Milford, Ct., son of Capt. Joseph born 1754, son of Joseph born November 13, 1724, son of Joseph baptized January 15, 1693. This Joseph was the son of Josiah baptized 1645, the son of Richard 1st.

Nathan Platt, above, gives these data of Joseph his father. He had ten children: David Miles, born May 12, 1802; Martha M., June 15, 1803; Joseph, Jr., January 15, 1805; Eliza, August 3, 1806; Charlotte, January 9, 1808; Nathan himself, 1809; Catharine, November, 1811; Emily, March 29, 1814; William, July 22, 1816, and Nancy Spencer, October 7, 1819. David Miles lived in Wisconsin, deceased; left sons and daughters. One is Lucius C. Platt of Chicago. Joseph jr., died in Michigan. His son, Nathan Platt, resides in Muskegon, Mich.

Henry N. Platt, lawyer, Buffalo, N. Y., is the youngest child of Nathan Platt, of Hornellsville. He married, December 12, 1887, Julia M. Peck, daughter of Myron H. Peck, of Batavia, N. Y. One son, Myron Nathan, born June 12, 1889. Nathan Platt married, January 7, 1842, Caroline M. Richmond, of Livonia, N. Y. Seven children: Richmond, Susan, Susan 2d, Annette, Lucia, Charles and Henry Nathan. Richmond J. Platt lives in Cedar Rapids, Iowa, and has a son Walter, also a second son.

Joseph Platt went to Hamburg, N. Y., about 1830. Three sons, Charles M., William and Horace, and three daughters, Mrs. Leach, Mrs. Walker and Fanny deceased. Charles M. married Asenath A. Dayton, of Eden, N. Y., now residing in Alden, N. Y. They have four children living: Frank L. in Richmond, Va.; Lewis D. in Alton, Iowa; Nellie Platt and Mrs. F. L. Barnet, of Alden, N. Y.

Joseph Platt above had brothers: Abel, who went to Dixon, Ill. (two sons and two daughters.) David died in Buffalo; James and Montgomery, who remained East. William, brother of Chas. M., has a son, Rev. Ward D. Platt, in Hornellsville, N. Y.

Horace resides on the old place in Hamburg. The father of Joseph above was James Platt, of New Fairfield, Ct.

—Charlotte Platt, born January 9, 1808, daughter of Joseph Platt, of Prospect, Ct., (?) married F. D. Benham, in that place, April 6, 1828. Their children were: Edward F. S. Benham, born September 14, 1832; O. J. Benham, September 22, 1834; George C. (died 1887); Daniel W., born December 13, 1837; Amelia C. and Florinda, Wm. W. and Robert B. Benham, the last born April 6, 1852. O. J. Benham resides in Cleveland, Ohio.

XXIX.

THE SCIOTO BRANCH.

———

This traces to the Josiah stock, by William Augustus, William, Benjamin, Ebenezer, John, son of John, son of Josiah 1st, son of Richard 1st, of Milford, Ct. Benjamin Platt, born in Danbury, Ct., January 3, 1757, heads this branch. March 31, 1776, he married Adah Fairchild, born September 28, 1758, died August 14, 1833. He removed to Lanesboro', Mass.; then to Ohio, and about 1817 made his home in Columbus, on the borders of the Scioto. His grandson, Wm. Augustus, born in Lanesboro', Mass., March 7, 1809, was with his grandfather in Columbus in early boyhood. Benjamin Platt was a worker in gold, silver and brass. He made clocks, and invented a surveyor's compass, movable, for running lines over hilly land. He was fond of medical studies, and among relatives showed much skill in applying his knowledge. He had nine children: Hannah, born February 20, 1778; William; Cyrus; Ely, October 8, 1784; Sarah, born June 6, 1778; Benjamin, May 24, 1791, died March 3, 1812; Augustus, born August 4, 1793, married Elsa Chase, November 24, 1816; Hiram, July 6, 1796, married Henrietta Summers, November, 1815, and Maria, April 22, 1805, married Erastus Luce, October 10, 1825. Sarah married Jarod Brace February 20, 1815. Hannah, the oldest, married Rufus Ferris, May 7, 1801. Their children were : Harriet, Hiram, 1805 ; Cornelia ; Dan, born November 26, 1810, and Rufus, March 4, 1813.

—William Platt, son of Benjamin, born November 19, 1780, married February 7, 1804, Pamelia Royce, of Lanesboro', Mass. Their children were : Pamelia, born June 25, 1805, married 1821 ; David Gregory, died March 24, 1885, in California ; Laura Ann, January 7, 1807, married Dr. Wm. C. Hicock, and is still living in Burlington, Vt. ; Wm. Augustus; and Sarah M. Platt, born August 27, 1811, who married Matthew J. Gilbert, died May 26, 1837, in Columbus, O. A second wife of Wm. Platt was Harriet Little, married December 4, 1817. Their children were : Cyrus, born 1818 ; and Harriet Little, October 17, 1820, married September 28, 1884, Theodore Sollace. Wm. Platt died January 7, 1814. His brother Cyrus, born 1783, married, June, 1812, Laura Royce ; he died September 7, 1824.

—William Augustus Platt, son of William, married in Delaware, O., September 2, 1839, Fanny Arabella Hayes, only sister of ex-President Rutherford B. Hayes. They had six children : Sarah Sophia, Laura, William Hayes, Fanny, Emily, and Rutherford Hayes Platt. 1. Sarah Sophia, born October 5, 1840, died in infancy. 2. Laura, born April 1, 1842. 3. William Hayes, born March 3, 1844, died January 27, 1851. 4. Fanny, born April 12, 1847. 5. Emily, born July 18, 1850. 6. Rutherford Hayes Platt, born September 6, 1853. A second marriage of William A. Platt was to Sarah Follet, of Sandusky, O. Their children were: Susan, Lucy, and Sarah. Susan married Hermon M. Hubbard, of Columbus, O.; two sons, Hermon Milton, and Platt. William A. Platt died August 8, 1882.

—Laura Platt, his oldest daughter living, married Gen. John G. Mitchell, October 3, 1862. He served in the Ohio Volunteer Infantry during the war of the Rebellion, and was made Brigadier-General while in active service. Their children are: Elizabeth, born October 2, 1864; Fanny, April 13, 1869; Jane Andrews, June 10, 1871; and John Grant, born June 17, 1874. The home of the family is in Columbus, Ohio.

—Fanny Platt, next daughter, married Dr. Erskine B. Fullerton, October 19, 1871. They reside in Columbus, O. Their children were five: William Platt, November 23, 1872, died January 28, 1873; Laura, born October 30, 1873; Dorothy, July 9, 1877; Rutherford, June 30, 1880; and Fanny, born December 2, 1882.

—Emily Platt, youngest daughter of William A., married Gen. Russell Hastings, June 19, 1878. The ceremony was at the White House, Washington, D. C. Their children are: Lucy Webb, born May 26, 1880; Fanny, born April 1, 1882; and Platt, born January 25, 1885. Gen. Hastings, during the Rebellion, was in the Ohio Volunteer Infantry, and reached his military honors in active service. The home of the family is in Hamilton, Bermuda Islands. It is one of the very charming places in the Island

group. Its lily gardens, oleander hedges, beautiful walks and drives makes it indeed a "fairyland."
I have heard of many who have enjoyed the hospi-
talities of their pleasant home.

—Rutherford Hayes Platt, only son living of Wm.
A. Platt, born in Columbus, O., September 6, 1853, a
graduate of Columbia Law School, New York, in
1879; married Maryette Smith, January 5, 1887.
Their son William Andrews was born December 24,
1887. Anne Swan, their four months old little daughter, died in mid-January, 1890. " He is a lawyer of
promise and good repute in his native city."

Cyrus Platt, of Delaware, O., grandson of Wm.
Platt, and son of Benjamin, born in Columbus, O.,
September 20, 1818, married November 9, 1847.
Jeanette Hulme, of Burlington, N. J., born February
25, 1816, (died August 21, 1877.) Their children
were eight: Ellen H., Howard, F. W. Platt, Jeanette
H., Harriet L., Franklin Cyrus, Martha Canfield,
and Clara I. Ellen born August 9, 1848, married
April 13, 1874, L. C. Sayre of Lawrence, Kansas.
Howard, born May 13, 1850, married September 30,
1875, M. R. Andrews. F. W. Platt, born July 29,
1852, married April 27, 1882, H. Cross; residing in
Delaware, O. Jeanette Hulme, August 10, 1854,
married December 12, 1877, A. C. Watson of London,
Ohio. Harriet, April 10, 1857, married November
23, 1881, R. J. Mitford, of Garden City, Kansas. F.
Cyrus, born November 14, 1859, is residing in Garden City. Clara I, born August 2, 1865, died August
25, 1866.

—Howard Platt, son of Cyrus, had four children:

Kennett A., born October 14, 1876, died September 19. 1880: Jeanette H., born December 25, 1877; Mary, born July 2, 1880; Clara D., April 26, 1882, died October 14, 1886. Howard Platt resides in Leadville, Col. He is a civil engineer.

—F. W. Platt, son of Cyrus, has four children: Warren Cumming, born December 6, 1883; Malcolm Cyrus, September 27, 1885, and Marguerite Alice, and Jeanette Hulme. The family reside in Delaware, O.

XXX.

LEROY BRANCH.

This traces to the Josiah Branch. Ezra Platt, son of Ezra, removed from Lanesboro', Mass., and finally settled in Leroy, N. Y., 1802. In the following year he was made first Judge of Genesse county, which office he held till his death, in 1811. The first Episcopal services in Leroy were held in his new barn. He married Lois Baldwin. No issue. A second marriage was to Margaret Bunnell, of Lanesboro', Mass. Nine children : Lois, who married Stephen A. Wolcott ; Oliver, who married Sarah Todd ; Ira, who died aged 30 ; Ezra 3d, who married Sally Depue ; Elijah ; Nancy ; George, who married Rachel Lyman (he died aged 84) ; and two who died in infancy. Elijah Platt, son of Ezra 2d, married Harriet H. Jordan in 1823. Six children : Lafayette, who married Caroline Spencer ; Martha, who married E. B. Hinsdale ; Horatio, who died aged 28 ; Margaret Platt, residing in Gettysburg, South Dakota ; Henry A., who died in infancy ; and George Norton. (See the Danbury Branch.) It was said of Judge Elijah Platt that " he was ever the friend of Religion, Education, Law and Order." He was 19 years a warden of the Episcopal church in Leroy. His son, George

Norton Platt, formerly of Leroy, N. Y., finally located at Vacaville, Solano county, Cal.   He married Elizabeth A. Wiard, of Leroy.   He has two sons : Ralph Hilton and Frank Lafayette, twins.   The latter has just graduated from the Dental College at Philadelphia.   This family traces its ancestral line through Elijah, Ezra 2d, Ezra 1st, Ebenezer 1st, John and John and Josiah 1st to Richard Platt 1st, of Milford, Ct. These data, in the main, were sent me by Miss Margaret Platt, of Gettysburg, S. D., and by Frank Lafayette Platt, of San Francisco.

XXXI.

LAKE SHORE BRANCH.

Miss Ella Mary Platt, of Cleveland, Ohio, gives the following data. Her father, Alfred Cowles Platt, seventeen years a resident of Sandusky, O., was born in Milford, Ct., April 3, 1828, in that part of the township now called Woodmont, lying between Milford proper and New Haven. The old log-house is still standing, on what is called "The Flat Iron," a lot between three cross roads near the Sound. He married Harriet Ella Paige, of Oberlin, O., September 30, 1857. She died March 6, 1864, leaving four children: Eriola Cowles Platt, Ella Mary Platt, Clayton Winfield Platt, and Harriet Paige Platt. A second marriage was to Lenora E. Shattuc, of Kipton, O. Two children by this marriage: Regina M. Platt and Frederick D. Platt. Mr. Alfred Cowles Platt died in Sandusky, October 2, 1884. His widow is still living in Cleveland, O. Her daughter, Regina M., born in Sandusky, February 22, 1869, married James O. Hamilton, of Cleveland; now living there. Frederick D. Platt, born in Sandusky, November 16, 1872, also resides in Cleveland. Of the older children, Eriola C., born in Oberlin, June 22, 1858, lives in Sandusky; Ella Mary Platt, born in former place, December 3,

1859, is a well-known artist in Cleveland; Clayton Winfield Platt, born in Oberlin, July 16, 1862, married Flora Palmer, of same place, in August, 1883. One daughter, Winnifred Harriet Platt. Their home is in Sandusky, O. Harriet Paige Platt, born in Oberlin, resides in Cleveland, O.

Isaac Smith Platt, of Fremont O., now over eighty years old, traces his line from Richard first, of Milford, through his son Josiah, and Josiah 2d—then his son Isaac, through two other Isaacs, to himself, the fourth. He chiefly gives these data. The first Josiah built a house near "Mortimer Tract," about 1700, still standing, though quite a ruin. (It has a very antique look, and would doubtless please Ruskin.) Josiah 2d lived in the old house. Then Isaac succeeded him, whose wife was Phebe. He died early. The children were Grace and Isaac 2d in this branch. Grace married Joseph Merwin, and they removed to New Milford, about which place and Merwinville North, many of the descendants still live. Isaac 2d married Amy Eells. Their children were nine: Isaac 3d, born 1783; Amy, Phebe, Asahel, Alanson, Abigail, Maria, Theresa, and Merit, the last born 1802. Isaac 3d in this branch married Abigail Smith, daughter of a revolutionary officer. A second marriage was to Rebecca Powell, of Washington, Ct. He removed to Franklin, N. Y., and died there in 1854. His children were: Abigail Gratia, born 1804. Isaac Smith, born July 22, 1806, and Harriet who died in 1811. Abigail G., married Jas. A. Grant in Franklin, N. Y., and died in Washington, Ct., 1879.

Her two surviving children live there. Amy Platt, oldest daughter of Isaac 2d married Elias Burwell. A second marriage was to Robert Burwell, whose son Robert M. lives in New Haven. She died in Mercer. Pa., where some of her family were living. Sidney Platt Burwell, her son, now lives in Cleveland, O. Another son went to Seattle, Washington. Phebe Platt, second daughter of Isaac 2d, married Amos Smith, of North Milford, and went to Coschocton, O. She had seven children. Asahel Platt, second son of Isaac 2d, went to Ohio, where he married Mary Barrett, and died there.

—Alanson Platt, third son of Isaac 2d, married Betsey, daughter of David Beach, of North Milford. They left the old homestead and went to Attica, N. Y., and then to Oberlin, O., where he died 1765 (?). Their children were eleven: Alanson S., Landra Beach, Lester Ward, Charlotte, Mary, Samuel Isaac, M. Fayette, Albert Cowles, Phebe, Gratia, and Henry M. Platt, the last born in Oberlin, the others in the old home. Alanson S., clockmaker in Bristol, Ct., died in Cincinnati, O. Lester Ward, printer in Cincinnati, went to Kcatskotoos (Indian name for Platte River), and died there in 1876. Charlotte married a Winters and lives in western Iowa. Clarissa, or Theresa, (?) married a Goodell, and she lives, too, in western Iowa. Mary married a Darwin, and she was for many years a teacher of Greek in the college in Burlington, Iowa. Samuel Isaac, born August, 1819, died in Oregon about 1854; his grave is marked at Oberlin. M. Fayette, a Congregational minister, lived in Lincoln, Neb.; but at last removed to Los

Angeles, Cal. Asahel died in Oregon about 1852. Phebe married Dr. Coxhead, and died in Oakland, Cal., 1886. Gratia married Mr. Mill, and she now lives in California. Henry M. Platt resides in Birmingham, Ala.

—Abigail, third daughter of Isaac Platt 2d, married Alfred Cowles, of Bristol, Ct., and died there 1836.

—Maria, fourth daughter, married Isaac Gillett, of Burlington, Ct., and died there about 1865.

—Merit, youngest son of Isaac 2d, was a scientist. He was an assistant to Professor Silliman in New Haven. He married Abigail Merwin in Milford, became a teacher there, and died in 1842. His daughter Abbie is the wife of Professor Henry Upson, of New Preston, Ct.

—Merit W. Platt, son of Alanson S., resides in Toledo, O.

—Herman Smith and his brother Willie reside in Baltimore. They are sons of Landra B. Platt.

—Lester, another son, is a Congregational minister in Flint, Mich. He has no children.

—Fayette Platt has six ; the oldest, Alfred C. Platt, is a lawyer in Lincoln, Nebraska. -

—Charlotte C. married Asahel Johnson, of Manlius, N. Y., at which place he died. She returned east, and died at Ferryville, Ct. Archer Platt and his sister Fannie (Mrs. Hull) reside in Toledo, O.; Merit W., their father, also. Clayton Platt, son of Alfred, resides in Sandusky, O.

Isaac S. Platt thinks the descendants of Isaac and Phebe Platt number at least one hundred; he has personally known seventy-five. Miss Ella M. Platt, of Cleveland, gives these additional data : Henry M. Platt, of Lakeside, O., has two daughters, Augusta and Frances. Gracia M. Platt married a Nash, living near Los Angeles, Cal. Betsey C. married a Ricketts, living in Iowa. Mary Abigail (Darwin) had children: Charles Carlyle, of Washington, D. C. ; Wm. P., of Keokuk, Iowa, and Mary C., of Waco, Texas. Alanson S. Platt, late of Cincinnati, O., left children : Ellen F. (Johnson) ; Merrit W. Platt, of Toledo, O., who has daughters, Jesse Platt and Fannie M. (Hull), of same place, and their brother, Archie W. Platt. Mrs. Phebe R. (Coxhead), of Oakland, who died in 1884, left four children : Minnie G. (Lynch), Ella Platt (Bouton), Ralph S. and Edith, all living in or near Oakland, Cal. It should be recorded of Mrs. Mary A. Darwin, late of Burlington, Iowa, that she was an accomplished and successful teacher and an effective and ready speaker. She died July 30, 1886. Her husband, Will L. Darwin, now resides in San Francisco, Cal. One of the main roots of this branch was Alanson Platt, born in Milford, Ct., January, 1792. He married Elizabeth Beach, daughter of Samuel, April 18, 1810. He died in Oberlin, O. He was a son of Isaac Platt 2d, in this branch, of the Jósiah stock.

Laudra B. Platt, of Baltimore, son of Alanson, born in Milford, Ct., September 8, 1812, married March 29, 1838, Harriet Hemmingway, born in East Haven, Ct., April 5, 1811. He died February 27, 1887. She died September 4, 1887. Their children are : Herman S., Harriet M., James B., Jane Esther, Lester Beach, and William D. Platt.

—Herman S. married Emily McComas, of Maryland. Their children are: James B., and Herman S.

—Harriet M. married Lyman R. Casey, late of New York, just elected U. S. Senator from North Dakota. Their children: Harry P., died May 21, 1863; Frank, Carl, and Theodora Casey.

—James B. Platt married Kate B. Hawley, of Maryland. Children: Ravaud C., died July 7, 1872; and Adele T., who died May 15, 1874.

—Lester B. married Lucy B. Tillotson, of Michigan. One son, Beach Platt.

—Jane Esther Platt married Marvin C. Stone, of Ohio. Their children are: Chester, died October 24, 1876, and Lester M. Stone.

—William D. Platt, the youngest, married Anna E. Washburn, of Maryland. Their children are: Anna, and William D. Platt. Their home is in Baltimore.

———

N. M. Platt, of Cleveland, O., gives these data. His father, David H. Platt, sixty-five years ago lived at North Fairfield, Huron Co., Ohio. He married Betsey Smith there. He is now residing at Cleveland, seventy-five years of age. The grandfather was Samuel Platt, born in New Milford, Ct., as his father before him. Samuel Platt died about 1880, aged ninety-four. His brother was Philo. David H. Platt had six sisters; all were married. He had one brother who died in Michigan without heirs. N. M. Platt was born at North Fairfield, O., December 5, 1844. In 1873 he married Ida McGuillicudy.

One little girl, Belle J., born May, 1883. He has a brother, Corwin H. Platt, residing in Cleveland. He married Mrs. Sarah Moulton near 1863; one son, William G. Platt. This family doubtless trace to old Milford, Ct.

XXXII.

FORT DODGE BRANCH.

———

JAMES LAWRENCE PLATT, of Fort Dodge, Iowa, is the son of Theodorus J. Platt, the son of Stephen, who came from Connecticut. Theodorus J. Platt was born in Alleghany County, New York. He married Mellissa Anne Bellinger, near 1798. Maria, the eldest daughter, is Mrs. R. G. Montony, of Aurora, Ill. John D. Platt, a son, resides in Richland, Kalamazoo County, Mich. Henry S. Platt, of St. Louis, is another son. Two other daughters are Emily, residing in Kewannee, Ill., and Julia A., residing in New York City. The father, Theodorus, died in Livingston Co., N. Y. James L. Platt, of Fort Dodge, is the President of the Chicago and Van Meter Coal Mining Co. The mines are at Van Meter, Iowa. There are several Stephen Platts in the Milford and Huntington Branches.

XXXIII.

JERSEY BRANCH.

———

THIS traces to the oldest Huntington Branch. Jesse 3d, son of Isaac Platt 3d, born September 15, 1762, died in Huntington, November 24, 1827. He married Debora Titus, born January 12, 1766, died December 30, 1849. Their children were: Isaac, born August 1, 1785, died October 30, 1880; Joel, born October 12, 1787; David born April 1, 1790, died June 27, 1822; Ira, born December 29, 1792, died 1795; Ira 2d, born March 5, 1795, died August 25, 1825; Daniel, born July 29, 1797, died January 17, 1831; Jesse 4th, born July 25, 1800, died December 24, 1857; Sally, born August 27, 1802, died February 17, 1851; Ansel, 1808, died in infancy.

—Jesse 4th, married November, 1828, Elizabeth J. Brown, of New York, and soon removed to Jersey City. These are his children born there: Jesse 5th, born August 24, 1829, Joel Stafford and Benjamin G.; Theodore S., born February 24, 1835, died at sea January 7, 1857; Charles P., born April 24, 1837, died from wounds received at battle of Gettysburg, July 28, 1863; Edwin Franklin, born in 1845, died 1875, was also at battle of Gettysburg; Frederick

G., born 1857, died 1878; and Ansel, born, 1841, died 1843.

—Jesse 5th and Amelia Adelaide Chazoth, born September 16, 1831, were married in Jersey City, July 5, 1853; living at Montclair. Their children are: Mary Isabella, Amelia Elizabeth, Grace Adelaide, deceased, Jessie Maude and Charles Wiltberger, born March 16, 1869. Mary Isabella, born 1854, was married to George I. Wichman, of Montclair, October 17, 1878; one son, Frank Maxwell. Amelia Elizabeth was married in Montclair to John N. Solomons, same day. They have two children: Grace Nelson and Kermeth Platt Solomons.

—Joel S., second son of Jesse 4th, married Harriet Eliza Downer, of New York, July 3, 1856. They are living in Jersey City. Their children are: Charles Henry, born May 5, 1857, died in his 14th year; Jesse Stafford and Harriet Amelia, died in infancy; Elizabeth Jane; Edwin Porter, born November 15, 1866; Grace Adelaide, 1869; George B., born March 24, 1872, died in his third year; Walter Gorton, died in his second year; Georgietta Emeline; Benjamin Franklin, died aged seven; Mary Bell; Harry Augustus, born June 3, 1881; and Alonzo Freeman, born January 3, 1883.

—Benj. G. Platt, third son of Jesse 4th, married Julia Lopez, April, 1857; residing in Jersey City. Their children are: Lottie Isabelle, 1861, married February 21, 1884, Wm. H. Armstrong, of Jersey City; Frederick Gorton, born April 14, 1864, married September 5, 1889, Addie Wake, of East Orange, N. J. A second marriage of Benj. G. was to Mary Frances

Higgins, of New York.   Children : Jesse Amelia and Florence Irene.

———

Abraham Platt located at Potter's Creek, Ocean County, N. J., early in the century.   His children were : William, Alexander, Amy and Elmira.   William Platt left one son, Job, and a daughter, Charity.   Job Platt left eight children : Andrew J., Wm. Henry, Job Hamilton, Debora E., Caroline L., Rachel A. and Sarah H.

—Charity married a Mr. Stockton, and had thirteen children.

Geo. C. Platt, son of Joel, of Huntington, married Sarah Allen, 1851.   Six children.   Living in New York.

XXXIV.

BURLINGTON BRANCH.

Thomas Platt, born 1740, is among the first of his name resident in Burlington County, N.J. John Platt, his son, formerly of New Hanover, married Alice Stevenson, September 23, 1784. Their children were: Elizabeth, born July 9, 1785, married John Irwin; Martha, born December 27, 1787; William, born March 13, 1790; Mary, born January 21, 1793, died 1871; George, born July 19, 1795; and John, born September 24, 1802. A second marriage was to Mary Conrow. Children: Franklin, born January 1, 1810, died August 19, 1871; Samuel, born July 11, 1811; and Clayton, born March 23, 1817, died October 21, 1879.

Franklin, son of John, married Clara Ann Greenough, of Sunbury, Pa., December 16, 1837. She is living in Philadelphia. Children: Helen Abigail, born November 18, 1839, died 1883; Annie, born February 10, 1841, died 1860; Ebenezer Greenough, born January 28, 1843; Franklin, born November 19, 1844; Clara Greenough, born November 13, 1848; Wm. Greenough, born June 9, 1851, died 1885; and Mary Eliza, born August 4, 1854.

—Clara Greenough Platt, married J. B. Canby, of

Philadelphia. Children : Clara Greenough, born March 15, 1881; Franklin Platt Canby, born April 25, 1884, and James Benjamin Canby, born September 22, 1887.

William Platt, son of John Platt, of New Hanover, married Maria Taylor. Children: Emily, born 1817; Clayton T., born 1819, died 1877; Sarah, born 1821; William, Jr., born 1827; Charles Platt, born 1829; and Fanny.

—Emily Platt, married David Pepper. Died 1876, leaving two sons, William Platt and David. William P. Pepper married Alice Lyman. Three daughters: Emily, Marian, and Martha. David P. married Sally T. Newbold. A son David and a daughter Mary, dec.

Elizabeth Platt, oldest daughter of John Platt, of New Hanover, married John Irwin. They had eleven children : Mary Ann, Elizabeth, Lydia, Alice, Maria, John W., George W., Samuel, Edwin, William Platt, and Charles Irwin. The last died in his youth. The family live in Ohio ; some in Indiana.

John Platt, second son of John, married Mary Jackson. He died 1854. His children were: George, Lavinia, Elizabeth, Alice, Susan, Franklin, Edward (died young), John 3d, Alfred and Charles, and two dying in infancy. Of these, George, from the fall of his horse, died in his 15th year ; Franklin married Ella B. Ford. John Platt 3d died in 1862, aged 21, from wounds in the battle of Fair Oaks. Charles Platt married Rachel H. Lincoln. Children : Mary, Florence, Bessie R., John Lincoln, and Helen Platt.

Clayton Taylor Platt, oldest son of William Platt, married Amelia Lockwood (née Cooley.) A second marriage was to Martha D. Lucas. By this, two sons, John, born 1875, and Clayton, born 1879.

—Sarah Platt, daughter of William, married William Pepper, 1840. Their children are: George, married Mehitable Wharton; died leaving George and Frances); William (who married Frances Perry; three sons, William, Franklin, and Oliver Perry Pepper); Maria (who married John S. Gerhard; four children); Emily (who married E. Watts; four children: Ethel, Marion, Henry, and Carlton); Rathaum (who married James B. Leonard; three children—one deceased, Sarah, and Rathaum); and Fanny (who married Sidney Wright; one child, Henrietta.

William Platt, Jr., died 1862, unmarried.

Fanny Platt married John D. Shaaff. No issue.

Charles Platt, born 1829, youngest son of William, residing in Philadelphia, married June 5, 1851, Laura Newbold. Their children: Clayton, who married Jessie Bates; Charles, who married Elizabeth Norris, (two children, Charles Platt 3d, and Henry Norris); William A., who married Christine Chambers; and Laura Newbold Platt.

George Platt, son of John of New Hanover, married Sarah Taylor, of Philadelphia. Both deceased. Their children were: Henry, Laura, Maria, Louis Taylor, George, and Emily. Of these, none are living but George and Emily. Their home is in Philadelphia. This branch in its founder is closely related to the one which follows.

XXXV.

BINGHAMTON BRANCH.

———

Rev. William Henry Platt, late rector of Trinity Church, Carbondale, Pa., is a descendant from Jacob Platt, who was born March 10, 1743, and who, with his brother Thomas, born December 28, 1740, appear to be the first settlers of their name in Burlington Co., N. J. His grandfather, son of Jacob, was Daniel Platt, who resided near New Egypt, in that county. Daniel married Mary Kirdy, of English parentage. She died aged ninety. Their children were: Elisha, Martha, Mary, Jacob, and Richard Platt. Jacob, the grandfather of these, died July 16, 1816, and was buried in Wrightstown, N. J. Elisha, son of Daniel, died at Wilmington, Del., 1860, aged seventy. Jacob Platt 2d died 1876, in his 56th year. Richard died 1865, aged about 42. Mary married John Holbert, of Philadelphia; died 1880, aged 68. Martha married Geo. Flemard, of N. J. She survives her husband.

—Rev. Wm. Henry Platt, son of Jacob 2d, married September 30, 1874, Francis Hart, daughter of Joseph Hall, of Philadelphia. Their children are: Dallas Hall, and Elizabeth Hall Platt. The head of this branch and that of Burlington beyond a doubt were brothers.

The distant ancestry of these two branches is not traced. The first "Jacob Platt" in the family was a son of Isaac 1st, of Huntington, his youngest son, Jacob, born September 29, 1682. Little is known further about him or his descendants. In the Milford or Huntington record, there is no trace of a Jacob Platt, born in 1743 or a Thomas Platt in 1740, or near these dates. These brothers were early settlers in Burlington Co., N. J. Franklin Platt, of Philadelphia, who has been searching into the history of the Burlington Branch of the family says : "There was another Thomas Platt of New Hanover, Burlington Co., N. J., because when my grandfather John was married in 1784, he was named in the wedding certificate, as the son of Thomas Platt, deceased. Whereas, Thomas, of 1740 married in 1770, and the last of his nine children, Charles, was born in 1787." He thinks that this Thomas Platt was probably the father of Thomas, Jacob and John, and born near 1718. "Thomas" in the early record of the family does not appear to be a common name.

It will be noted, that the Rev. Charles Henry Platt, of the Plattsburg Branch, was five years a resident and a rector in Binghamton, N. Y. The Rev. Wm. Henry Platt above is now the rector of the Episcopal church in this city.

XXXVI.

VERMONT BRANCH.

It is stated, in Orcutt's History of New Milford, that "Epenetus Platt, of that town, was one among the first ten on the tax list in 1802–9. He was at the time the wealthiest man in Lower Meryall, owning hundreds of acres of land."

Epenetus Platt, son of Gideon and Mary (Buckingham), born February, 1738, married Susannah Merwin, daughter of Joseph. They had a son, Epenetus, born at Milford, August 13, 1760; also, Gideon, Fowler, and Sheldon, and Susannah, Mary, Mabel, and Margaret. Epenetus married Molly Stone, August 10, 1783. Their children were: Laura, married to Nathan Terrill; Avis, who married Sylvester Wheaton, of Camillus, N. Y., 1809; Hervey; Polly, who married Silas Hill, 1813, and Elmore Platt, late of Glens Falls, N. Y. A second marriage was to Sarah Lobdell, March 17, 1803. By this marriage, one child, Marshall Platt, who married Tryphena Merwin, of Milford, March 20, 1825. Elmore Platt, late of Glens Falls, born in Milford, Ct., August 18, 1797, married Betsey Peck, February 2, 1825. He died July 26, 1880, leaving four children: Myron, Sarah Tryphena, Harriet, who married O. L. Baldwin, May 1, 1855, and Harvey Platt. Myron Platt, born August 15, 1830, married Sarah Elizabeth Larrabee. They live at Larrabee's Point, Vt. They have children : Fred. Elmore Platt, born June 28, 1859 ; Nellie Ray Platt, of same place, and Mary Larrabee Platt, born August 22, 1857. The latter married Robt. O. Bascom, a lawyer of Fort Edward, N. Y., December 20, 1882. Their children are : Wyman Samuel, born February 14, 1885, and Robt. Platt Bascom, born December 29, 1886, both at Fort Edward.

—Harvey Platt, youngest son of Elmore Platt, born at Glens Falls, February 23, 1838, married Anna W. Morgan ; now residing in Philadelphia, Pa. They have : Alonzo Willoughby Platt, born at the Falls, June 22, 1868 ; Harvey Elmore Platt, born at same place, February 18, 1870; and Anna Bessie Platt, born at Philadelphia, 1879.

This Epenetus stock traces to the Gideon Branch ; then to Joseph 1st, youngest son of Richard 1st, of Milford.

———

Victor M. Platt, son of Isaac Platt, lately of Kingsbury, N. Y., and grandson of Epenetus of same place, formerly of Milford, Ct., had a brother, Royal B., and three sisters, Emma S., Caroline A., and Jane Platt. Victor M. Platt married Jemima Brown. He died 1877 at the residence of his son, Charles W. Platt, at East Shoreham, Vt., leaving five children ; two only are now living: Carrie P. and Charles W. Carrie P. married Mr. Treadway. They are now living at Grand Rapids, Mich. They have three sons : Howard, John and Alfred Treadway. Charles

W. Platt married Florence A. Wright, of Shoreham, March 10, 1864. Their children are: Clarence W., Phebe E., Emma A., Thirza A., Mary I., Lucius W., Eugene B., and Florence. Of these, Emma A. married Geo. P. LeBrocq, of Nasbeth, Pa. One child, a daughter. Clarence W. married Delia Sweeny, of Whiting, Vt., now living at East Shoreham. Charles W. Platt was two years in the union army during the civil war.

———

James C. Platt, a merchant of Winooski, Vt., is the son of James Satterlee Platt (the latter died August 16, 1889, aged 73). His grandfather was of Poultney, Vt., also James Satterlee Platt, originally from Connecticut. James C. Platt, born May 27, 1842, married Emma A. Allen, of Winooski, May 24, 1870. His children are: William E., born February 22, 1872; Arthur E., born September 27, 1878; Stella A., born November 6, 1880; Martin H., born February 23, 1886.

His uncle, Col. L. B. Platt, raised and equipped, by order of the U. S. Government, the first Vermont cavalry regiment for the late war, the only one— 1,200 strong—from the State. His son, L. B. Platt, resides in Winooski.

———

Miss Eloise C. Platt is in the class of '91 in Smith's College, Northampton, Mass. Her grandfather was Samuel B. Platt who died in Burlington, Vt., in 1879. Her father was Zephaniah Platt, born in Colchester, Vt. He married Susan Chubbuck, born in Wellsborough, Pa. The home of his daughter is Burlington, Vt. Her sisters, Ada and Clara, are in the class of '94 in Smith's college.

———

Edward Webster Platt, of Worcester, is the son of D. R. Platt, Barre, Vt.

Alanson Platt, of Highgate Springs, Vt., the son of James H. Platt, late of Swanton, Vt., had two uncles named John and Nathan. Alanson Platt had three brothers younger, Hiram, Daniel, and George, and a sister, Lorina. His grandfather lived in Clarenden, Vt. Alanson has a daughter, Ella M. Platt, who is now Mrs. Lovell, of Brockton, Mass. She has one daughter. Daniel Platt resides in Cresco, Iowa. His children are: Carrie Louise, now Mrs. Martin ; Mattie Irene, and James Leroy.

XXXVII.

QUEECHE BRANCH.

EDWARD R. PLATT, son of James, late of Queeche, Vt., born in Burlington, 1826, graduated at West Point, 1849, served in the artillery on frontier to 1855; assistant Professor in French at West Point four years to 1859; Captain Second Artillery, May 15, 1861; commanded his battery at Bull Run; brevetted Major for gallantry; Judge Advocate-General Army of Potomac from November, 1863, to July, 1865; brevet Lieutenant-Colonel for gallantry at Fredericksburg; transferred to staff as Assistant Adjutant-General with rank of major. Died June 17, 1884, at Ft. Leavenworth, Kan.

Jas. H. Platt (son of James, late of Queeche, Vt.), born 1837 at St. Johns, Ca., his parents being temporarily there; graduated from the Medical School of the University of Vermont in 1859; served during the civil war as Captain of Fourth Vermont Volunteers; on staff of General Sedgwick as acting chief quartermaster Sixth Corps; a prisoner of war May 30 to December, 1864; appointed Lieutenant-Colonel and chief quartermaster, which he declined; at the close of the war he settled in Virginia. He was a member of the Petersburg City Council; member also of the State Constitutional Convention ; in 1869 he was elected to Congress, and re-elected for three following sessions. He is now a resident of Denver, Col. He married Sarah Sophia Chase, of Holyoke, Mass. He has one son, George F., born 1867, and a daughter, Florence, by a first marriage to Sarah C. Foster in 1859. His second marriage was in 1884. One daughter. His grandfather was of Plattsburg, removing to Sandy Hill, where he died about 1800. His only sister living is Mrs. Geo. P. Bugbee, of Hartford, Vt. His sister Ella Sophia, wife of Rev. Levi Rogers, of Georgetown, Mass., died 1883, without children.

XXXVIII.

BETHEL BRANCH.

JAMES D. PLATT, of New York City, traces to his grandfather, Ebenezer, born in Bethel, Conn., August 23, 1764, who married Anna Hoyt, 1788. Ebenezer Platt died November 17, 1834.

—Dennis Platt, son of Ebenezer, was born in Danbury or Bethel, September 25, 1800. He graduated from Yale College in 1824. He married, June, 1828, Caroline Dwight, of New Haven, Ct. He was ordained to the Christian ministry. His first charge was at Willimantic, Ct., 1827 to 1829. He preached at Canterbury, Ct., 1830 to 1833; at Homer, N. Y., 1834 to 1842; at Manlius, N. Y., from 1842 to 1845; and at Binghamton, N. Y., from 1846 to 1853. He resided at South Norwalk, Ct., at his death, in 1878. His widow is now living there, at ninety years of age. His children are James D. Platt, and Eliza G. The daughter is living with her aged mother in Norwalk.

—James D. Platt, son of Dennis Platt, was born February 24, 1836. He married Augusta M. Morgan, September 17, 1863. He resided at Barbadoes, in the West Indies, twelve years. He has two children, a son and a daughter: Dwight M. Platt, born September 21, 1864, and Caroline M. Platt. They were both born in Barbadoes. The family reside in Lenox Avenue, New York City.

XXXIX

DANBURY BRANCH.

———

EBENEZER PLATT, son of John, son of John, jr., son of Josiah 1st, of Milford, resided some time in Newtown. Born 1708, in Milford, he married Miss Hicock, of Danbury, where he made his home. She was born 1719. They left eleven children : Molly, who married Thaddeus Bennett, of Weston, Ct.; Phebe, who married Daniel Crofut, lived at the West ; Ebenezer 2d (1738), who married Sarah Andrews, dying in Danbury, 1775; Ezra, born 1740 ; Abial, 1745, who married Rhoda Hall, of Lanesboro', Mass., where he died ; Joseph who married Lydia Elsworth or Elmore, of Sharon, Ct.; Benjamin, of Scioto Branch ; James, born 1760, who married Olive Benedict, dying at Green River, N. Y., now Hillsdale ; and Hannah, who married Ely Taylor. She died at Bethel, in Danbury. Ezra has the unique distinction of having been a tory in the Revolution. He went to Fort Moultrie, Charleston, S. C., where he died 1776. There must be some black sheep in the flock. His wife was never known to mention his name after he left to join the English forces. His wife's children were : Ezra 2d, Levi, Ithiel, Eli, and

Ebenezer 3d. Ebenezer 1st lived some years in Lanesboro', Mass., where he died.

The Ebenezer Platt who married Miss Hicock was a son of John Platt 2d, of Newtown, where he lived till he removed to Danbury. John Platt, sr., son of deacon Josiah, of Milford, baptized September 9, 1677, was an early resident of Newtown. At a session of the General Assembly, May, 1711, "Capt. John Hawley, Benjamin Sherman, of Stratford, and John Platt, of Newtown," were appointed a "committee to lay out divisions of land in said Newtown." His home lot was on the west side of the village street, and on the corner next north of where the Congregational Church now stands. His father, Josiah, mentions in his will (proved July 1, 1724-5, vol. 5, Probate Records) these children : John, Josiah, Richard, Joseph, Sarah Bryan, Mary Clark, Hannah Merwin, and Abigail Briscol. John Platt, of Newtown, conveyed land to his brother Richard, of Milford, April 20, 1725, vols. 3 and 4, p. 461. John Platt conveyed land to his son John, jr., May 18, 1741. Also, to his son Moses, same date. Richard Platt, of Milford, conveyed land to his nephew, Ebenezer Platt, of Newtown, April 18, 1740. Also, John Platt, of Newtown, conveyed land to his son Ebenezer, January 17, 1744. This Ebenezer Platt, of Danbury, whither he had removed after his marriage, made a will dated September 14, 1764, proved November 19, following, in which these children are named : Ebenezer, Ezra, Abial, Daniel, Joseph, Benjamin, James, Mary wife of Thaddeus Bennett, Abigail, Phebe, and Hannah.

It is well to state that the Probate Records of Danbury show beside this one, three other Ebenezer Platts. Daniel, son of Ebenezer 1st, was born August 27, 1747; he died April, 1798. Mary (Mrs. Bennett) had three children: Jabez, Platt, and Irena. Abial and Rhoda had two sons, Hall and Abial Platt. Joseph, born February 15, 1750, and his wife Lydia, had two sons and a daughter, Joseph, Ely, and Polly Platt.

SAYBROOK BRANCH.

JOSEPH C. PLATT, of Waterford, N. Y., has given many data of this branch. The first name is that of Frederick Platt, who, it is thought, settled in Killingworth about 1790. There are no very early records. He married Miss Fox, of New London, Ct., and left six children : Samuel, who settled in Putchaug, now Westbrook ; Ebenezer, of same place, who married Dorothy Post ; Obadiah ; Mary, who married Samuel Stevens, of Killingworth ; and Lydia, who married David Kilsey.

—Obadiah, third son, born 1709, married Hannah Lane, of Clinton, Ct., December 21, 1737. He located in the western part of Saybrook, what the Indians called Pettipang, now Winthrop, Ct. His house was ten rods from the school-house. He died aged sixty-four. His widow married Caleb Chapman, of Saybrook.

—Captain Dan, of the revolutionary army, son of Obadiah above, born 1735, married Jemima Pratt, January 12, 1763 ; died aged eighty-eight.

—Joseph Platt, another son, born June 1, 1740.

died, aged twenty-one, at Crown Point. He was in the old French war.

—Noah Platt, third son of Obadiah, born September 4, 1742, married Lucretia Chapman, 1772; then Mrs. H. Wright, 1800; died October 1 ;, 1811. He was the father of Col. Obadiah Platt, 2d.

—Hannah, daughter of Obadiah, born 1745, married William Hill; died aged seventy-six.

—John Platt, a fourth son, born 1746, married Lucy West, of Chester, October 12, 1779; died at the age of ninety-one. He had a son, Capt. John Platt.

—Elizabeth, a second daughter, born 1749, married Benj. Burr; died aged about ninety.

—Sarah, a third daughter, born 1751; married Isaac Post; died at the age of seventy-eight.

—Mary, a fourth daughter, born 1753; married Michael Spencer; died aged seventy-eight.

—Lydia, last child of Obadiah, born 1756; married Josiah Post; died aged eighty.

Dan Platt, son of Capt. Dan, known as deacon Platt, born June 21, 1764; married Catherine Lane, December 20, 1787. A second marriage was to Mrs. Cynthia Evarts, of Madison, Ct.; he died in Madison over seventy-eight.

—Jemima Platt, daughter of Capt. Dan, born 1766; died aged twenty.

—Hannah Platt, a second daughter, born 1769; married John Lane; died nearly sixty-six.

—Joseph Platt, a second son, born 1774; died aged five.

—David, third son of Capt. Dan, born 1777; married Lydia Wilcox.

—Sarah, third daughter of same, born 1781; married George Havens. After his death she married Bela Stannard; she died over sixty.

—Lucretia Platt, fourth daughter, born 1785; married Gaylord Coan.

John Platt, fourth son of Obadiah 1st, had five sons: John, called Capt., Jared, Curtis, William, and Alfred, and seven daughters: Lucy, Lucinda, Anna, Julia, Hannah, Polly, and Lydia. They married: Lucy, Ezra Barker, of Chester; Lucinda, Elisha Kilsey, of Killingworth; Anna, Elisha Rice in 1808; Hannah, Joseph Chittenden; Polly, Friend Phelps, of Killingworth; Lydia, Ezra Jones; Alfred, Sophia Williams. Jared died in New Haven, and Curtis was killed by a railroad accident, 1871.

Deacon Dan Platt had five sons and five daughters: Joseph, Jemima, Hezekiah, Dr. Dan, Catherine, Austin, Ezra, Eunice, Abigail, and Harriet.

1. Joseph Platt, eldest, was a lawyer, born in 1789; he married Lydia Pratt; he died aged thirty-seven. He was an associate of the father of the late Chief Justice Waite. 2. Jemima, oldest daughter, married Jonathan Scranton; then Ebenezer Dudley, of Madison. 3. Hezekiah Lane Platt, second son, married Sarah Mills. 4. Dr. Dan Platt, third son, born 1795, married Abby Lathrop. He married twice afterwards, and lived at Key West, Fla. 5. Catherine Lane Platt, second daughter, born 1797, married John Buckingham; a second marriage was to Gilbert Gaylord, of West Springfield, Mass. 6. Austin Platt, born 1799, married Eliza Hinckman; he is buried in Elizabeth, N. J.

7. Abigail, third daughter, married Jeremiah Russell, of old Branfort, Ct. 8. Ezra Platt, fifth son, born 1803; died in New York, aged twenty-five. 9. Eunice Platt, fourth daughter, born 1805; in 1871 was residing in Fair Haven, Ct. 10. Harriet Platt, youngest, born 1808; died in New York at the age of twenty-three.

Jerusha T. Platt, daughter of Joseph Platt, of Deep River, Ct., married Mr. Allen. Three children: George William, Caroline J., and J. Platt Allen, of New York.

———

Lozelle J. Platt, of Deep River, Ct., son of Obadiah 2d, born on the farm he now occupies, April 5, 1819, married Mary Augusta Albee, February 19, 1844, born in Lyme, Ct., December 17, 1824, her family being from Dudley, Mass. Their children are five : Mary Eva, Jennie Ella, Ada Lillian, Jessie Corinne and Edith Jerusha. 1. Mary Eva, born December 7, 1846; married Herbert Z. Doane, August, 1870. Their children are : Eva Herbertine, born July 28, 1870, and Clara Estelle, born April 7, 1882. 2. Jennie Ella, born March 5, 1849; married Charles Augustus Northend, of New Britain, June 18, 1876; now residing there. Their children are : Grace Evelyn, born December 6, 1878, and Allan Platt, born October 3, 1887; Arthur Platt died May 4, 1883, aged 2 months, and Robert also in infancy, 1884. 3. Ada Lillian, born March 18, 1857 ; residing in Hartford, Ct. 4. Jessie Corinne, born November 14, 1860; married Clarence E. Lamb, August 27, 1883; residing at the homestead. Two children :

Louise Albee, born May 12, 1885, and Gladys Margaret, born December 16, 1889. 5. Edith Jerusha, born May 18, 1869; residing with her sister in Hartford, Ct.

Lozelle J. Platt's brothers and sisters were: Noah, Obadiah, Samuel W. and Temperance Amelia. He was a grandson of Noah Platt, and one of the sons of the Obadiah Platt who died in 1841. He writes that he thinks the Saybrook Branch is of German origin, but that the early records of the family in New London were burnt by Arnold in the revolution. He admits that there is no reliable proof, and well says that "traditions, like scientific theories, are good to set the mind on an enquiry, but they will not do to swear by." The writer of this has had occasion to hunt down a good many traditions, and his opinion is that they are very often "such stuff as dreams are made of." The recurrence of so many names so frequent in the Milford Branch would seem to show an undoubted connection; and the Biblical names, without exception, among the first descendants of Frederick, is a decided argument against a German origin. The Teutonic race do not follow Scripture so closely. Among the early children we ought to find a Fritz, a Wilhelm, or Heinrich, a Johann, a Ludwig or a Karl. But they are not there. The inference is that, in large probability, one of Isaac's sons, about whom we know little (John, Joseph or Jacob), may have crossed the Sound from Huntington and established this branch in the last decade of the 17th century; or some other of our name, of whom we know little, may have been the first in this branch in the first decade of the 18th century. Tradition will not even give us the right names, when it fails in so many other points. It is to be regretted that the ancestral line is not more clearly traced. The discussion above is by no means conclusive, only suggestive. If the records indeed went far enough back, there would be unity doubtless in some sturdy Saxon's home, before the Teutonic tribes swarmed over Britain.

XLI.

SCRANTON BRANCH.

———

THIS is an offshoot of the preceding. Joseph Curtis Platt, son of Joseph Platt lawyer, was born in Saybrook, September 17, 1816. He married Catherine Serena Scranton, daughter of Jonathan Scranton, of Madison, Ct., April 2, 1844. Mr. Platt was a merchant in Fair Haven, Ct., but at length became a manufacturer of iron. He removed to Scranton, Pa. in 1846. He was one of the firm of Scrantons & Platt, which firm at length grew into the Lackawanna Iron and Coal Co. They were among the very first to use coal in this country for smelting purposes. The enterprise and success of this company in reality resulted in the building up of the City of Scranton. Mr. Platt died at the age of 71, in that place. He had two brothers and two sisters: Geo. Washington, who died in childhood; Wm. Henry, born September 8, 1821, residing in Scranton, Pa.; Temperance J. who married Edward C. Allen, of Meriden, Ct., and Lydia M. who married Charles F. Mattes, of Scranton. She lived to the age of thirty-five only.

Joseph Curtis Platt 1st, of Scranton, Pa., was instrumental in giving the name to the city where he resided. He was public-spirited and influential. His "Reminiscenses of the Earlier History of Scranton," an address delivered before the Lackawanna Institute of History and Science, is a valuable narrative of enterprise and venture in the neighborhood, showing how the foundations of present property were laid. He died in Scranton, November 15, 1887. His wife had preceded him, July 4th, the same year. Their children are : Joseph Curtis Platt 2d, now of Waterford, N. Y. ; Ella Jemima Platt, and Frank Elbert Platt.

—Joseph Curtis Platt 2d, son of the late J. C. Platt, of Scranton, was born at Fair Haven, Ct., January 9, 1845. He married Kate Judd Jones, of Penn Yan, N. Y., December 8, 1869, born April 28, 1846. Their home is in Waterford, N. Y. He graduated at Philips' Academy, Andover, Mass. 1862, and at the Rensselaer Polytechnic Institute, Troy, N. Y., in 1866, a civil engineer. He is a manufacturer in iron. He resided in Scranton from childhood, then at Franklin Furnace, N. J., till 1875 ; then at his present home. He was President of the Mohawk and Hudson Manufacturing Co., and of the Eddy Valve Co., but he has lately retired from business. He is proprietor of the Button Boiler Co., Waterford. He has children : Frederick Joseph Platt, born at Franklin Furnace, July 23, 1871 ; Llewellyn Jones Platt, born at same place, July 23, 1873 (died July 15, 1876, while on a visit to his grandfather at Scranton) ; Elbert Scranton Platt, born December 21, 1876 ; and Edward Howard

Platt, November 5, 1878, who died in infancy. The father, Jos. C. Platt, is a trustee of the Rensselaer Polytechnic Institute, Troy, N. Y., where he received the degree of C. E. His oldest son, Frederick Joseph, is in the class of '92, at Cornell University, Ithaca, N. Y.

—Frank Elbert Platt, second son of Joseph C. Platt (1st), born February 21, 1859, resides in Scranton, at the old homestead. He married Elizabeth Augusta Skinner, of Guilford, Ct., born 1860. Their children are: Joseph Curtis Platt 3d, born at Cold Spring, N. Y., November 18, 1887; Margaret Scranton, born in New York city; and Philip Skinner Platt, born in Scranton, Pa., November 26, 1889. He is engaged in carrying on the industries of his father, the original "Iron Works" in the Lackawanna Valley.

Wm. Henry Platt, of Scranton, son of Joseph Platt, lawyer, married Emily Mabel Hopkins, of Naugatuck, Ct. His children are: Geo. Hopkins; Amelia Lydia, who died in her fourth year; Wm. Henry Platt 2d, of Brooklyn, L. I.; Emily M. and Catherine S. Platt. Geo. Hopkins Platt, born March 2, 1850, married Frances E. Lowell. He was General Superintendent of the Clearfield Bituminous Coal Co. at Peale, Pa., at the time of his death, January 1, 1887. He had before been Superintendent of the McIntyre Coal Co. His widow, with one remaining child, Florence May, is living at Elmira, N. Y. Emily M. Platt, second daughter, born November 3, 1861, married Dr. L. C. Millspaugh, of Vine Valley, N. Y. Catherine S., third daughter of W. H. Platt, born

June 8, 1864, married Albert E. Jenkins, of West Superior, Wis.

—Wm. Henry Platt 2d, of Brooklyn, L. I., born in Scranton, September 5, 1858, married Ida F. Drury, of Elmira, N. Y., October 3, 1883. They had one son, Robt. Drury, born at Atkinson Kas., who died in infancy. He is in the office of the Rome, Watertown & Ogdensburg R. R. Co., New York.

XLII

NORWICH BRANCH.

ELY PLATT, third son of Nathan Platt, born at Newtown, Ct., July 3, 1793; married Levia Beckley, of Naugatuck, daughter of Dr. Daniel Beckley, a soldier under Washington at Trenton. He lived some years at Washington, Ct., then at Utica, N. Y.; was several years in the public service. Died at Norwich, February 13, 1867, aged seventy-four. His children were: Rufus D., George Lewis, Adaline M., Nathan Ely, Emily L., Charles Beckley, and Helen Theresa Platt. At one time, under the old state constitution, it became his duty as a coroner of Oneida County to arrest the sheriff. His widow survived him many years, residing with daughters in Albany, N. Y.

—Rufus D. Platt, oldest son of Ely, born March 17, 1817, married Frances J. Whiton, of Troy, N. Y., June 12, 1845. Their children are: Evelyn, Cornelia, and one son, Frank. Cornelia M. married Nelson C. Marcellis, March 28, 1871. R. D. Platt was several years in charge of the manufacturing fur department in the late A. T. Stewart's store. He died at his home in Montclair. N. J., August 15, 1885, in his sixty-ninth year.

—Adaline M. Platt, oldest daughter of Ely Platt, born September 25, 1821, at Washington, Ct., married William T. Rudd, of Albany, N. Y., November 9, 1848. Her only son living is William Platt Rudd. His brother, Charles Beckley, died in babyhood. The only daughter living is Adeline, who married George Parker Howlett, of West Newton, Mass. They have one daughter, Marion. William Platt Rudd was born in Albany, N. Y., June 9, 1851. He graduated at Union College, in the class of '73, also at the Albany Law School, with the degree of L.L.B. He is a member of the Alphi Delta Phi fraternity; and now, of the law firm of Harris & Rudd, Albany. He married, October 25, 1883, Aimée Pierson, daughter of Henry A. Allen, of Albany. They have one son, Tracey Allen, born September 16, 1884. Mrs. William T. Rudd, his mother, died at the age of sixty-two. Her husband is still living, in Albany, at times visiting his daughter in the neighborhood of Boston.

—Nathan Ely Platt, third son of Ely Platt, born in Washington, Ct., May 1, 1823, lived in boyhood and early manhood in Utica, N. Y. In 1858 he established iron works at Marquette, Mich., on Lake Superior, but in 1861 removed to Chicago, Ill. He married, December 14, 1843, Mary Eveline Colburn, of Utica, who was born December 15, 1823. They had one daughter, Mary Eveline, who was born at Utica, September 15, 1847. She married, December 14, 1866, Ira S. Younglove, of Chicago, who was born in Vernon, Vt., November 10, 1835. She died November 28, 1873, in her 27th year, leaving an only son, Ira Platt Younglove, born October 7, 1867. He is now in Yale College in the class of '91. Mrs. Platt, his grandmother, died June 11, 1882, in her 59th year. It should be stated that Nathan E. Platt was President and Manager of the Lake Superior Foundry Co. at Marquette. He was a member of the first board of aldermen of the city. At Chicago he was in the iron commission business twenty odd years. He is a member of the Chicago Board of Trade, and at one time was a director in the Board. He has retired from business, but is still living in Chicago.

—Emily L. Platt, second daughter of Ely, was born at Washington, Ct., in 1825. She was a teacher in Albany, devoted and beloved for upwards of twenty-nine years. She seemed to have special gifts for her chosen work. There is no higher function than that of teaching. "Let not ambition mock at such useful toil." Her death was sudden, in Lynn, Mass., August 12, 1880. Her remains were buried in the beautiful cemetery outside of Albany, near her mother's grave.

—Charles Beckley Platt, the youngest son of Ely, born in Utica, March 8, 1827, lived in Geneva, N. Y. some time, then in New Haven; but finally he established himself in Norwich, Ct. He was concerned in the publication of the Norwich *Tribune* and also in that of the *Bulletin*. He became a merchant and was successful. He had a remarkable memory, was well read, and under the *nom de plume* of " Karl Beck," he wrote many excellent pieces of poetry and prose. He married Frances J. C. Dey, December 14, 1848,

A son, Allen, who died in his 24th rear; and a daughter who died in infancy. A second marriage was to Olive W. Barstow, of Norwich, February 6, 1860. Two of their children died young. His death was at his beautiful home, "Rocklawn," September, 8, 1883, in his 57th year. His widow still resides there, where, October 9, 1889, the only child remaining, Helen Barstow Platt, was married to Channing Moore Huntington, son of the late Rev. G. Huntington, and a nephew of Daniel Huntington, the artist. He is a graduate of Hamilton College, and is the literary editor of the Utica *Herald*, residing in that city. He has an infant son, born March 19, 1891.

—Helen Theresa Platt, the youngest, born in Utica, July 17, 1834, married John N. Byron, of New York, August 2, 1864. Their children are: Emily Lois, born in 1865; David Platt, born December 4, 1867; George Lewis, born April 27, 1870; Charles Ely, born January 16, 1873; Fred Russell, born March 7, 1875; all Albanians. Their home is in Albany, N. Y.

XLIII.

TIVOLI BRANCH.

———

This comes from the Norwich Branch. Rev. G. Lewis Platt, son of Ely Platt, has been Rector of St. Paul's Church, Tivoli-on-Hudson, N. Y., now (1891) over thirty-one years. Born at Washington, Ct., February 8, 1819, prepared for college at Utica under Dr. David Prentice, his early friend and adviser, he graduated at Hobart College, Geneva, N. Y., in 1841, taking the second honor in his class. In 1889 he received the degree of S.T.D. from his Alma Mater; he was ordained in the Episcopal Church in Charleston, S. C., 1848; called as assistant to Rev. Dr. Cutler, St. Anns, Brooklyn, L. I., in 1850; in '53, Rector of the Church of the Mediator, Philadelphia; in 1855, Rector of St. James, Great Barrington, Mass; some months in charge of Christ Church at Bridgeport, Ct.; and September 1, 1859, called to his present rectorship. New and beautiful stone churches, during his ministry, have been built at Great Barrington and Tivoli. He has published "Out of the Shadows Into the Light," "Beautiful on the Mountains," "Life-Work," "Life-Work of the Early-Called," "Light on the Cloud," "Good from the

Great Crime," "A Heroic Life," "True Patriotism," and other occasional sermons. He is a member of the Greek letter associations of Alpha Delta Phi and Phi Beta Kappa. He married Sarah D. Willard, of Greenfield, Mass., May 26, 1848. Four children by this marriage: Mary Memminger, born on Waccamaw, S. C.; Helen Levia, born at same place; George Willard and Frederic H. Pierrepont, born in Brooklyn, L. I. (Frederic died in Savannah, Ga., April 27, 1874, in his twenty-second year, after spending two years at Cornell University, and receiving his degrees of M.D. and Ph.D. from the University of Pennsylvania, Philadelphia.) A second marriage was to Clara Gibson, of Great Barrington, Mass., June 26, 1856. Two children living by this marriage: Clara Amelia and Estelle Gertrude Platt; Joseph G. and Herbert Winthrop died in infancy.

—Mary Memminger Platt, the first daughter, was married in St. Paul's Church, Tivoli, N. Y., August 19, 1890, to Kenyon Parsons, of London, now residing in New York. He was educated at the London University College School, and lately held an appointment in Ceylon. An importer. His wife was educated at the Packer Collegiate Institute, Brooklyn, L. I.

—Helen Levia Platt, the second daughter, born 1850, educated at Mrs. Cary's school, Philadelphia, married J. Melvin Thomas, of Albany, September 17, 1873. He graduated from Union College in the class of '72. He is a member of the Alpha Delta Phi. They have one daughter, Nellie May, not yet ten years old. They reside in Spokane Falls in the new State of Washington.

—George Willard Platt, son of G. Lewis Platt, born in Brooklyn, L. I., September 8, 1851, was some time at St. Stephen's College, Annandale, N. Y.; then at Cornell University; took a course of lectures at the College of Pharmacy, Philadelphia, Pa., 1873; married Edith, daughter of Judge Royall Tyler, of Brattleboro', Vt., September 5, 1877. They have two daughters and a son: Gertrude Tyler, Royall Tyler, and Laura Willard Platt. These children number the eleventh generation from Richard 1st, of Milford. The home of the family is in Great Barrington, Mass. The father is well established in the drug business.

XLIV.

WESTERN BRANCHES.

H. PLATT CUSHING, of Mankato, Minn., gives these names and dates: Mary Ann Platt was an only child of Abial Platt, who was one of a family of seven: Tirzah Platt, born March 30, 1771; Jabez H. Platt, July 30, 1772; Rhoda Platt, born November 20, 1774; Adah P., July 26, 1776; Mary, April, 1779; Abial Platt, born February 7, 1781, and Hannah, July 7, 1783. Mr. H. P. Cushing is the great-grandson of Abial Platt on his grandmother's side.

—G. W. Platt, of Cincinnati, O., is the son of A. J. N. Platt, and grandson of Zephaniah Platt, formerly of New York, latterly of Springfield, O., where he taught a law school. G. W. Platt had an aunt, Amelia (widow of Daniel P. McLaron.) He has three children: George W., Mumford, and Mary Platt.

—Rev. Abram Platt lived some years at Greenville, Mich., and died there.

His brother, Joseph Platt, resides in Brooklyn, L. I., and his daughter-in-law also resides in Brooklyn. She has a daughter in Denver, Colo. Walter F. Platt, of New York, is a grandson of Rev. Abram Platt.

———

—In the Le Roy Branch, we noted the residence of G. N. Platt, at Vacaville, Solano Co., Cal.

—John Meade Platt, son of Dr. W. H. Platt, of Petersburg, Va., resides at Annacortes, Washington.

—J. Melvin Thomas, who married Helen Levia Platt, late of Albany, N. Y., is residing at Spokane Falls, in the new State of Washington.

—Howard Platt, son of Cyrus, resides at Leadville, Colo.

—Frank Platt., dental surgeon, son of G. Norton Platt. is a resident of San Francisco.

XLV.

HUNTINGTON MARRIAGES, BAPTISMS AND OTHER DATA.

———

Epenetus Platt and Sarah Scudder were MARRIED October 31, 1723.

Philip Platt and Phebe Rogers, December 15, 1725.

Amos Platt and Zerviah Whitman, July 3, 1729.

Samuel Stratton and Ruth Platt, April 22, 1728.

Eliphalet Wicks and Hannah Platt, March 26, 1730.

Zephaniah Platt and Hannah Sexton, of Smithtown, March 21, 1730.

Samuel Bagley and Phebe Platt, of Smithtown, January 11, 1731-2.

Micajah Townsend and Elizabeth Platt, April 23, 1732.

Joseph Platt, widower, and Jane Blatchley, widow, May 21, 1733.

Richard Allison and Elizabeth Platt, September 19, 1733.

Robert Arthur and Tabitha Platt, December 23, 1734.

Isaac Platt, widower, and Abigail Baylis, widow, August 15, 1736.

Josiah Wheeler and Mary Platt, September 1, 1736.

Zophar Platt and Rebecca Wood, November 19, 1738.

Nehemiah Palmer, of Greenwich, Ct., and Abigail Platt, January 28, 1738-9.

John Platt, widower, and Mary Wood, widow, August 16, 1739.

Archibald Greenfield and Mary Platt, October 1, 1740.

Eliakim Smith and Mary Platt, April 4, 1743.

Isaac Smith, of Islip, and Jemimah Platt, December 28, 1743.

Philip Platt, jr., and Temperance Smith, November 14, 1744.

Joseph Platt, jr., and Mary Barker, January 10, 1744-5.

Isaac Platt, jr., and Esther Ketcham, February 22, 1744-5.

Treadwell Brush and Hannah Platt, May 14, 1746.

Rev. Nathan Tucker and Sarah Platt, of Smithtown, June 18, 1747.

Epenetus Wood and Mary Platt, widow, October 25, 1746.

Amos Willets and Keziah Platt, July 24, 1749.

Jacob Brush and Sarah Platt, October 4, 1749.

Joseph Wicks and Mary Platt, November 20, 1749.

Jacob Platt and Mary Bryant, December 13, 1750.

Jesse Platt and Mary Brush, January 24, 1750-1.

Obadiah Platt and Mary Carll, February 17 1751-2.

Stephen Kelsey and Anna Platt, March 31, 1752.

Richard Platt and Elizabeth Jarvis, April 30, 1752.

John Wheeler and Phebe Platt, December 7, 1752.

John Sammis, widower, and Phebe Platt, widow, January 14, 1753.

Jonas Platt and Rebecca Bennett, December 12, 1754.

Zophar Platt and Sarah Platt, April 11, 1757.

Solomon Platt and Hannah Wood, June 8, 1757.

Eliphalet Platt, of Smithtown, and Elizabeth Scudder, December 19, 1757.

Daniel Tucker, widower, and Elizabeth Platt, widow, August 10, 1758.

Epenetus Platt, jr., and Hannah Marvin, August 13, 1758.

Israel Wood, widower, and Vashti Platt, May 1, 1762.

Capt. Isaac Platt, widower, and Mary Smith, widow, May 11, 1762.

Jedediah Raymond, of Norwalk, and Elizabeth Platt, November 28, 1763.

John Sammis, jr., and Mary Platt, August 5, 1764.

Jesse Carll, widower, and Temperance Platt, widow, January 22, 1772.

Nathaniel Buffett and Zerviah Platt, October 27, 1774.

Henry Titus and Phebe Platt, December 31, 1774.

Nathaniel Brush and Hannah Platt, January 1, 1775.

Timothy Conklin, jr., and Mary Platt, February 15, 1776.

David Rusco, jr., and Hannah Platt, March 31, 1776.

Ezra Conklin and Sarah Platt, October 4, 1778.

Solomon Ketcham, jr., and Rebecca Platt, March 7, 1779.

Joseph Platt and Rebecca Gildersleeve, November 28, 1769.

Obadiah Platt and Mary Platt, February 5, 1770.

Zebulon Platt and Phebe Bennett, widow, August 23, 1772.

Philip Platt and Mary, February 7, 1773.

Isaac Platt, of Huntington, and Eunice Platt, of Connecticut, October 18, 1786.

Israel Platt, of Huntington, and Hannah Oakley Hunt, of Huntington, January 24, 1787.

———

There are many marriage "licenses" found recorded in the Secretary of State's office at Albany, N. Y. Among them are Benjamin Platt and Hannah Wooley, August 6, 1783 ; Charles Platt and Caroline Adriance, May 22, 1773 ; Nathaniel Platt and Phebe Smith, November 10, 1766; Uriah Platt and Sarah Treadwell, January 21, 1761 ; and Zephaniah Platt and Mary Van Wyck, November 23, 1761.

———

The baptismal records in the old church were kept by Rev. Ebenezer Prime, (the first one is in 1723); by Rev. John Close from 1768 ; by Rev. Nathaniel Woodhull from 1786 ; and by Rev. Joshua Hartt, at different dates.

The following persons of our name were baptized in the town of Huntington, L. I. The records, unfortunately, do not give generally the parentage of the baptized, and do not go far back :   Jesse Platt, 1723; John Platt, February 14, 1723–4; Hannah, November 8, 1724; Philip, November 6, 1726; Mary, June 5, 1726; Phebe, June 10, 1726; Vashti, October 23, 1726; Jonas, December 3, 1727 (died December 10, 1804); Solomon, June 2, 1728; Obadiah, September 1, 1728; Jesse, October 20, 1728; Margaret, October 20, 1728; Keziah, November 24, 1728; Epenetus, September 13, 1730;   Amos, December 30, 1730; Zophar, January 10, 1730; Stephen, March 21, 1730; Philip Smith, March 5, 1731; Phebe, May 2, 1731; Sarah, April 2, 1732, Zerviah, November 25, 1732; Mary, January 28, 1732–3 ; Uriah, March 31, 1734; Zophar, October 30, 1734; Ann, June 10, 1733; John, February 1, 1735–6; Mary, May 18, 1735; Thankful Skudder Platt, same date ; Naomi, August 22, 1736; Zephaniah, January 1, 1737–8; Israel, May 26, 1738; Samuel, June 3, 1739; Elizabeth, September 23, 1738; Israel, November 30, 1740; Nathan, November 30, 1740; Hannah, January 13, 1739; Epenetus, January 27, 1741-2; Sarah, January 27, 1741-2; Phebe and Mary, same date ; Elizabeth, August 15, 1742; Charles, March 11, 1743-4; Selah, June 20, 1744; Jeremiah, August 26, 1744; Zebulon, November 6, 1744; Rebecca, March 23, 1746; Elizabeth, March 25, 1746; Obadiah, March 23, 1745-6; Mary Platt (adult), October 19, 1746; Mary, January 4, 1746; David, July 13, 1746; Joseph, October 14, 1746; Elizabeth, September 4,

1748; Phebe, September 11, 1748; Elizabeth, September 18, 1748; Zerviah, February 25, 1749-50; Sarah, November 11, 1750; Philip, March 17, 1750-1; Mary, June 9, 1751; Gilbert, April 11, 1753; Hannah, August 5, 1753; Ebenezer, May 9, 1754; Phebe, October 27, 1754; Bathsheba, January 11, 1756; Mary and Sarah (twins), August 1, 1756; Hannah, November 7, 1756; Hannah, January 3, 1757; Rebecca, January 23, 1757; Daniel, (of Smithtown) August 7, 1757; Scudder, April 23, 1758; Gilbert, September 17, 1758; William, February 25, 1759; Amos, July 8, 1759; Mary, May 27, 1759; Bathsheba, June 17, 1759; Phebe, August 24, 1760; Elizabeth, same date; Elizabeth, October 19, 1760; Jesse, August 30, 1761; Mary, October 16, 1761; Stephen, July 25, 1762; Treadwell, September 12, 1762; Ananias, October 17, 1762; Richard, November 21, 1762; Henry, May 1, 1764; Isaac, June 14, 1764; Mary, June 3, 1764; Israel, November 14, 1764; Hannah, September 30, 1764; Keturah, October 21, 1764; Phebe, September 1, 1765; Judith, March 5, 1765; Experience, December 9, 1766; Zephaniah, August 9, 1772; Mary, July 22, 1770; Charity, October, 23, 1770; Mary and Hannah, sisters, March 11, 1775; Elison, November 15, 1775; Zerviah, December 17, 1775; Epenetus, Stephen and Peleg (brothers) March 11, 1775; Zephaniah, August 9, 1772. The following baptisms were by Rev. Joshua Hartt: Rebecca Platt, August, 1774; David, May 20, 1790; Phebe, November 27, 1775; Elizabeth, same date; Hannah, June 2, 1799; Jacob, April 29, 1781; Joseph, June 8, 1783; Zophar, June 20, 1784; Dorcas, March 7, 1787.

Phebe Platt, wife of Epenetus Platt 1st, by will left to her son Epenetus, one of the three Bibles left by his grandfather. The other two, one to each of her daughters, Hannah and Elizabeth.

The land records show that five acres of land were laid out to Isaac Platt, Huntington, L. I., February 20, 1724; one acre adjoining his home lot, and that of Jonas Platt.   Land laid out to Isaac Platt, 1722-3. Land laid out to Amos Platt, 1730.   Land laid out to Isaac Platt in 1737 and 1739.   Land laid out to Philip Platt, 1732. Joseph Platt died before 1755. Jonas Platt, sr., gave a release to John Platt of all interest in his father's estate, December 18, 1713. Highway laid out by Isaac Platt and others, May 1, 1744.

It is to be noted, that there was a John Platt and a Jacob Platt in Huntington, in 1668.   John Platt in that year sold land "formerly in the tenor and occupation of John Budd." Jacob Platt was one of the owners of "ye seventh farm," with five others, in 1672.   It does not appear that they were the sons of Isaac, for his children, by the record, were not born then. Were these Isaac Platt's sons by his first marriage? There is no trace of any in any records. Isaac 1st was married in Milford before he went to Long Island. The names we have of his children are only by his marriage in Huntington.

"Isaac Platt and Joseph Platt were magistrates in Huntington, 1673."

"Eunice Platt, born February 9, 1767, died August 22, 1862." Eliza J. Conklin's family Bible.

The will of Isaac Platt was dated May 22, 1695 (?) as recited in a quit-claim from the eldest son Jonas to his brothers, John, Joseph and Jacob, of his (Jonas') interest in his father Isaac's estate ; which quit-claim is dated September 7, 1696. But Isaac Platt died 1691.

The will of Epenetus Platt 2d, the Major, mentions children, Epenetus, Uriah, Zophar, Elizabeth (married Micajah Townsend), Phœbe, wife of Benjamin Treadwell, and Mary, wife of Timothy Treadwell.

Land laid out to Joseph Platt and Isaac Platt, 1732.

Isaac Platt and Joseph Platt were witnesses to a deed, November 1, 1684.

Isaac Platt was President of the Board of Trustees Huntington, 1746 to 1750.

Capt. Isaac Platt, son of Jonas, born 1699, died February 5, 1763, aged sixty-four. His second wife was Abigail Baylis, widow.

Jesse Platt, of Hempstead, baptized 1728, married Mary Brush, January 24, 1750.

XLVI.

MILFORD RECORDS OF OUR NAME.

Given by N. G. Pond, Esq., drawn accurately from various sources ; brought down to 1820. s, son ; d, daughter ; b, born ; m, married ; di, died.

John, s Richard and Mary, of Norwalk, m Hannah Clark, d George.

Isaac, s same, of Huntington, L. I., died 1691.

Sarah, d " m Thos. Beach, 2dly Miles Merwin.

Epenetus, d " b July, 1640, of Huntington, di 1693.

Hannah, d " b Oct., 1643, m Christopher Comstock, of Norwalk.

Josiah, s " b Nov., 1645, m Sarah Canfield, d Thomas, Dec 2, 1669.

Joseph, s " b Apl., 1649, m Mary Kellogg, d David, of Norwalk, in 1693.

Josiah, s Josiah, b June, 1671, m Sarah Burwell, d Nathan, June 8, 1707.

Sarah, d Josiah, b Sept., 1673, m Richard Bryan, s Richard; think she married 2dly Jas. Green.

Mary, d " b Nov., 1675, m Joseph Clark, s Thomas, died Oct. 28, 1755.

John, s Josiah, b Sept., 1677, not in will, 1721.

Richard, s   "   b Aug., 1682, m Esther Buckingham, d Samuel, Nov. 7, 1706.

Hannah, d   "   b Nov., 1685, m Jonathan (or John?) Merwin Feb. 7, 1706.

Abigail, d   "   b March, 1688, m Sam'l Briscol, s Nathaniel, July 3, 1712, di 1773.

Joseph, s   "   b Jan., 1693, m Mehetable Fenn, d Benj., June, 1720.

Josiah, s Josiah, jr., b Oct., 1707, m Mary Newton d Thomas.

Nathan, s   "   b July, 1709, m Elizabeth Peck, of Newtown, June 5, 1740.

Isaac, s   "   b April, 1711, m Phebe Smith, d John, March 12, 1744.

Sarah. d   "   b March, 1713, m Joseph Beard, s Joseph, children: Sarah, Abigail and Mary.

Abigail, d   "   b Oct., 1716, not named in will.

Frances, d   "   b Feb., 1717, m Jeremiah Peck, s Jeremiah, Oct. 26, 1743.

Sarah, d John Platt, b March, 1704.

Phebe, d   "   b Aug., 1705.

Ebenezer, s   "   b Jan., 1708.

John, s   "   b April, 1711, m Sarah Peck, d Ephraim.

Esther, d Richard and Hester, b Feb., 1708, died unmarried, Dec. 24, 1728.

Ann, d same, b Nov., 1710, m Camp. Children: Jonathan, Richard, Abram, Isaac, Sarah, Esther and Mary.

Mary, d   "   b Sept., 1711, m Thomas Clark, s

Thomas.   Ch.: Mary, Thomas and
           Martha, di May 6, 1740.
Richard, s same, b Feb., 1715, m Mehetable Fisk, d
           Ebenezer, March 1, 1737, di May
           3, 1756.
Samuel, s   "   b Nov., 1720, m Hannah Prudden,
           Mar. 13, 1762.
Jonas, s Josiah, sr. and Sarah Burwell, b Nov., 1725,
    wife Sarah.
Joseph, s Joseph and Mehetable Fenn, b Nov., 1724,
           m Hannah Buckingham, d of
           Thomas, di Aug. 30, 1806.
Mehetable, d same, b Sept., 1727, m Joseph Whit-
           more.
Sarah, d   "   mentioned in will, m John Peck,
           s Jeremiah, 1751.
Mary, d Joseph and Mary Kellogg, b Sept., 1681, m
           John Woodruff, s Matthew, Dec.
           22, 1698.
Joseph, s same, b Feb. 16, 1684.
Phebe, d   "   b March, 1686, m Sam'l Newton,
           s Sam'l, Nov. 29, 1705.
Samuel, s   "   b Sept. 1690, m Sarah Beard, d
           Jeremiah, 1744.
Hannah, d   "   b Ap'l, 1693, m Fletcher Norton,
           s Roger.
Epenetus, s   "   b May, 1696, di Ap'l 10, 1723.
Elizabeth, d "   b Feb., 1698, m Nehemiah Smith,
           s Benjamin.
Gideon, s   "   b Sept., 1700.
Sarah, d Joseph, b March, 1703.
Mary, d   "   b May, 1704.

Joseph, s Joseph and Sarah, b May, 1711, di 1776.

Abigail, d same, b Nov., 1712, m Noah Plumb, s •
        Joseph, went to Stratford.

Ebenezer, s "   b July, 1713, m Hannah Green, di
        Aug. 13, 1790.

Stephen, s   "   b Dec., 1717, m Hannah Wood-
        ruff, d John, of Woodbury, 1748·

Phebe, d   "   b Aug., 1721, m Jonah Newton,
        2dly Oliver Sanford, of Wood-
        bury, says brother's will.

Sarah, d   "   b Sept., 1721.

Jeremiah, s Samuel P. and Sarah Beard, b Oct.,
        1718, went to New Milford.

Samuel, s same, b March, 1723, m Anna Welch, of
        New Milford, Aug. 17, 1749.

Epenetus, s "   b Feb., 1736, of New Milford, di
        1760.

Mary and Ann, twins, ds Gideon and Mary Bucking-
        ham.   Mary m Benj. Ball, s Benedict, Ann m Dan.
        Ives April, 1754.

Phebe, d same, b May, 1731, m Samuel Miles,   s
        Theophilus.

Gideon, s   "   b March, 1734, prob. m Mehetable
        Platt, d Richard, of Waterbury, 1784.

Sarah, d   "   b Dec., 1736, m Wm. Nott, says
        mother's will.

Epenetus,   "   b Feb., 1738, m Susanna Merwin, d
        Joseph.

Nehemiah,   "   b July, 1741, m Thankful Merwin, of
        ˙N. Milford, 1782.

Abiah, s   "   b Jan., 1750.

Isaac, s Isaac and Phebe Smith, d Joseph, b Jan.,
            1755, m Amy Eells, says I. Platt.
Phebe, d same, m Joseph Merwin, N. Haven.
Mehetable, d Richard and Mehetable, b May, 1738,
            prob. m Gideon Platt, s Gideon
            (law records, vol. 8.)
Richard, s same, b March, 1742, m Sarah Camp, d
            Caleb, 2dly Ann Rogers, d Jo-
            seph.
Stephen, s Stephen and Hannah, b May 17, 1749;
            think he went to Woodbury.
Hannah, d Sam'l and Hannah, b May, 1743.
Samuel, s same, b Oct., 1744, m Sybil Strong, d
            Ephraim, March, 1765.
David, s   "   mentioned in mother's will.
Sarah, d   "   mentioned in mother's will, m
            Elias Camp, s Samuel.
Esther, d   "   b May, 1747, m David Clark, s
            Samuel.
Mary, d   "   b Jan., 1749, m Smith (papers disc.
            in Strong's garret.)
Grace, d   "   b Aug., 1750, m Richard Clark, s
            Samuel.
Anna, d   "   b 1754 (in will), m Nehemiah
            Clark, s Thomas, di 1810.
Jeremiah, s Jeremiah and Hannah, b Dec., 1747, m
            Mary Merwin, d Miles, settled in
            Bridgewater.
Sarah, d same, b Nov., 1751.
Newton Sam'l, s " b March, 1752.
Nathan s Nathan, b Oct., 1741.
Elizabeth, d "   b March, 1749.

Sarah, d Nathan, b June, 1758, died 1762.

Asa, s Gideon and Mehetable, b May, 1769, m Martha Woodruff, April 6, 1791.

Gideon, s same, mentioned in will.

Mehetable, d " b March 5, 1762, m Isaac Treat, s Joseph, 1785.

Abigail, d Stephen, b April, 1768.

William, s Jonah and Hannah Clark, b Oct., 1797, m Mary A. Baldwin, d Thaddeus, Oct. 18, 1821.

Clark, s same, b April, 1800, m Sybil Stow, d Jared or Jedediah, Nov. 17, 1825.

Patta Maria, d " b Sept., 1802, m Isaac Treat, s Isaac, Oct. 20, 1820.

Amelia C., d " b Oct., 1805, m Charles Merwin.

Jonah, s " b April, 1808, m Comfort Baldwin, d Beard.

Charles, s " b May, 1811, m Emeline Bushnell, of Deep River.

Eliza Ann, d " b Dec., 1813, m Abm. Marks.

Mary Jerusha, d " b Nov., 1815, m Jerry Mervin, s David.

Nehemiah, s Nehemiah, b May, 1773. Had sons: Jireh and William.

Polly Esther, d same, married Fisk Durand, s John.

Abigail, d Jonas and Elizabeth, b Aug., 1772, m John Partree.

Phebe, d same, b Jan., 1774.

Sibyl, d " m John Gillette, Jr., 1781.

Jonas, s " and Elizabeth d., b Nov. 1774.

Mary, d " b 1778.

Sarah, d " mentioned in will, m Samuel Bryan.

Mary, d " b 1778.

Mary, d Ebenezer, b May, 1777, m Thomas Stow,
2dly Joseph J. Minor, April 8,
1814.

Ebenezer, s " b June, 1780, m Sarah Smith,
April 30, 1800.

Johah, s " b 1774, m Hannah Clark, d David,
Nov. 5, 1796, di 1843.

Clarissa, d Jeremiah Platt, b Sept, 1784.

Mehetable, d Joseph and Mabel, b Apl. 4, 1771, m
David Treat, s Joseph, May
24, 1792, di Feb. 22, 1857.

Joseph, s same, b Feb. 1786, m Martha Miles, d
David, Mar. 28, 1801, di 1859.

Mabel, d " b Jan. 31, 1781, m Rd. Fenn, s
Benjamin, Aug. 15, 1802, settled
in O.

Elizabeth, d " b Apl. 28, 1785, m Robt. Treat
s Robt. and Content, March 28,
1811, di June 6, 1852.

Charlotte, d Capt. Joseph, b Dec. 21, 1789, m D.
Clark, s Samuel, Dec. 24, 1812.
Settled in Middlebury.

Nathan, s same, b Jan. 29, 1791, m Sally Fowler, d
Nathan, Jan. 12, 1812, di 1867.

Susanna, d Joseph, jr., b March 17, 1794, m Merwin
Andrew, s William, Apl. 23, 1812, di
Apl. 20, 1872.

Dan, s same, b Nov. 26, 1796, m Emily for 2d wife
Feb. 6, 1817.

Richard, s Richard and Sarah Camp, b 1766, m Margaret Fowler, d Nathan, June 6,
1796.

Fisk, s same, b 1768, m Sarah Newton, d Jonah
    and Phebe, Aug. 8, 1792, di 1847.
Sarah, d   "   m Nathan Fowler, s Nathan, July 9,
    1788.
Rogers, s   "   b 1779.
Joseph, s Joseph and Anna Rogers, b Sept., 1794, m
    Sarah Stone, d Samuel, Feb. 3,
    1804; 2dly, Elizabeth Baldwin,
    d Elisha, Aug. 23, 1829.
William, s same, b Dec., 1792, m Anna Stow, d Jede-
    diah, Nov. 21, 1821.
Isaac, s Isaac and Amy Eells, b Oct., 1783, m Abi-
    gail Smith, d Rich-ard, May 8,
    1803; 2dly, Rebecca Powell, of
    Washington.
Phebe, d same, m Amos Smith, Dec. 11, 1803; set-
    tled in Coschocton, O.
Amy, d   "   m Elias Burwell, s John; 2dly,
    Robert Burwell, of N. H.
Asel, s   "   m Mary Barrett, lived in Ohio.
Alanson, s   "   b Jan., 1792, m Elizabeth Beach, d
    Samuel, Ap'l 18, 1810, di Ober-
    lin, Ohio.
Abigail, d   "   b Sept., 1794, m Alfred Cowles,
    Bristol, Ct.; died there.
Abigail, d Benj. and Abigail Green, b 1784 (?), m
    Eliphalet Sanford, s Elisha,
    March 10, 1799.
Benjamin, s same, b 1795, m Nancy Bristol, d Na-
    than, Jan. 22, 1802, di 1870, at
    Prospect.
Daniel, s   "   b 1795, m Betsey Higby, d

Sam'l, Nov. 25, 1804, settled in Skeneateles.

Sarah, d   same, b before 1795, m Miles Smith, s Theophilus, 2dly Wm. Bush of Eng., di 1818.

Nancy Sacket, d"   m Garret Gillett, s Benj., Oct. 23, 1808.

Elisha, s   "   b bet. 1790 and '95, went to Prospect.

Hannah, d   "   b Aug. 11, 1794, m John W. Sanford, s John, Nov. 5, 1815.

Maria, d   "   b May, 1797.

Mary, d   "   m Garret Gillett, (2d wife).

Polly Esther, d Jireh and Keturah Smith, b May, 1805.

Minerva, d   same, b Jan. 4, 1807.

Hannah Smith, d "   b Sept. 12, 1792, m J. Stevens.

Clarissa, d   "   b July 26, 1794.

Keturah, d   "   also Jireh, b March to June, 1798.

William, s   "   b June to Sept., 1799.

Harvey, s   "   b bet., Oct., 1801 and Feb., 1802.

Mary A., d Asa and Martha Woodruff, b 1791.

Enoch Woodruff, s same, b Nov. 4, 1793.

Patta, d   "   b May 23, 1796, m Raymond Baldwin.

Hetty, d   "   b Nov. 9, 1798.

Asa Gideon, s   "   b June 23, 1801, di May 12, 1832.

Esther Maria, d   "   b between Jan. 31 and Apl., 1804.

Laura and Lucretia, ds "   born in Orange.

Newton, s Fisk and Sarah Newton, b 1795, m Anna

Clark, d Abraham, Oct. 18, 1821, di 1863.

Sarah, d same, b 1797, m Jireh Treat, s Jonathan Oct. 7, 1813, di May, 1867.

Richard, s " m Mary A. Baldwin. d Eisha, May 26, 1820.

Catherine, d " b 1802, di Nov., 1868, not m.

Jonah, s " b 1804, m Sarah Fowler, d Wm. H., March 22, 1829.

Susan, d " b Apl. 26, 1806, m Hull Allen, s Gabriel, Westport, Aug. 16, 1825.

Phebe Maria, d" b June, 1814, m Samuel Miles, s Sam'l, di July, 1858.

Abigail G., d Isaac, b Feb. 27, 1804, m Jas. A. Grant, of Franklin, N. Y., di 1879.

Isaac Smith, s " b July 22, 1806, not married.

Alanson S., s Alanson and Elizabeth, b near 1806, di Cincinnati

Orlando B., s same, b near 1807 (?) went to Baltimore.

Lester W., s " b June, 1814.

Betsey Charlotte, d " b 1816.

Amy Clarissa, d " b 1818.

Samuel Isaac, s " b Aug., 1819, di Oregon.

Mary Abigail, d " b May, 1822.

Merit Fayette, s " b Sept., 1824.

Asael Edwin, s " b July, 1826.

Alfred Cowles, s " b 1828, of O.

Sally, d Nathan and Sally Fowler, b Aug. 22, 1810, m Abel R. Hines, s Joel.

Nathan, s,   same, b May 30, 1812, m Sarah S. Platt, d Joseph, 1839.

Martha, d   "   b Oct. 28, 1815, m D. L. Hubbel; also Susan, 1813, m W. Andrew.

Phebe Rebecca, d   "   b June, 1830.

Elizabeth Ann, d Joseph and Sarah, b Jan. 18, 1806, m Eliakim Fenn, s Wm.

Joseph Rogers, s   same, b Nov. 3, 1807, m Mariette Smith, West Haven.

Mehetable Maria, d   "   b July 22, 1809, m David Nettleton, Nov. 4, 1832.

Mary Naomi, d   "   b Jan. 26, 1812, m Jonah Clark, s Elias.

R'd Willis, s   "   b July 3, 1815, m Abigail Clark, d Luke.

Sarah Stone, d   "   b Feb. 16, 1816, m Nathan Platt, s Nathaniel, 1839.

Elliot Baldwin, s Joseph and Elizabeth, b April 2, 1833.

XLVII.

ENGLISH BRANCHES.

———

Wm. K. Platt, of Philadelphia, the son of William, of Saddleworth, West Riding, Yorkshire, Eng. (who was the son of John Platt), was born in Saddleworth, 1829; came to this country in 1854; married Emma H. Ellis; has three daughters living: Anna B. (now Mrs. Eugene P. Jancks); Evaline Victoria, Helen Eugenia, and Bertha Virginia. Their home is in Camden, N. J. His business office is in Philadelphia.

——

Joseph Platt, son of the late Charles L. Platt, of Brooklyn, L. I., traces to his great-grandfather, Richard Platt, of the Island of Curacoa, the first of the family who came to this country. His grandfather is Joseph Platt, now seventy-five, Commissioner of Buildings in Brooklyn; he has six children.

———

Mamie E. Platt, of Baltimore, has an uncle William Platt, and a sister Mattie. Her father was the late Thomas M. Platt.

———

F. C. Platt, Worcester, Mass., is a son of James Platt (whose father was John, of Saddleworth, Eng.),

who was captain of a vessel, and who went to
California in 1849; but was not heard of since.

———

Willard H. Platt, of New York, born June 12,
1854, traces to his great-great-grandfather, an Eng-
lish merchant in New York. His grandfather, Hezekiah Doolittle Platt, was born in Saratoga Co., N.
Y., his great-grandfather being resident there in his
closing years. His father, Willard Platt, was born in
Elmira, N. Y., March 24, 1830. Hezekiah D. Platt
had a brother William who moved to Lewiston, N. Y.
Of his large family, there are now living: Mrs. Sarah
Allen, Mrs. Abbie Wright, Miss Louise Platt, Geo.
Washington Platt, Augustine E. Platt, and James
Platt. Mr. Willard H. Platt, who gives these data,
has three children: Mabel, Willard Rice, and Harold
Birdsall. His father's cousin, Miss Louisa Platt,
resides in Brooklyn, L. I.

———

David Mills Platt, of South Norwalk, whose
grandparents came from London; born in Redding,
Ct.; married Elizabeth Squires, of Weston, Ct., July
18, 1839. Five sons and one daughter: Samuel
James, Charles Henry, David Arthur, George Wal-
lace, and Albert Everett. All married but George.
D. M. Platt was seventy-two in December, 1890.
Samuel J. was fifty in September, 1890. The father
had an uncle, Mills Platt, who settled in Washington,
Ct., and who had quite a family.

———

Jay L. Platt, of West Dryden, N. Y., writes that
his great-grandparents came from Holland. Daniel

Platt had four daughters and three sons, namely:
Alonzo, John L. and Daniel W. Platt. This last was
his father, who, April 1, 1860, married Rheba C.
Labar.

Harry Platt, of Germantown, Pa., is a son of
John Platt, of Saddleworth, Eng. His grandfather,
James, married Sarah Bradbury, of Weakly, Eng.
His aunt, Mattie E. Platt, is living with him.

Horace H. Platt, of Manayunk, Philadelphia, is
the son of John Platt; his grandfather, William, was
of Saddleworth, Yorkshire, Eng. He has brothers,
Frank and John, here, and sisters, Mary and Sadie.

Chas. J. W. Platt, of Philadelphia, son of Jas.
W. Platt, of Oldham, Lancashire, Eng., married
Annie Gray, October 27, 1889.

Geo. C. Platt, of Philadelphia, son of Robert
Platt, West Virginia, was in the late war; wounded
at Gettysburg; was in over twenty engagements.
His brother, John H. Platt, served in the 10th N. Y.
Volunteers.

James Platt, of Boston, Mass., born in Yorkshire, Eng., married Magdalena Bogardus. Children
living: Martha A., Walter and Helena. The last,
married and living in Detroit, Mich. Martha A.
Platt is living in Boston. The father, James, died
1878. He came to our country in 1842.

There are Platts in Salem, Mass., who spell

their name with a final s. Their connection with Richard Platt, of Milford, is not traced. A Samuel and a Jonathan Platt were early settlers at Rowley, Mass.

———

Wm. Platt, of Philadelphia, son of Thomas Platt, of Londonderry, Ireland. His mother was of the Ewing stock. An ancestor went to Ireland from England, and was at the battle of the Boyne, under William of Orange.

———

Chas. E. Platt, of Philadelphia, son of James Platt, of Thorp Lane, Eng., had three uncles die in this country. Lives with his mother and sister.

———

Edgar M. Platt, of Boston, is a son of Thomas Platt, of English parentage.

———

August Platt, of Cleveland, O., says his father was born in Alsace. Five children. Two brothers are with him.

———

Alfred Platt, of Roxborough, Pa., whose father, John Platt, was killed in our civil war, has a son Alfred. His daughter Amelia married William Tyson.

———

Charles C. Platt, of Philadelphia, was born in Rotterdam, Hol. He thinks his great-grandfather was Spanish.

———

John Platt, son of John Platt, of Heyside, Roy-

ton township, Eng., came to this country in 1864;
living in Philadelphia.

———

George Platt, of Philadelphia, whose father was
from Silverdale, Staffordshire, Eng., married Wilhelmina Staitle; has two children: George Elmer
and Estella.

———

E. K. Platt, of Long Island City, N. Y., traces to
his grandfather, James Platt, of Saddleworth, Yorkshire, Eng.   The grandfather was a nephew of James
Platt of that place, born 1725.

XLVIII.

VALUABLE ENGLISH DATA.

EDWARD HENCHMAN married a daughter of John Platt, son of Sir Hugh Platt, knight.

Richard Moseby married Judith, a daughter of Sir Thomas Playter, of Soterby, in County Suffolk, knight and baronet.

Sir Stephen Soame, of Hayden, County Essex, knight, married Elizabeth, daughter of above Sir Thomas.

These records are taken from the "Visitation of London," 1633-4.

The following record is from "The Visitation of Cheshire," dated 1580 :

" Alice, daughter of John Birchells, of Birchel, married Richard Platt, of London. Sons : Hugh Platt and John Platt."

The following is from "The Visitation of Essex," dated 1634 :

" George Gent, Esq., of Moyns, married Anne, daughter of Sir Thomas Platters, in Soterby in County Suffolk. Second wife."

In "Visitation of Oxford," dated 1566–74, and 1634, are the following :

"Francis Gates, of Bent, married Elizabeth, daughter of Bartholomew Platt, of Spershott, in County Berks." "Elizabeth, daughter of John Platte, of Hanney, County Berks, married John Stompe, of Newnam, Morryn, Gent."

———

The "Visitations" above are a series of books, made up of various pedigrees, published by the Harleian Society, in 1869. The records, in some sense, are official, as persons appointed for this purpose visited the localities, and copied from the official documents.

———

From Le Neve's "Knights," a book of pedigrees, we take the following :

" Rebecca, daughter of Sir Thomas Stringer, married to Sir John Platt, son of John Platt, of Godalming, Surrey. (Probably about 1700.)"

"Sir John Platt, of Westbrook Place, knighted at Whitehall, July 6, 1672."

———

The following is from "Burke's Dictionary of Landed Gentry" :

"Tudwell of Wales. Thomas Tudwell, minor canon of Windsor, some time of Bradfield Hall, in Essex, died about 1672, leaving by Anne, his wife, fifth daughter of Richard Platt, Esq., eldest son of Sir Hugh Platt, knight, of Bidwell Green, County Middlesex, etc."

———

"Thomas Dale, Esq., of Penwick, in County of Derby, born in 1603, married Mary, daughter of Thomas Platts, of Flagg."

"Thomas Platt, Esq., married, May 2, 1839, to Anna, daughter of John Hugh Smyth Pigott, of Brockley Hall and the Grove, County of Somerset.

"Diana, daughter of Thomas Little, Esq., married in 1816 to James Platt, Esq., of Bolton, and died in 1819, leaving a daughter, Mary Ann, who was married, first to George Newman Hardy, Esq., and secondly to William Alsop, Esq., of Liverpool.

————

In a book of "Marriage Licenses," published by the Harleian Society, London, in 1886, there are many curious records. We take from it the following:

"Marriage Licenses issued from the Faculty office of the Archbishop of Canterbury at London:"

"February 10, 1573-4, Hugh Platt and Margaret Younge."

"1663, November 3, Henry Woolnough, of Shelley, County Essex, Clerk, Bachelor. 24, and Elizabeth Platt of Godalming, Surry, Spinster, 16, daughter of John Platt, of same, Clerk, who consents at All Hollows the Less, Thames Street, or St. Smithins, London (Rev. John Platt)."

"1632, Dec. 18. Henbanbrigge, of St. Dunstan, in the East, London, Gent., bachelor, 23, and Mary Platt, of St. Clement Danes, Midd'x, about 26, widow of Richard Platts, late of Barwicke, Co. Sussex, draper, to marry at St. Brides, London."

"Thomas Platt, Esq., of the town of Hague in

Holland, Bachelor, 36, and Susanna Bressey, of Dort, in Holland, whose parents are living in Dort and consent at the Hague, or Dort, aforesaid."

"1672, June 12. John Platt of Godelming, Co. Surrey, Esq., Bachelor, 22, and Rebecca Stringer, Spinster, about 18, daughter of Sir Thomas Stringer, Kt., at St. Andrews, Holborn, or Enfield, Co. Middlesex, or Barnett, Co. Herts."

"1697, June 24. Jeremiah Platt, of Folkingham Co. Lincoln, Gent., bachelor, 28, and Miss Elizabeth Wallett, of Weston, said Co., spinster, 22, at her own disposal, her parents dead; at St. Giles-in-the Fields, Middlesex or"——

The following are Marriage Licenses issued by the Bishop of London:

"1559, Jan. 22. George Tychet, Kt., Lord Audeley, and Joanna Platt, widow, of St. Andrews in Eastcheap, London, to marry anywhere in the diocese."

"1577, Sept. 25. John Platt, of St. James, Yarlick Hithe, and Elizabeth Longe, Sp'r, of All Hollows Barking, at Barking, County Essex."

"1616, Aug. 30. Isaac Gilbert, of Rayley, County Essex, yeoman, and Sarah Platt, of Rochford, said county, spinster, dau. of Robert Platt, of Foulness, dec.; at St. Thaxted.

"1626, Dec. 9. Francis Chamberlaine, of St. Andrews, in the Wardrebe, London, yeoman, and Elizabeth Platt, of St. Clement Danes, Midd., widow; at St. Clement Danes, afsd."

1625, June 6. Hugh Platt, and Clara Mirriull, widow.

1612, July 31. John Bailey, of St. Mary's, Whitechapel, Midd., yeoman, and Anne Platts, of Westham, County Essex, spinster, daughter of Robert Platt, late of So. Wingfield, County Derby, yeoman, dec., at Little All Hollows, Thames St., London.

The following marriages are from the Register of St. Georges, Hanover Square, published in two volumes by the Harleian Society, London :

"1764, Sept. 26. Evan Kinsey, B., and Mary Plats, S."

"1727, Jan. 26. Alexander Gurnly and Ann Platt."

"1729, April 7. Richard Platt, B., and Elizabeth Adams, S., both of St. James, Westminster."

"1756, January 2. Samuel Platt, W., and Elizabeth Kippling, S."

"1756, Feb. 22. Thomas Evans of this parish, B., and Ann Platt, of Putney, Surrey, S."

"1766, Dec. 19. Alexander Stanhope, B., and Sarah Platt, S."

"1778, Nov. 11. John Richardson and Mary Platt."

"1781, Nov. 18. John Nicholas Durand, of St. Catharine Cree, London, and Mary Ann Platt, of this parish."

"1785, Nov. 11. John Baldwin and Mary Louisa Platt."

"1789, April 28. John Salmon and Ann Platt.

"1795, June 6. Richard Norfolk and Ann Platt.

"1796, Sept. 24. Joshua Platt and Sarah Alger."

"1800, Oct. 5. William Platt and Ann Wilkinson."

"1802, Nov. 6. George Kidd, B., and Mary Platt, S."

"1802, Dec. 25. James Platt and Ann Morgan."

"1804, Sept. 27. John Jarvis and Elizabeth Platt."

"1807, Jan. 1. Charles Platt, Esq., of Rotherham, County York, B-, and Judith Ann Ramsden, of this parish."

———

In "Dod's Book of the Peerage" there is a full account of Hon. Sir Thomas Joshua Platt, son of the late Thomas Platt, Esq., of Brunswick Square, solicitor (who died in 1842.) The son was knighted 1845. "He was educated at Harrow School, and at Trinity College, Cambridge, where he graduated B.A. 1810 ; M.A., 1814. Entered as a Student of the Inner Temple, and was called to the bar by that Society in Feb., 1816 ; went the Home Circuit ; became a King's Counsel, 1834 ; was raised to the Bench as a Baron of the Court of Exchequer in 1845. Retired 1856. Residence, 59 Portland Place, London, W."

———

In Manning and Bray's "History of Surrey" the following data are recorded :

"John Platt, of West Horsley, baptized Dec. 26, 1649, was knighted. He died June 17, 1705, at Wickham Abbey, in the parish of Wickham Skeith. His father was John Platt, some time Rector of West Horsley." In the pedigree of the Platts, in Godelming, this following is given in the history named above. "Hugh Platt, of Aldenham. His son, Richard, Alderman of London, married Alice, daughter of

John Birchells, of County Chester. Died 1600. His son, Sir Hugh, of Bethnel Green, married a daughter of Justice Young. A second marriage was to Judith, a daughter of Wm. Albany, a merchant of London. He died 1605. His sons were Richard, Hugh, John, William of Highgate, and Robert. William was a great benefactor of St. John's College, Cambridge. He died 1637, without issue. He gave extensive lands and valuable rents for the support of fellows and scholars. There is a distinct building in the college appropriated to this foundation. The college, in memory of their generous benefactor, repaired and beautified his monument in Highgate chapel, 1713, and again in 1743. Under arches are busts of Mr. Platt and his wife, and among the monuments are many "escocheons."

John Platt, of Rickmensworth, married Rebecca, daughter of Sir Hugh Cole, of Lee's Court, County Worcester, Kt. His son John was Rector of West Horsley. *His* son John of Godelming was knighted. *His* son was John of Thurlow, Suffolk. *His* sons were Joseph and William. An interesting pedigree.

There was a Richard de Playz, also a John de Playz, cousin and heir of Aveline, wife of Edmund, Earl of Lancaster, who lived in the reign of Edward III.

Richard Platt, of London, was a benefactor to the parish of St. Alban's, by the endowment of a free grammar school for sixty scholars, in 1597; also six houses built of brick, for six poor persons, at the same time. At the end of the school-hall, there is a portrait of the founder. The school is on the road leading from the village of Oldenham to that of Elstree. This Richard Platt, was an Alderman of London, a high distinction in his day. See "Cluterbuck's History of Hertfordshire."

John Platt, England, politician, born 1817, a magistrate of the County of Lancaster, high sheriff of County Carnarvon, 1863, was a member of parliament for Oldham, 1865, and many years afterwards.

XLIX.

ANCESTRAL TABLETS AND INSCRIPTIONS ON TOMBSTONES.

———

WE go back to old England for a few. In Cansick's Epitaphs of Middlesex, the following is found, in old St. Pancreas Church :

"Dedicated to the Memorie of William Platt, of Highgate, in the Countie of Midd., Esq're, sonne and heir of Sir Hugh Platt, of Kerlie Castle, who married ye youngest daughter of Sr John Hungerford, of Downamay, in the Countie of Gloucester, Knight. He had one brother of the whole blood, and three sisters, viz : Robert Platt, Ann Platt, Judith Platt, and Mary Platt. He departed this world upon the eleventh day of November, one thousand six hundred and thirty-seven, aged five and forty yeares."

This is followed by an inscription on the same stone in memory of his widow, who married " Ed. Tucker, of Madingly, in the Countie of Wilts, Esq., by whom she had one only daughter married to Sir Thomas Gore, of Barrow, in the Countie of Somerset, Knight." She died 1687, in the 86th year of her age. This monument was restored at the expense of St. John's College, Cambridge, 1848. It was removed from the old chapel at Highgate, A. D. 1833.

In Highgate Cemetery, County Middlesex. (From Cansick's Epitaphs of Middlesex), is the following :

" Here repose the remains of

THOMAS PLATT

late of St. Georges, Bloomsbury, Esquire,
who was born on the 4th of January, 1760,
and admitted an Attorney and Solicitor
in the Supreme Court at Westminster, 1780,
served the office of Chamber Clerk
under the Right Honorable Lords
Mansfield, Kenyon, and Ellenborough,
Chief Justices of England,
and enjoyed the confidence of these noble Lords
to the time of their respective deaths.

After his retirement from office he received
from a large number of his professional Brethren
the united and public expression of their gratitude
for the upright, able, and courteous
manner in which he had discharged its duties,
and having retained
the esteem and respect of the members of his profession
and acquired the veneration and attachment
of his private friends.
closed his useful and honorable life
on the 8th day of October, 1842.

'Thou shalt come to thy grave in a full age, like
as a shock of corn cometh in his season.'

Job, v. :26.

' A good man leaveth an inheritance to his children's
children.'

Prov., Chap. xiii., v. 22."

In Highgate County (from Cansick's Epitaphs of Middlesex) is the following :

"I believe

in the

communion of saints.

To the beloved and revered memory of the

Hon. Sir THOMAS JOSHUA PLATT, Knight,

many years one of the Barons
of Her Majesty's Court of Exchequer.

He was the eldest son of Thomas Platt, Esq're,
of Brunswick Square ;
educated at Harrow School and Trinity College,
Cambridge,
he was called to the bar 9th Feb'y, 1816,
and having, on the 27th of Dec'r, 1834
received his patent as one of His Majesty's Counsel,
was raised to the Bench on the 27th Jan'y., 1845.

He died on the 10th Feb'y.. 1862, aged 73 years.

' The souls of the righteous are in the hands of God,
and there shall no torment touch them,
In the sight of the unwise they seemed to die ;'
and their departure is taken for misery ;
And their going from us to be utter destruction ;
but they are in peace.'—Wisdom iii.'

Angelica Helen, died 14th May, 1860.
Georgina, died 15th July, 1860.
Emily Octavia, died 12th June, 1860."

The following are found in the cemetery in Huntington, L. I.:

"Ester, wife of Scudder Platt, who died August 22, 1806, in her 47th year."

" Here lies ye body of Capt. Isaac Platt, who departed this life Feb. ye 5th, A.D. 1763, in ye 64th year of his age."

"In memory of Dr. Zophar Platt, who after a long and successful life died in peace, Sept. 23, 1792, aged 87."

"In memory of Zophar Platt, Esq., who died March 27, 1811, in his 77th year.,"

A "Zophar Platt, died November 4, 1812, aged 27."

" In memory of Mrs. Mary Platt, relict of Obadiah Platt, who died January 9, 1795, aged 64."

" In memory of Sarah, wife of Zophar Platt died May 10, 1811, in her 77th year."

" In memory of Scudder Platt, who died November 29, 1828, in the 70th year of his age."

The following data are " derived" mainly from a striking volume on "The Tombstones in Milford, Ct.," by N. G. Pond, Esq., of that place :

Mrs. Sarah Beard, wife of Joseph Beard, was the daughter of Josiah and Sarah (Burwell) Platt, born March, 1713, died August 30, 1751.

—Sarah Platt, daughter of Josiah and Sarah (Canfield) Platt, was the wife of Richard Bryan, son of Richard the Settler in 1639.

—Capt. Joseph Bryan, who died 1783, was the son of Richard and Sarah (Platt) Bryan. He married

Elizabeth, daughter of Zachariah and Hannah (Allen) Whitman.   On his tombstone:

> " Let not the dead forgotten be
> Lest men forget that they must die."

—Gideon Buckingham, son of Daniel, died June, 1, 1719.   His widow married Joseph Platt.

—Mary Platt, daughter of Deacon Josiah and Sarah (Canfield) Platt, married deacon Joseph Clark. She died October 28, 1755, in her 81st year.

Hannah, daughter of Joseph and Mary (Platt) Clark, married Jonathan Fowler, son of William, January 9, 1728.

—Sarah (Platt) Fowler, wife of Nathan, lost her only son William, September 3, 1799.   On the tombstone :

> " Stop, children dear, as you pass by,
> And see you're not too young to die."

—Phebe Newton, daughter of Joseph and Mary (Kellogg) Platt, wife of Samuel Newton, died November 12, 1727, in the 42d year of her age.

—Elizabeth, daughter of Joseph and Sarah Platt, first wife of Serg't. Jonah Newton, died July 5, 1734.

—Phebe, daughter of Sarah and Joseph Platt, married Serg't. Jonah Newton, who died April 19, 1756.

—Hannah, daughter of Joseph and Mary (Kellogg) Platt, married Lieut. Fletcher Newton, son of Roger and Abigail (Fletcher) Newton.

—Epenetus Platt, son of Joseph and Mary (Kellogg) Platt, died April 10, 1723, aged 27.

—Hester Platt, daughter of Richard and Hester Platt, died December 24, 1728, in the 21st year of her age. Her mother was Hester, daughter of Samuel and Sarah (Baldwin) Buckingham.

—Serg't Richard Platt, son of Josiah and Esther (Buckingham) Platt, married Mehetable, daughter of Ebenezer Fisk ; he died May 3, 1756, in his 42d year.

—Richard Platt, son of Serg't Richard and Mehetable (Fisk) Platt, died January 11, 1799, in his 57th year. On his tombstone :

> " A loving Husband, a tender Father,
> Left this world to enjoy the other."

—Hannah, daughter of Fletcher and Hannah (Platt) Newton, was the wife of John Prudden, son of John and Mary (Clark) Prudden. He died September 3, 1786. She, October 7, 1790, aged 73.

—Polly, second wife of Captain Samuel Tibbals, was the daughter of Benjamin and Ann (Platt) Bull. She died March 17, 179–, in her 38th year.

—Mary, daughter of Thomas and Mary (Platt) Clark, the wife of Robert Treat, died August 29, 1799, aged 66.

—Mehetable, daughter of Joseph and Hannah (Buckingham) Platt, was the mother of Mrs. David (Mehetable) Treat. Her grandson, David Treat, two years old, died February 3, 1797.

—Mary, daughter of Joseph Platt, married Capt. John Woodruff, December 22, 1698. Her husband died July 23, 1726, in his 53d year.

—A stone in the Waterbury Cemetery reads:

"Nathan Platt died July 30, 1815, aged 84."
A soldier of the revolution."
" Them also that sleep in Jesus, will God bring with Him."

He was the grandfather of the writer.

—Gideon Platt, son of Lieut. Gideon and Mary (Buckingham) Platt, died September 24, 1796, in his 63d year.   On his tombstone:

" In hopes of a glorious immortality,
  Behold, my friend, as you pass by,
  Returned to dust—I here do lie,
  As I am now, so you must be,
  Prepare for death, and follow me."

L.

FACTS, TRADITIONS AND DATES.

This chapter is to pick up disconnected threads and weave them into the narrative. It is a good rule to gather up the fragments that nothing be lost. The family record in the Revolution was creditable. Its members generally were full of the spirit of a wise liberty; and often contributed to mould our free institutions, in that position in life in which Providence placed them. Capt. Nathaniel Platt, as recorded, held his commission from Washington, and did effective service. Many on Long Island, which was under British rule, suffered and were imprisoned because they were loyal to the principles of human right. Four of the sons of Zephaniah Platt (1709), of Long Island, were in the U. S. Army in the Revolutionary war. Many others were soldiers in that army.

Mrs. A. T. Redfield relates that she visited Long Island and obtained pieces of the "Platt" tree, to which her great-grandfather, with fifty others, was chained till taken to the Jersey prison ship, where most of them died. He lived but two days after he reached home, and was buried near this tree. This was Zephaniah Platt, of Long Island.

Judge Charles Platt, of Plattsburg, was a year in the patriot ranks. Dan Platt, of the Saybrook Branch, was a captain in the Revolution. Many lost their lives in the Union ranks in the civil war.

———

Abigail Platt, mother of Benj. Sanford, of Milford, remembered that her father, Capt. Benjamin Platt, of Milford, went to Huntington, L. I., to visit their relatives there, and that he brought home some apple grafts. This Captain Benjamin Platt was an officer in the Revolutionary war, and was at Danbury. He died in April, 1808. This was related by Benj. P. Bush, of West Haven.

———

Bancroft in his invaluable history of the United States, speaking of the determined spirit of liberty in the early settlers of our country says, that the people "demanded power to govern themselves. Discontent (on Long Island) created a popular convention; and if the two Platts, Titus, Wood, and Wicks, of Huntington, arbitrarily summoned to New York, were still more arbitrarily thrown into prison, the fixed purpose of the yeomanry remained unshaken."

———

The coat of arms granted by Edward III, in 1326 is described thus: Per pale, gule, or, lion passant, armed, motto—"Merit has its reward"—which I have rendered into Latin "Virtus suum praemium habet."

———

The capstone to the memory of Richard Platt 1st, on the memorial bridge in Milford Ct., is three feet long, 22 inches wide, and 15 inches high. It is located on the south wall of the bridge, in the place of honor, next to the stone in memory of Peter Prudden, "the first pastor in Milford." Each stone stands out distinctly from the others, giving to the top of the bridge on each side the finish of a turreted battlement.

———

The date, respecting the "baptism in Bovingdon, Hertfordshire, Eng., of Richard Platt, son of Joseph, in 1603," cannot be verified, for the church records there now, only go back to 1675. This word is sent me by my friend, Dr. W. H. S. Aubrey, of London, Eng.

———

Dr. Daniel Beckley, of Naugatuck, Ct. the writer's maternal grandfather, who served under Washington, at Trenton, died at Utica, N. Y., at the age of 85. He was 70 years a member of church. He told his grandson, that, his enlistment having expired, on his return home from the army, he paid sixty dollars for his lodging and breakfast, in the Federal greenback corrency of the revolutionary day.   Fiat money!

———

Admiral Theodorus Bailey, the types on page 108 make to be engaged, in command of a U. S. ship, in "the capture of slaves!" Slavers. He was capturing ships that were capturing slaves. Would that there had been some such American Admiral doing that work a hundred years and more before—when England having the monopoly of the slave trade was eager to fill our colonies with the kidnapped ship-loads of these sons of bondage. England afterwards did the just thing in freeing the slaves in her part of the West Indies.

———

Richard Platt of New Haven, has two children residing there : George H. Platt, and Mrs. M. A. Barnes.

———

Eliza A. Platt, daughter of G. W. Platt, of New York, married E. W. Stoddard of Succasunna, N. J.

———

Oliver Platt, was a graduate of Hamilton College in the class of 1823.   He has not been traced.

———

C. C. Platt, of Ithaca, N. Y. is the son of the Rev. Wm. K. Platt, who was born in New York City. He is a druggist.

———

Mr. George Cornwall, banker of Po'keepsie, N. Y. has a place in this Lineage.   His mother Eliza Antoinette Morey was the grand-daughter of James Platt, of the Oswego Branch.

———

Mrs. Wm. Floyd Platt, née Woolsey, of the Oswego Branch, was lost at sea.   She was a passenger on the ill-fated Ville de Paris.

———

There is a Jonas Platt in Smithland, Louisiana, of the Plattsburg Branch.

———

Chas. Easton Platt, late of Detroit, Mich., is in Berlin, Germany.   He is perfecting his knowledge of the art of music.   His mother resides in Waterbury, Conn.

———

Mrs. Chas. Wales, of St. Andrews, Canada, is a Platt descendant.   Her daughter is Mrs. Wm. Drysdale, of Montreal, whose husband is a publisher in that city.

———

Ellen Gray Johnson, of Up. Red Hook, N. Y., married Henry L. Underwood, Oct. 1, 1872.   She was born Nov. 29th, 1845.   They had one daughter Mary Platt.   Her father removed to Birmingham, Alabama.

———

Channing M. Huntington, of Utica, who married Nellie B. Platt, of Norwich, has lately published a handsome little volume entitled "A Bachelor's Wife and other Poems."   It shows ability in that gifted kind of work.

———

Wm. Platt Merritt, of Grand Union Hotel, is the son of Wm. C. Merritt, who married Rachel, a daughter of Joseph Platt, of Bedford.   Deacon Joseph was a son of Charles, son of Jonathan, son of Benoni Platt 1st, of the Westchester Branch.

———

Albon Platt Man, late of New York City, born at Constable, Northern New York, Jan. 18th, 1811, a son of Dr. Albon Man, of the neighborhood of Plattsburg, was a grandson of Capt. Nathaniel Platt, who served under Washington in the Revolution.   He studied law under Judge Parkhurst in Plattsburg, and under Judge Kent in New York, and was admitted to the bar in 1832. He was sixty years a lawyer, successful and prominent. He was a member of the N. England So. and of the Union League Club. He was a brother of Mrs. Hugh McCulloch of Washington, D. C. He married Mary L. Brower of Wilks-barre, Pa. A second marriage was to Mary E. Hubbell, of Utica. He died at his home in New York, March 30th, '91, in his eighty-first year; a long and honorable life. Seven sons, a daughter and his widow survive him. His oldest, William, was born June 5, 1839; Frederick H.; Albon P. Jr.; Henry H.; Alric H.; Edward, and Arthur the youngest son, born July 18, 1871, and the only daughter living, Mary Man. William and Henry were associated with the father's law firm in Wall Street. He was a member of the Madison Square Presbyterian Church, where his funeral was attended.

Theodore W. Parmele, of the Judge Jonas Branch, of New York, married Emily F., daughter of Gen. Charles Room. Two children living, Charles R. and Helen Livingston. Bertha died young. A second marriage was to Mary Platt, grand-daughter of Judge Jonas Platt. One son, Henry Livingston, who died in infancy, Holmes Agnew, of the same branch, married, April 6, 1891, Isabelle de Puys Foote, grand-niece of ex-Governor Randolph, of New Jersey. He resides in Tacoma, Washington.

Thomas Platt, who was a resident of Chazy, N. Y.,

during the war of 1812, and who died there about 1824, had two daughters, Edith and Priscilla Platt. There were other children : Mary, Marian, Elizabeth and Releafie, and Nelson and Daniel. Mrs. Mary M. Wilder was the daughter of Edith, (who married Matthias B. Miller, May 15, 1830), and she was the grand-daughter of Col. Thomas Miller of Plattsburg, who won so brilliant laurels in the battle of Lundy's Lane in the war of 1812. Mrs. Wilder, the widow of J. Spencer Wilder, now resides in Clinton, Wis. He died June 6, 1883. Two of her father's sisters (Millers) married Platts, cousins, of Plattsburg, both named Zephaniah, and the wedding was on the same day. The presence of hundreds of guests made it what the Germans call a "Hochzeit," a high time. Thomas Platt was from Vermont, and he or his father was from Conn., possibly from New Milford or Norwalk. There is no Thomas Platt from Milford, according to the records in the old township. Mrs. Wilder's sister is Mrs. Geo. Cooper, née Charlotte E. Miller, who now resides in Manitowoc, Wis.

———

Hon. B. Platt Carpenter, formerly of Po'keepsie, N. Y., now of Helena, Montana, was the last territorial Governor of that new state. His mother, Maria Bockée, daughter of Jacob Bockée, was a granddaughter of Margaret Platt (Smith) who was a daughter of Maj. Epenetus Platt, of the younger Huntington Branch. His father was Morgan Carpenter, of Po'keepsie. Before he went West, he was nominated on the Republican ticket for Lieutenant-Governor in N. Y. He was prominent in his party in the state. Born in Stanford, Duchess Co., May 14, 1837, he graduated from Union College in the class of '58. Admitted the following year to the bar in Duchess Co., he held various positions in public life. Among them, he was state senator and county judge. His oldest brother, the Hon. Jacob B. Carpenter, who has been a member of the legislature, mayor of Po'keepsie, and has held other honorable positions, is now residing at Little Rest, Duchess Co. A sister, Miss S. M. Carpenter, resides in Po'keepsie. Mr. Morgan Carpenter had other children : Benjamin, dec'd, Catherine, Mary, Isaac Smith, and Louisa. B. Platt Carpenter was the youngest son. In his new home in Montana, during his governorship, he was elected a member of the Constitutional Convention, and afterwards a member of the Code Convention. He married Esther Thorn. They have three children: Nina, Katherine, and Steven. Nina married Edward Tower, of Poughkeepsie. They have one son, Albert Tower.

———

Obadiah, eldest son of Abel, blind in one eye, was cutting a tree, and it fell on him and killed him. This was in Redding.

———

Eunice Platt used to say that both of her grandmothers were Molly Smiths ; one married Obadiah Platt, the other a Scudder.

———

Thankful Platt's mother, Molly Scudder, died when she was only one year old, and she was adopted by

Thos. Jarvis and his wife, Abigail, they having no children.

———

Sturges Selleck, of Danbury, had six silver spoons with "T. S." on them. He died 1871. He married a grand-daughter of Polly Hull. Her daughter is Mrs. Chas. Benedict.

———

Mrs. Hugh McCulloch, of Washington, D. C., writes : "My grandmother's silver tea-set is with my sister, Mrs. Lawrence Myers, Colorado Springs. Old Mrs. Woolsey, née Livingston, inquired of me, many years since, if I had it, for she said they used to have tea from that pot on grandma's round tea table, when tea was a proscribed beverage. My grandmother had kept a little with which to treat old friends."

—She also writes : "The wives of the early settlers of Plattsburg were very well educated women, I have always heard. Charles Platt married Caroline Adriance, of Fishkill, who was beautiful even in extreme old age; and her daughters, whom I remember, were handsome women. My grandmother, the daughter of Richard Smith, of Smithtown, now King's Park, L. I., was also beautiful. My cousin, Mrs. Collins, has a portrait painted when she was past middle age."

———

"The World's Encyclopedia of Wonders and Curiosities," published by J. B. Anderson, now sold by J. B. Alden, of New York, was compiled and written by I. Platt, D.D. It takes a wide range through nature, art, science and literature.

There is an interesting " Life and Letters of Mrs. Cyrus Platt," of Delaware, O. Her religious character, and her effective good works are herein admirably delineated. Her name before marriage was Jeanette Hulme, of Burlington, N. J. The book was compiled by her husband. There are letters in it from E. H. Canfield, D.D., and Stephen H. Tyng, D.D., late rector of St. George's, New York. Hers was a bright and beautiful Christian character. "That she hath done shall be spoken of for a memorial of her." "She walked beside the sad and weary with words of cheer and comfort." It is a choice volume of Christian biography. Her numerous letters are bright, thoughtful, frank, interesting, and gracefully worded.

James Platt, F.S.S., of London, Eng., distributed gratuitously, in 1873, 30,000 copies of an essay on Business. He has lately expanded it into a rich and interesting volume, entitled "Business." It is a stirring and admirable work on wise living. It has gone through seventy-five editions in London. He has also written a book called "Life," which has gone through twenty-one editions. His volume entitled "Money," has reached nineteen editions. Without question, they all may be characterized in general as timely, incisive, inspirited, and abounding in words of admirable suggestion. These three have been reprinted by Putnam's Sons, here. The same author has published volumes on "Morality," "Progress," "Economy," and "Poverty," and no doubt they will do good in our work-day world, and give richness and effectiveness to life. We are glad to call attention to these books. His themes, in his works on "Life" and "Business," show how valuable they may be when handled with force and freshness. Some of them are: "Is Life Worth Living?" "Culture," "Common Sense," "Thrift," "Marriage," "Happiness," and "Health;" "Industry," "Perseverance," "Punctuality," "Prudence," "Tact," "Truthfulness," "Integrity," and "A Few Hints what to do with Money." It is readily seen that these topics, though old, may be even new in an earnest-minded thinker, who writes with ability and fervor. His views of life are realistic, specially adapted to the life of to-day. The future life has a limited weight in his scales. Hence we must say of him, as of all, that the written thoughts of men need to be sifted before we adopt and assimilate them. Many writers have views that are their own, and ought not to belong to any others.

The works of the Rev. Dr. Wm. H. Platt, of Petersburg, Va., which are named at close of Chapter X., have been favorably received by the public.

In the seventh chapter we have spoken of "Old Times in Huntington," by Henry C. Platt, Esq., of New York.

Mr. Jos. C. Platt, of Waterford, N. Y., writes, November 10, 1890: "I lately met Mr. James Platt and daughter, of Gloucester,.Eng. In conversation with them, I learned that they saw in me and my brother many family peculiarities which reminded them of their own relatives, and they thought we must have sprung from a common stock." They informed him, that "in Saddleworth, Eng., in Yorkshire, about ten miles E. N. E. of Manchester, there are large numbers of Platts, and the name appears very frequently on the stones in the cemetery."

The estate of the late Nathan C. Platt, of New York, was sold in March, 1886, for the sum of $375,000. In the *New York Herald*, of the 3d of March that year, we read this statement: "When the Platts—Nathan and George—made their thousands in New York, there was no assay office there. The mint was in Philadelphia, nearly a hundred miles away, and those who had made their return trip from California, around Cape Horn, after a four months' voyage in the famous clipper ships of the time, did not care to make another railroad trip to sell their 'ore.' They carried it around their waists, had it sewed in the lining of their clothes, or in satchels, or in their pockets, and even before they divested themselves of their mining clothes, or indulged in the luxuries incident to a return home, they tramped down Liberty street three or four hundred strong, and sold their 'diggings.' Old Mr. Platt weighed the ore, figured the value, and gave the Californian his check for the amount. At that time it was well known that the Platts kept a large cash balance on hand in the growing business of the city. Nathan and George, when quite young, came to the city about 1810, from Huntington, L. I., and engaged in the manufacture of gold and silver thimbles, in a small shop in what is now known as Chatham square. They met with success there, manufactured other articles, and had so expanded their business, that, about 1830, they purchased 4 and 6 Liberty street, a part of the well-known Grant Thurburn estate, whose seed store and garden form part of the history of New York. It was here in Liberty street that they became prominent jewelers in New York. They opened an assay office just previous to the California excitement, and their stamp on a bar of gold was considered, here and abroad, as good as that of the U. S. mint. The 'forty niners' from California rapidly increased their business, and in a few years they owned additional property on Maiden Lane and Nassau street." The old-time Platt establishment, 4 and 6 Liberty street, was sold to Henry Platt for $123,000. David Platt was a brother of Nathan and George above, all children of Elkanah Platt, of the older Huntington stock. David, in the first years of their business in New York, was interested with his brothers.

———

A kinsman, of the Waterbury branch, lately deceased, left an estate estimated, his brother told me, at $300,000.

———

There are twenty-six Platts, whose wills are on record in the Surrogate's office in New York city.

The tradition that Richard Platt 1st and a brother arrived with the Salem colony, went west to Springfield, Mass., and then south to Windsor, Ct., and that the brother tarried there, while Richard went on to New Haven, Dr. H. R. Stiles, the historian of Windsor, disposes of in these words to me: "No trace of Platt—either Josiah or Fisk—in Windsor. If he stopped there over night undoubtedly he stayed with the 'reputable householder' appointed by the town, 'to entertayne ye stranger,' as was the custom of ye day—but the hotel register had not been invented, and hence cannot be produced in evidence. The land records show that he settled not at Windsor; nor do the town records hint that he was drummed out of town, or in any way harrassed by the constable. So, tradition be hanged!"

———

As a balance to this, I insert the following:.

A brother kinsman sends me this newspaper clipping: "The Woolseys, of New Haven; the Platts, of Plattsburg; the Bowdoins, founders of Bowdoin College; the Hon. R. C. Winthrop, who made the address at the dedication of the Washington Monument, are descended from Leoffric, one of the kings of Wales." He well says: "This may be a revelation to some. For myself—

   ' Higher still my proud pretentions rise—
   The son of parents, passed into the skies.' "

———

Here is no fancy, but a stray fact. Samuel Platt was one of the original proprietors of Bridgewater,

Ct. He died there July 22, 1785, in his sixty-first year.

Alrick H. Man, Esq., of New York, writes this to Prof. Platt, of New Haven: "In the history of Virginia, 3 vols., it is recorded that Richard Platt and his wife were killed in the Virginia massacre in 1623." This adds another to the many English Richards.

Here the writer parts with the reader. An honorable record this. Let us maintain it on our part. My mother used to say to me when a youth,

> "Count that day lost whose low descending sun
> Views from thy hands no worthy action done."

Let it be a transmitted message. One of our gifted bishops has written:

> "We are dwelling,
> In an age on ages telling,
> To be living is sublime."

Let us really find this out, and do our part to make it so. And what our hands find to do, let us do with our might. If you are as good as your fathers, strive even to be better. There are higher standpoints before us all. Let us press towards them.

> "Heart within and God o'erhead."

ERRATA.

On 7th page, ninth line, read "Jonas" for Jonah.

"　　　"　　eighth "　　　"　"I." for T. Hull.

On 21st "　fifth　"　　"　"removed" for returned.

" 30th " thirteenth line, read "Andros" for Andrews.

" 38th page, sixth line from bottom, read "second" for record.

On 49th page, third line from bottom, read "Martha" for Margaret.

On 51st page, third line from bottom, read "1891" for 1890.

" 57th " fifth "　"　　"　　"　"Morris" for Huntington.

On 68th page, seventeenth line, read "Almon" for Almore.

" 69th " third line from bottom, read "Josiah and Louise, his children."

On 72d page, last line, leave out "branch."

" 103d " top line, read "Binghamton."

" 108th " second line from bottom, read "slavers" for slaves.

On 119th page, eighth line from bottom, read "Manette" for Manetta.

On 123d page, ninth line, read "Weston" for Westen.

" 124th " eleventh line, read "Andariese" for Andarine.

" 128th " thirteenth line from bottom, read "Isidora" for Isidor.

On 141st page, ninth line, read "Platt" for Pratt.

" 214th " second line, " "make" for makes.

LI

INDEX

OF

PLATT NAMES IN THE BOOK, FOUND

ON THE NUMBERED PAGES.

A

Arthur Livingston, 124.
August, 330.
Augustus, 26.

Aurelia, 76.
Austin, 275.

B

Benjamin, 49, 50,175, 211, 267.
Benjamin G., 238.
Benoni, 191.
Bertha, 180, 186.

Bessie, 83.
Betsey, 89, 134, 147 8.
Bleeker, 105.
Brewster W., 32.

C

Cansten, 149.
Carrie F., 87.
Carrie P., 254.
Caroline, 33, 38, 51, 111, 112, 149, 186, 263.
Caroline Child, 46.
Catherine, 49, 149, 275.
Catherine S., 283.
C. Adams, 142.
C. Easton, 358.
C. Grenough, 243.
Charles, 26, 71 6, 105, 195, 330.
Charles A., 142.
Charles Beckley, 289.
Charles C., 111.
Charles D., 57.
Charles E., 105, 180.
Charles H., 86.
Charles Henry, 33.
Charles J. W., 329.

Charles, Judge, 45, 111.
Charles M., 87.
Charles S., 33, 39, 67.
Charles Sandford, 185.
Charles Sellers, 128.
Charles T., U.S.N., 101 2.
Charles W., 8, 71, 254.
Charles Z., 105.
Chas. Henry, Rev., 102.
Charlotte,38,89,200 3,208.
Chauncey, 26, 137.
C. Heminway, 7, 86, 88.
Clara, 255.
Clara A., 294.
Clarence W., 88.
Clarissa, 83.
Clark, 76.
Clark Murray, 185.
Clayton, 244 5.
Clayton Winfield, 223.
Cornelius, 26.

F

G

H

I

J

K

L

Nathaniel, Capt., 45, 107.
N. Dwight, 70.
Nettie D., 87.
Nehemiah, 203.
Newton, 44.

Nicholas, 82.
N. M., 228.
Noah, 274–7.
Norman S., 70.

O

Obadiah, 31, 36, 81–3, 167, 273.
Obadiah 2d, Col. O., 31.
Obadiah H., 84, 90.
O. H., 90.

Oliver, 36, 39–40.
Orrin, 88.
Orton W., 186.
Orville H. (U.S.S.), 167, 169.

P

Paulina, 82.
Peleg, 133.
Peter M., 106.
Phebe, 32, 36, 43, 107.
Philetus, 32, 36.
Philip, 49, 95, 283.

Philo N., 82.
Philo R., 90.
Philo, Toussey, 82, 163.
Phineas, 71.
Phoebe, 49.
Polly, 36, 82, 84.

R

Rachel, 105, 195.
Ralph Hilton, 220.
Raymond, 151.
Rebecca, 32, 57.
Regina M., 223.
R. Goodman, 142.
R. H., 72.
Rhoda, 96.
Richard, 63, 70, 164.
Richard 1st, 13, 65, 357, 368.
Richard, Col., 46, 48.

Richard Morris, 57.
Richard, of London, 341.
Robert, 105–6, 168.
Robt. Drury, 284.
Robert Treat, 76.
Robert (U. S. N.), 39.
Royall Tyler, 295.
Rufus D., 287.
Ruth, 134.
Ruth Ann, 168.
Rutherford Hayes, 212.

S

Sally Rusco, 96.
Samuel, 24, 26, 39, 75, 95, 106, 112, 129, 225.
Samuel B., 255.
Samuel Floyd, 128.
Samuel Keyes, 105.
Samuel R., 134.
Sanford Hall, 35.
Sarah, 15, 19, 32, 36, 45, 50, 59, 63, 65, 67, 88, 137, 253.
Sarah A., 68, 87, 108.
Sarah E., 35, 50, 105.
Sarah F., 147.
Sarah S., 150, 211.
Sarah Walworth, 102.

Seabury B., 187.
Selah, 49.
Sherman, 83, 91.
Silas, 88.
Simeon D., 169, 170.
Sir Hugh, 10, 336.
Sir John, 336.
Sir Thomas, 340 7.
Solomon, 45.
Stephen, 36, 105, 134, 193.
Stephen H., 35.
Susan, 26, 106, 149.
Susannah, 120.
Sydney, 33, 44.
Sylvester, 89, 156.

T

Timothy, 31, 81-5.
Theodora H., 181.
Theodore, 76, 88, 337.
Theodorus, 101, 105.

Theron E., 163.
Thomas, 243, 250, 360.
Thomas C., 203.

U

Uriah, 45, 48, 306.

Uriah 2d, 49, 55.

V

Van Zandt, 105.

Victor M., 254.

W

Wakeman, 84, 90.
Walter, 7, 180, 300.

Ward D., 87.
Warren Cumming, 215.

Z

INDEX OF NAMES

OF MOST

OF THE COLLATERAL BRANCHES,

PREPARED BY

JAMES M. BLACKWELL.

A

B

D

E

Earl, Olive, 86.
Edwards, Paulina, 82.
Elmon, Charlotte, 101.

Elseffer, Katherine, 143.
Eyre, Martha, 129.

F

Fairchild, Henry, 88.
Feltham, Julia H., 175.
Fenn, Mehetable, 75.
Ferris, Hannah, 212.
Fields, J. C., 88.
Fisk, Mehetable, 64.
Fitch, Wm., 121.
Fleet, Stephen, 36.
Flint, M. B., 49.
Floyd, Eliza, 127.
Floyd, Mrs. Nichol, 55.

Foote, Dr. Lyman, 111.
Ford, Jennie M., 68.
Fowler, Jonathan, 64.
Fowler, Charles, 89.
Fowler, Dr. Samuel, 59.
Fox, Wm. B., 37.
Freligh, Elizabeth, 104.
Frost, Lucy, 170.
Fuller, W. H., 69.
Fuller, Wm. A., 105.
Fullerton, Fanny, 213.

G

Gaines, Elias, 56, 59.
Gantz, Eliza, 37, 38.
Gaylord, Lucy, 136.
Gerard, Urania M., 39.
Gerhard, Maria, 245.
Gibson, Clara, 294.
Gilbert, Sarah M., 212.
Gillett, Jeremiah, 64.
Gilman, Sarah, 124.

Goldthwait, H. M., 39.
Graham, Charlotte, 113.
Grant, Abigail G., 224.
Grant, Pamela, 112.
Graves, Miss, 135.
Green, Hannah, 76.
Green, Thomas, 101.
Griggs, Fanny, 135.
Grinzeback, Ella, 34.

H

Haines, Elias, 56, 59.
Hall, Abigail, 95.
Hall, Parmelia, 35.

Hall, Volutia, 67.
Halsey, Maria P., 111.
Halsey, Rev. Frederic, 111.

I

J

Jackson, Col. Joseph, 59.
Jackson, Mary L., 102, 244.
Jacobs, Mary, 88.
Jenkins, Catherine S., 283.
Jenkins, Cornelia, 122.
Johnson, Charlotte C., 226.
Johnson, Rev. John G., 58.
Johnston, Robert, 143.
Johnston, Samuel B., 38.
Jones, Elizabeth L., 106.
Jones, Kate Judd, 282.
Jones, Walter R. J., 109.
Judd, Asahel, 70.

K

Kellog, Mary, 75, 179.
Kellogg, Samuel, 24.
Kennard, Grace, 201.
Kent, Cornelia G., 103.
Kent, Hannah, 103.
Ketcham, Amos P., 37.
Ketcham, Andrew J., 38.
Ketcham, Esther, 31, 83.
Ketcham, Rebecca, 37.
Keyes, Sarah, 105.
King, Sarah Jane, 187.
Kirk, Harriet E., 37.
Kirtland, Eliza, 185.
Kissam, Benj. Treadwell, 49.
Kissam, Daniel, 49.
Knowles, Abigail Hart, 143.

L

Lane, Hannah, 273.
Lansing, Richard R., 120.
Lansing, Susannah, 120.
Larned, Judge Sylvester, 121.
Lawrence, Maria, 103.
Leach, Dr. L. R., 88.
Lee, Thankful F., 180.
Leonard, Rathaum, 245.
Lewis, Abigail, 56.
Lewis, Jennie V., 136.
Lewis, Jerusha, 168.
Livingston, Helen, 117.
Lockwood, Sarah, 23.
Logan, Helen M., 170.
Lorillard, Eliza M., 109.
Lovell, Ella M., 256.
Luce, Maria, 212.

M

N

O

P

R

Rathbun, Charles, 112.
Raymond, Ann, 26.
Raymond, Hannah, 83.
Reilly, Manette, 121.
Reynolds, Ruth, 134.
Riddle, Carrie, 110.
Robert, Adelbert, 87.
Robertson, Dorcas, 135.
Rodman, Emily L., 40.
Rogers, E. P., D. D., 57.
Rogers, James, 57.
Rogers, Jesse, 36.
Roshore, Eliza, 32.
Ross, Eliza, 112.

Ross, Jane, 82.
Ross, Sadie, 110.
Royce, Abi, 156, 212.
Rudd, Adeline M., 288.
Rudman, Phebe, 35.
Rudman, Wm., 35.
Rundell, Cynthia, 192.
Russell, Capt. Samuel, 105.
Russell, Fanny, 185.
Russell, Mary C., 163.
Ruthren, Marion E., 134.
Ryerson, Judge Thos. C., 59.

S

Sailley, Julia, 101.
Sailly, Frederick C., 105.
Sanders, Jabez, 25.
Sammis, Content, 36.
Sammis, Jonas, 36.
Sandford, Mary, 64.
Sanford, Elizabeth, 168.
Sanford, Joseph, 64.
Sanford, Lemuel, 82.
Sanford, Sarah, 64.
Saxton, Hannah, 45.
Sayre, Ellen, 214.
Schermerhorn, Margy, 135.
Scherzer, Annie E., 143.
Scudder, Elizabeth, 133.

Smith, John, 69, 103.
Smith, Jonathan, 43.
Smith, Lorilla, 135.
Smith, Margery, 85.
Smith, Mary, 49, 72, 81, 151, 167.
Smith, Miss ——, 36.
Smith, Nathaniel, 36.
Smith, Phebe, 31, 37, 107, 225.
Smith, Ruby, 66.
Smith, Capt. Sidney, 108.
Smith, Temperance, 48.
Smith, Willard, 120.
Suydam, Miss ——, 35.

T

Y